THOSE
TWO
LITTLE
WORDS

by
Samantha Keathley

See, I have placed
before you an open door
that no one can shut.
Rev 3:8

Open Door Publishers, Inc
P.O. Box 2871
Malta, NY 12020 (518) 899-2097
http://www.opendoorpublishers.com

Printed in the United States of America

First Edition

ISBN: 978-1-937138-04-2

Backgroud picture cover by Margaret Stapleton.

Cover design by Jami LaCasse.

For Him

Chapter 1

"The honeymoon is over," I yell to Janice as I clench the phone tightly in my fist.

"What do you mean it's over?" Janice questions in an octave higher than her normal whine. "You were supposed to be away for two more days. What happened, April?"

"I did my best. Well, that's a lie, but I DON'T love him and he does not love me. We both tried, and after two days I needed to go home. He wanted to spend every waking moment by my side. He even tried to follow me into the bathroom when I had to go, well, you know. I had to go! I couldn't take another minute of that. We had our flight changed and arrived at his house, my new home about an hour ago. So, when can I come over?"

"Wait, what do you mean, you came home early because Ryan, the man you just married, wanted to spend all of his time with you? Isn't that every bride's dream?" Janice asks.

"Not mine, I need my space. When can I come over?"

"When your honeymoon is officially over, which would mean not for another two days. I am not going to help you out of this, your crazy need for space. Do you think you're single? I'm sorry to inform you April, but you are married now, and I'm not going to come between the two of you, so stop acting like you're single when you're not."

"Okay. I'll just call Sara then."

"Run, run, run, but you will still wake up every morning married," Janice states.

"I know, and what am I supposed to do about that?" I say as I slam the phone shut. My hand shakes as I move to put it on my night stand. I can't believe she isn't going to help me through this, one of the hardest times of my life. I thought she was my best friend.

The tears fall as unwilling sobs control my body. I've only been married 48 hours and I'm crying already, I thought as I throw myself on my bed. How could I marry someone without loving them? That was my one rule. If I ever married, which I never planned to do, it would be because his presence made my heart skip a beat. My mind would be consumed with warm fuzzy thoughts about him. My feet would barely touch the ground as I walked, but, no, instead I want to be away from him. My fog filled vision has, apparently, muddled my common sense. What was I thinking?

Colossal is too small a word for this mistake. Confusion has become my new mental state, whereas before I was proud to say I worked best under pressure, always making clear intelligent decisions. Why did this one seem right at the time? It was a quick decision. I slept maybe three hours the night before it and when he showed up the next morning we decided to elope. To both of us it seemed that there was no other choice. Marrying seemed to be our only option.

As I roll over to get under the blanket, I see Ryan standing in the doorframe and his grinding jaw muscles cue me that he must have heard my conversation with Janice. There's anger in his glare and something else I can't quite place.

He'd said on our way back to his home, which I'd never seen before, that he was going to work. I assumed he'd left already because we'd arrived back about an hour ago. Even though it was lunch time, neither of us was hungry. He will be in for a surprise when he learns I don't know how to cook at all. I can't even make coffee.

He opens his mouth, but closes it hastily before turning back down the stairs. Where am I anyway? How many times in an adult's life can someone say they don't know their own address? Here I am, and I don't even know what my house looks like. It was a blur when I came in. All I asked Ryan to do was lead me to the guest room. And that was where he brought me. And that is where I've stayed. I know it's only been an hour since I arrived, but I should have been more prepared. I could start to unpack the little I have here, but my mind is telling me to hold off because maybe there is a way to reverse my marital status. I don't want to unpack either. That gives the room a more permanent feel.

Ryan supplied the furnishings. It has a queen size bed with a pretty floral comforter. The furniture is solid mahogany wood with intricate designs running along the perimeter, very stylish and unique. The walls are a light blue that match the curtains, which cascade all the way to the floor. I wonder what the rest of the house looks like? There's no time like the present to go and find out, but first I have to at least wash my face and change my clothes. And, of course, I need to give Ryan enough time to leave.

Two full days is how long I've been married, and I still haven't spoken much to him. We talked more before we were married. How ironic. Every time I had the opportunity, my voice suddenly disappeared. Whether it was that I had no desire to communicate with him or that I already knew we had nothing in common. So why bother to talk, I am unsure. Why doesn't really matter, right? By his odd departure, I'd say he has the same problem too. Maybe we have one thing in common then.

This is difficult, living with a man, I mean. The last time I lived with a man, it was my father and that didn't go very well. Marrying Ryan seemed to be the right decision, but maybe there was another way. Why did I say, "I do?" How could I have made such an impulsive mistake? I'm not even an impulsive department store shopper!

On our honeymoon, he told me his home had four bedrooms and two and a half bathrooms with white brick covering the whole outside, along with a big fenced-in backyard. It was perfect for children. Children? Did I hear him correctly? Whose children was he talking about? I'm not planning to have his children. How could I bring children into a loveless marriage? Urghh. Anyway, the house that he was describing sounded like my picture of a dream house. Then he said he and his mother did all the decorating. I almost laughed out loud. He decorated? Shockingly, now as I walk from room to room, I realize that it is very well festooned. It's beautiful; even the curtains are colors that I adore. I never would have thought that a man would let lavender enter his bathroom but, there it is, my favorite color. Still, I don't feel happy seeing it, only sad because of my flawed connection to the man who owns it.

As I continue on down the stairs, the room I come to next appears to be a family room, a room that Ryan must spend a lot of time in. The couches look very comfortable and the computer area. Wow! It must have cost a lot with two large flat screen monitors and a custom designed desk with exhaustive storage. I need to have a seat in the chair to see if it is as comfortable as it looks. It is! And there are a number of buttons on the side of the chair and, Oops! I knocked the mouse off the desk when I was… "Oh, what's this?" Ryan left his email on. It looks like he didn't finish writing this one. Normally, I'm not a nosy person, but how else am I going to find out more about this man that I now live with?

Mom and Dad,

The past few days have been a blur. Life has been moving at a very fast pace. You know what happened at the beginning of the week, but I haven't had time to tell you about the rest of the week. Please read all of this first before you jump up and run to your truck to come over here. That might not be the best idea right now anyway because of all that has changed in such a short period of time. I wish I could come over to explain this to the both of you in person, but you will understand why I can't, soon enough. Also, I would like it if you both read this together. This is going to be hard for you to read, but first I want you to know I feel I did the honorable thing. I also believe that God has a hand in this. I'm not sure how, but I know He does. With that said I am not going to recap what you already know, but I will start right from where we last talked. But first, in the mean time can you please do me a favor because I am presently unable to? Can you send a message to my girl and let her know I miss her immensely and can't wait to see her. Let her know that I need to sort out some things first before I can see her. Thank you. My heart is more at peace knowing you will help me.

After we talked the other day, I decided to spend the night fasting and praying. I stayed up the whole night seeking God in what to do next. Only one thing came to mind, and that was to marry April. God gave me a peace about it even though we hardly know each other and she obviously can't stand the sight of me. I tried to talk God out of it and I struggled most of the night but still, I believe it is what God wants. I know you have both waited a long time for me to get married and give you more grandchildren. I also know this is not the way you would have wished me to do it and for that I am sorry. Mom, I hope the tears you are shedding now are happy ones. I hope you do not feel that you

THOSE TWO LITTLE WORDS

did a bad job raising me and that my decision does not cause a wedge in our relationship. I love you both very much and hope with all my heart you still support me, and now my wife. I truly believe that in time, we will find a way to love each other and hopefully it resembles the loving bond in your marriage. You have both been wonderful parents to me, showing me what a marriage should be and I long for that myself. Please pray for me to make the right decisions and to love April the way she deserves to be loved.

You both know how I have been stubbornly in love, for most of my life, with

That was it. Who did he love and why would he marry me if he was in love with someone else? I didn't think this could get any worse, but…

"Are you feeling okay, April? You don't look so good," Ryan asks.

Where did he come from? I quickly look down so he doesn't notice me looking at the screen. My hands are shaking. What if he noticed I was reading his email? What would he do? Yell a lot? Throw something? Maybe he will walk out and never come back. That wouldn't be so bad. The harsh reality rushes in. I do not know this man. It's like I rolled the dice and picked a man at random. I haven't really talked to him since middle school. I have heard about him from a couple of people, one being my sister. They have only said nice things, but they never lived with him, so how would they know? There's a throbbing in my ears as I start to panic. Deep breathes. That is what I am supposed to do when I feel a panic attack coming on, but how do you do that when you can't breathe?

"April?" Ryan says in a calm voice.

As he said my name, I look up at the computer and thankfully see that the screensaver is on. Then I look at his face and only see concern. As my mind registers that he didn't know that I secretly invaded his privacy, a mammoth weight lifts, and I'm able to get a full breath this time. A few more like this, and I should be okay.

"April?" he asks again.

"Oh. Yes, I am alright. Just a little lightheaded or something, but it's already passed."

"Are you sure that was it? You looked like you were terrified. Did I scare you when I came in?"

"Yes, you did. I thought you went to work."

"That was why I came up before. I was going to work when I realized I had other things to do around the house first. You seemed like you needed to be alone so I left. I'm sorry I startled you. That was not my intention. I thought you were still upstairs, but I'm glad you're down here now. Have you had a chance to look around yet?"

"Yes, a little bit. You did a great job decorating."

"Thanks. It was mostly mom. She didn't want me to paint every room the same color, so she picked out the colors, and I painted the rooms. Then we ordered curtains to match. She had fun. Would you like me to show you around?"

"I think I've seen everything but the kitchen."

"That would explain why I didn't see you because that's where I was. Follow me, I'll lead the way."

As I follow him, I hope our conversation leads into my not knowing how to cook. I want him to know that as soon as possible so he can get used to the idea of ordering take out or whatever it was that he usually eats. As we turn the corner and enter the kitchen, my jaw drops. It's breathtaking.

Ryan waves his hand as he says, "This is where my creations transpire. Cooking is something I love to do when I have the time. I spent a good amount of time designing this room. I hope you like it."

"It's beautiful, really!" Did he just say he likes to cook?

"Great." The satisfaction reflects in his eyes.

"Did you just say you like to cook?" I question.

"Yes, I did and yes, I do. My grandmother was a chef and so was her father. My dad and I didn't professionally follow in my grandmother's footsteps, but as a hobby I enjoy it. I love food and experimenting with different flavors. I would love to cook dinner for you tonight, if that's ok? I was hoping you could tell me what your favorite foods are so I could make them for you from time to time."

"Um, do you mind if we do that a different night. I'm hoping to run over to my apartment and pack up the rest of my things. I have a lot to do there. I need to have everything out within the next two weeks. I'm glad that I was able to get out of the lease on such short notice. I think I'll go over there now, so don't worry about dinner. I'll just pick up something on my way back here tonight."

"Alright, but would you like some help? Pack or haul boxes, I could do whatever you want. I'm all yours. Then we could go out to eat - your choice."

"Ryan, that's kind of you to offer, but I think this is something I need to do by myself. Today I want to pack most, if not all of the boxes, then maybe in a couple of days you could help me move them here."

"Okay, you just tell me when and I'll be ready to help. I don't know what furniture you have, but whatever rooms you want to put it in is up to you. I don't mind if you change things. I want this to be your home too, so you can tell me where you want it to go and I'll put it there."

Is this guy for real? There has to be a catch. He likes change? My home too? He is being too compliant and very eager to help. In time, I'll figure out what he's up to. Until then, I think its best I don't talk too much to him. It's almost as if he wants me to like him. I don't tolerate fakeness. In time, the real Ryan will come out, and then I will be happy I didn't spend my precious time getting to know him. I think I'll help him along. How about I change a lot of his things and make myself at home like he said to do. I'm glad he suggested that because I am moving here, and I do want to feel like it's my home too.

"Thanks. That's a great idea. I would like to make some changes here and there. In answer to your other question, I don't have a favorite food. See you later." I comment over my shoulder as I walk toward the door, grabbing my coat.

"Uhh. Okay. Yeah, see you later," he says, as his shoulders drop.

I turn to see the look on his face and I mentally give myself a high five. He's quite perplexed. I don't think he knows what to make of me now. I shouldn't have acted friendly those past few minutes. It gave him the wrong impression. I am not a girl that is willing to be wooed by a man, even if he is my husband. I was not meant to marry. I hope my abruptness helps him see that I'm an independent woman who needs space.

* * *

Packing is one of those activities that can feel never ending. As I survey my dismal surroundings, the reality of my future decorative plans fold. I don't own anything worth saving except some clothes and a few odds and ends. My bed is about twenty years old. It was the one my parents bought me for my 8th birthday. Every time I see a mattress commercial, I quickly flip the channel. I don't want to see a picture of those nasty dust mites. The first time I saw one all the way through, I stayed up for hours scratching and letting my mind run wild. Never again.

All my furniture was given to me when friends and family bought new pieces. I wasn't ungrateful nor am I complaining. Their generosity helped me immensely. I don't know if anyone would want it. It wouldn't be sad to throw this all out, but maybe I'll ask Janice first.

Isn't it amazing that after being in Ryan's home for a mere two hours, my living standards have changed. I am blessed to have a home with all new furniture along with each room tastefully decorated. I went from poor girl to snobby rich woman in three days, actually snobby isn't my style. It will be nice to not have to struggle to pay my bills. I'm glad I can find some positive things about this. Ever since I was twelve years old, money or lack of it has ruled my life and mind, never thinking I would be in a situation where I didn't struggle. Struggling to get by is a part of who I am. Now I don't have to wish for a nice comfortable house to live in, I have one. Maybe I can do this marriage thing after all. There are some benefits to our arrangement, but I'm still swaying back and forth between the pros and cons. It doesn't help that when I close my eyes, I can see him standing in front of me with that sideways grin he flashes often. He's several inches taller than me and I'm 5'6", so he must be around 6'. He has brown hair streaked lighter by the big star and green eyes that hint at a ray of other shades, depending on what he is wearing. Also, when he's nervous, he shifts his weight from one foot to the other as his head tilts to the side. Some might describe it as adorable, but I'm not one of those people. I need some sleep. If I was well rested, my thoughts wouldn't be on Ryan!

I thought on my way to my apartment that I was going to take my time packing, or maybe skip the packing all together and relax in front of the television, but as I glance at the couch with the holes in the arms and the stuffing coming out of it, I've reconsidered. It's best to continue packing and then enjoy watching a movie on the huge flat screen, reclining in the comfort of those black leather couches.

Wiping the perspiration from my brow, I long for a shower. Finishing is, unfortunately, my utmost goal. Scanning the apartment, I take in the size of my piles. My throw away pile has now grown larger than the one to keep and the pile to give away, is a combination of the two. There is so much that I don't need now, thankfully. My dishes are chipped, my towels are discolored from a bleach brawl (but that is a story for another time), my socks have holes in them…. Hmm, I wonder what month Ryan turns the heat on? I wait as long as possible. I try to hold out until the middle of December, but when the first of that month rolls around, I usually have a pretty bad cold along with frozen toes and fingers! I have a cheap bill though! It occurs to me, what a weight that has been lifted! I will still have some bills to pay, but now I don't have to worry about any house purchases, or water coming in from the leaky roof, or the toilet over flowing. I can't wait to call Janice and tell her how magnificent Ryan's house is. Oh, I forgot about our last conversation. It would be good to wait several days before I talk to her again.

Chapter 2

Silence seems to be my best companion, but initially it was not by choice. This is the time in my life where the people I want to talk to aren't available and the ones that are would prefer to hear themselves talk about my situation, instead of giving me the help I need, a listening ear! That's one reason why I haven't called my mother yet. I can't blame her, my decision affects her too. But right now, I don't want to hear about that.

For two straight days, instead of focusing on my real problems, my thoughts were about Janice. Thoughts like, "She was supposed to be my best friend and she won't even talk to me. What type of support is that?" "You are supposed to be able to rely on your best friend." "A best friend is someone you can talk to no matter what comes out of your mouth."

On I went until the second day passed, when I realized that I was the one to say, "I do" NOT Janice. A good friend disagrees gently instead of letting the other walk down the wrong path. That is what Janice was trying to do for me, but instead of listening to her, I had an adult temper tantrum. And, I missed out on possibly forming a friendship with Ryan, which was what she was trying to accomplish. She was trying to help me, not hurt me, like I originally thought.

Asking for forgiveness is not a strong attribute of mine. I am not quite sure how to repair this. I also can't believe that in these past couple of days I have not said a single word to Ryan. I don't even know if I saw him. I know I have some major personality flaws and no idea how to solve them. How do you talk to someone you hardly know and you really don't care to get to know? And now he is my... I can't even say the word. I reach for my phone and dial as fast as I can.

"I need to talk to you," I say as fast as I can and continue, not allowing Janice to get a word in.

"Why didn't you talk me out of this? I can't believe you agreed with me that this was the only way. I should have brain stormed more to find another way to solve this. It's too late now. I am married and there's no way out of it!" I meant to start off with an apology, but I am a woman with warring emotions and unfortunately my selfishness has become my first priority.

"April, I know I said you couldn't come over until after your honeymoon has ended, but I've changed my mind. Come on over to eat and then talk or watch a movie, whatever you want. If you want to spend the night, please let Ryan know first." Her tone is comforting.

"Okay, I don't want to be rude to him. I'll let him know if he's here." I add.

"What do you mean, if he's there? You don't know?" Janice questions.

"No."

"When was the last time you saw him?"

"I can't remember, but I do know I didn't see him yesterday," I say as quietly as I can, forgetting that it doesn't matter because Janice has great hearing.

"I am not going to comment, but I do want to know what you've been doing."

"Janice, I couldn't even tell you. I know I need to apologize to you, but I can't now. What I do know is that I'm hungry. I'll be right over. And I hope you have a lot of food. See you in ten."

"See you," Janice sighs.

As I hang up the phone, I start packing way more clothes then one night requires. Thinking little about Ryan's feelings, I run downstairs hoping he already left for work or something so that I could just leave a note. I didn't slow down when I landed at to the bottom of the steps, and sure enough the klutz that I am runs right into him, knocking him and myself down to the ground. The fall knocks the wind out of me. I'm immobilized as I look down into his eyes which are only two inches from mine. "I'm really sorry," I whisper as I attempt to get to my feet, but instead end up tripping over my suitcase, falling again. My cheeks grow warm and my mouth quickly loses its moisture. In desperation, I start to crawl.

It's easy to figure out that Ryan isn't hurt. I can hear him trying to hold it in, but the laughter wouldn't stay.

"What are you laughing at?" I question.

"You have to admit that there was some hilarity in that."

"Well, maybe a little." I did start to see the humor in it, but as a little chuckle escapes my mouth, I realize who I'm laughing with and I make myself stop. This is not appropriate, laughing with him. This is just a business arrangement and nothing more.

"Ryan, I'm going to Janice's for the night. Tomorrow our honeymoon will officially be over. What time do you want to get together so we can discuss our situation?" I ask as I rub my elbow. I must have banged it on the way down.

"I have the day off tomorrow, so I'm available all day. When are you free?"

"I can be back here by 10:00 a.m. I think it's better to get our arrangement solidified. Then we will know what our proper roles are," I say, turn, and walk out the door. Maybe my feet stomp a little, but he is so frustrating to talk to that I have to leave then, before I open my mouth and say something I'd regret. He can't make a decision on his own, wanting to add that he would have to be stronger and more firm tomorrow, but I was already out the door going to my car. His wishy-washy personality is driving me crazy. This can't be a good sign. I already found something about him that really irritates me.

Seeing my car lightens my mood slightly, it's one of those hybrids. It was the best choice I ever made, especially now that gas costs $3.89 a gallon. That seems to be the one thing that hasn't changed in the last week. I love my car. It's reliable, fast, and new. Well, I guess two years old isn't new anymore, but it's mine and no one else can drive it or take it away from me, like my apartment and my privacy and....

Oh, I miss my apartment. Not the physical look of it, but how everything had a place and a purpose which made it neat and organized and most importantly, mine. I'd painted each room myself. I'd even made the curtains and they looked great, which is saying a lot for me because I can't cut a straight line. Disappointment nestles its head on my shoulder as thoughts of my own space vanish, but it'll be worth it, I hope.

* * *

"Janice, this is the best chocolate cake ever! Can I have the recipe?" I want to know, but expect her to say no. She's a little weird about not wanting to share recipes.

"It's a secret."

"You have to tell me." We've been down this road many times before and she usually tells me. She thinks I'm not going to make it anyway because I don't know how to cook, but she doesn't know I, sort of, bake. My attempts are my secret.

"I'll tell you April, but only if you make it for Ryan."

"That's not fair. In more ways than one, starting with the fact that you know I can't cook," I say as my hands go naturally to my hips. After a look at Janice's face, I see there's no changing her mind.

"Alright, I don't hate the man you know. I just don't love him, but I will, with your help, make him the cake on his birthday, whenever that is. So, where did you get that recipe?"

"It's on the side of the Hersey's cocoa powder box." Janice whispers, as if other people are in the room.

"Really?" I'm not sure if she was serious.

"Yes, but don't tell anyone. I want to bring this to the church dinner next week," she says as if someone would want a recipe from me.

"Okay. Thanks. Tomorrow will be better, right, Jan?" I ask as my eyes start to tear up.

"Tomorrow will make you feel like it was all worth it," she says, hugging her friend and praying that her words would be true.

"That's what I think too." A tear escapes down my cheek.

"When do you and Ryan discuss the details?"

"Ten o'clock. One minute I wish I said to meet earlier so that I could know my fate sooner. But in the next minute, I'm glad it's not scheduled earlier because what if my situation gets worse? Do you think it can get worse?"

"How could it get worse with Ryan as your husband now? He is so nice and good-looking. You know almost every single woman at church has hoped he would show interest in them and he never has. It has been one of those confusing conundrums. I don't think he's ever even dated someone from church and now he is married to you. I think it's rather amazing and dreamy."

"Dreamy? You have got to be kidding me! He is dull and he can't make up his mind about anything. Maybe that's why he never dated anyone. He couldn't figure out whom to pick. Unfortunately, I was the one picked for him and he just went along with it." Sighing, my shoulders sink low expressing my very real depression. I was not depressed a few weeks ago. It's mind-boggling what time, circumstances, and two little words can do.

"April, think of it this way, now you don't have to complain about men asking you out all the time. You are taken now, so you no longer have to think of a reason to say no."

"That's a good point." Taken? I'm not a possession.

"I still would like to know why you always said no."

"Jan, I didn't ever want to get married. You know that, so why date? It made no sense to me."

"Yes, April I know that part, but you never told me why you didn't want to get married."

"Let's just say that it seemed easier. And you're not married, why not?"

"Nice change of subject. You know I want to get married. I'm not a beauty queen. They don't care that I have blond hair and stunning blue eyes, along with my dimples. It's this extra weight I carry that every man I've met sees, and not me. I wish I knew how to lose it. My health is starting to be affected. But you didn't come over here to talk about me. I do hope that one day you will trust me enough to let me know why you never wanted to get married. I know most of the reason, but there's still more that you haven't shared."

"It doesn't really matter now, does it?" I say turning quickly.

"I guess not." But her eyes say otherwise.

"Janice, I do trust you. I'm just not ready to talk about it yet," I sigh.

"Alright, whenever you do want to talk, I'm here for you," she says earnestly.

"Let me see if I understand you," I say, my jaw clenching. "You will be here for me like you were two days ago? Because that kind of help I can get anywhere and I can just save some breath too." Speaking truthfully without tact has been the glue for the strong walls around my heart and the lack of friendships in my life.

"Ouch. That hurts. I know I wasn't there for you two days ago, but you were on your honeymoon. And when you told me you were going, you insisted that it was your idea and that you wanted to go. Besides, I was honoring your dream."

"What dream are you talking about?" I ask.

"Remember about two years ago, we had our only conversation where you opened up about marriage? You said, with tears in your eyes, 'If I ever get married, I need to have a honeymoon I'll remember. I want to go to Hawaii or the Caribbean, just the two of us, with no interruptions.'"

"Janice, do you really think I meant that? I mean under these circumstances with Ryan?"

"Yes, I did. When you called to say you were getting married and that you were going on a honeymoon too, what was I supposed to think? I know why you got married and I also know that you didn't love him, but I thought you were trying to sort that out. That was the reason, I thought, for the honeymoon. I am sorry that I didn't let you talk more on the phone the other day. I should have found out more details before I jumped to conclusions, but I really didn't want you to run away from your situation either. I was trying to help. I thought refusing your request to come over would help you, not hurt you, by giving you and Ryan time to get to know each other. I'm sorry for hurting you. I wish I could go back and restart that conversation. I would let you talk more and let you come over so that we could try to figure out what the best thing to do next should be. Can you forgive me, please?"

"Definitely." Janice has taught me a lot over the years, humbling herself and saying sorry sincerely, is just another great way that I can learn from her. Her example brings me closer to unselfishness.

"You are my best friend and I don't ever want to cause you more pain, ever."

"I know. I'm sorry too. First, I shouldn't have yelled at you on the phone, or hung up on you, and lastly for all the unkind thoughts I had about you. I know none of them are true and I think I used you as my punching bag. Every time I remembered my state of affairs, I let my mind wander with thoughts like, 'She's supposed to be my best friend,' stuff like that. I know you are my best friend and I can see your heart in trying to help me. I'm sorry too. Can you please forgive me?"

"Yes, I forgive you." I embrace her like a little child embraces their mom after being lost from her in a store. Being at odds with Janice is emotionally taxing. I feel so much better now that our disagreement has been settled and we can move on to having fun, but only after I clarify a couple of things.

"Selfishly I wanted to go on a honeymoon. You're right that I had that dream and I did hope that we might become friends during it, but mostly I wanted to go to Hawaii. The only other thing I am going to say about it is that it was horrible."

"I really don't understand how Hawaii could be dreadful."

"Another time I will tell you what happened, but tonight I want to enjoy myself, so let's watch that movie. I hope you picked out a comedy, I really could use a good laugh."

"Great, let me get it."

Chapter 3

The darkness in the clouds presses in, mimicking her emotions and thoughts. How was she going to continue taking care of this precious little girl? She knew God would let her know what to do next, God always did, but honestly she was afraid for Alyssa's future. For now, God wanted Alyssa to stay with her and for that she was very thankful. Her day today truly is brighter because of this girl's presence. She's determined to cherish each day she has with her.

Watching her sit in the grass, she wonders what she should do next. She's really tired and knows she can't take care of her much longer. Her heart aches so much with that thought. She loves Alyssa with all her heart and wishes she had the strength to take care of her granddaughter.

Alyssa has had a series of tough, challenging trials in a short period of time. She's only six years old and now has to face the hard fact that she cannot go home again. She doesn't have to face it today though, because Agnes hasn't told her yet. There hasn't been a good time, nor has she found the right words, comforting words. How does she comfort, when she herself needs to be comforted? She hugs her and talks to her and tries to answer all her questions. She hides her tears when Alyssa enters the room. She feeds her and tells her she loves her. She takes her to church and lets her friends come over. They visit family, but she knows that isn't enough. She needs security. She needs laughter and most importantly she needs her mother.

As day starts to turn into night, the words still don't come. She hopes that someday soon, before someone else tells her, she finds a way to explain what has happened. Agnes decides the answer to this dilemma is for tomorrow or the next day. God will handle that, because today is where God is telling her to focus. Pondering this, she quickly maps out the rest of the days' plans.

"Alyssa, Honey, come here please," she calls out the window, hoping the girl hears her and comes, because her legs have been moving slower and the less walking she has to do the better.

"Yes, Grandma, what is it?"

"How about we go out and watch a movie?"

"Yeah, I would love that, Grandma! Can Mommy come too?"

"Not today, sweetheart. Please go get ready."

"OK. Maybe she'll come next time. That's what I'll pray for," Alyssa says over her shoulder as she leaves the room.

Grasping for the kitchen chair, Agnes falls into it hard hitting her back on the way. She cannot control the silent sobs that shake her body. How did this spiral out of control? She leans forward as she takes slow but unsteady breathes, trying to calm her heart down. She can't believe Alyssa is going to pray for her mother to go to a movie with her. That's impossible, and it's all Agnes' fault that she still thinks it can happen. It's all because Agnes hasn't talked to her yet.

What am I going to do, God? Please give me wisdom during this time. I am unsure of what I need to do and say, so I have said nothing and now I know I was wrong. Forgive me, God. Help me hear your voice in this painful and confusing time. I feel that Alyssa needs to be here today, but that is all I know. I wish you would give me a glimpse of her future. Why won't you reveal it to me? Please guide me, Jesus.

"Grandma, I'm ready. Let's go. Can we get pizza too? That would be so much fun, and ice cream, Grandma! I know how much you love ice cream because I love it too. Please Grandma, please?"

"Sure, Alyssa. That sounds great!"

She would give her granddaughter almost anything just to see her beautiful smile. An infectious smile, she realizes, as she feels the corners of her mouth twitch upward for the first time since the letters started arriving. This is just what the two of them need. Last week she was struggling to figure out how she was going to pay the bills now that her savings account was depleting at a rapid pace. But that problem pales from this one.

"Grandma, can we watch the movie about the cat that does karate? It looks funny." Alyssa pleads.

"Some levity sounds wonderful right now." With that said, they sit in soothing silence, listening to the whoosh of each car as they pass them. The theatre's location has been in the same spot for over forty years. Agnes pulls into a parking spot and is taken aback by strong memories. Her first kiss was three spots over. More memories flood her mind and before she knows it, she is standing in front of the theatre.

"Alyssa, I need you to help me by reading the next playing time, I forgot my eye glasses."

"Sure. The movie starts at five o'clock."

"Great. That gives us time to enjoy a pizza next door at Ma Ma's Pizzeria." This is the place where she knew, with all her heart, she was going to marry her Charlie. That night she remembered watching the cool breeze sweep his hair over to the side as he opened the door for her. He was so handsome and sure of himself. He was a sweet talker too. The way he said her name as if she were a queen, and there was something about that twinkle in his eye as he watched her walk toward him. He won her heart that night, but she didn't let him know that 'till years later.

As they start walking to the restaurant, Alyssa starts complaining.

"Grandma, my leg hurts."

"Did you hurt it when you fell down the last two steps this morning?" Agnes asks.

"I don't think so. I didn't get hurt from that. That was fun."

"Where does it hurt?" Agnes wonders, as they reach the pizzeria.

"Here, here, and here." Alyssa groans as she points to her ankle, hip, and under side of her knee.

"Honey, it is probably from when you fell this morning. After a good night's sleep, you should be as good as new. Now, how about that pizza you have been wanting with ice cream on the top, was it?"

"No, Grandma not on top! I want ice cream after I finish the pizza!" Alyssa giggles as she looks up at her grandma.

"Ok, let's see if I have your order right, you want onions and pickles on top with sprinkles?"

"Ha ha, Grandma, very funny. You can get that on your pizza, but I want pepperoni on top of mine."

"That sounds good. I think I'll get the same. Let me order for us."

As they sit eating their pizza, Alyssa seems to have forgotten all about her leg pain. School is the topic that fills their dinner conversation. Mrs. Larwiski is the most loved teacher in the whole school and she is going to be Alyssa's 2nd grade teacher next year, hopefully. It all depends on... Agnes decides not to dwell on tomorrow.

"Grandma, are you listening to me? I was asking you if you think I will love Mrs. Larwiski or not? I know I still have to finish first grade, but you know I don't like Mrs. Hanson."

"Yes, sweetie, I am listening and I do think you are going to love her. Mrs. Hanson should have retired already. She is a good teacher, just tired."

"Do you think she will love me like Mommy loves me?"

"Oh honey, how could anyone not love you?" Agnes feels her tongue instantly loose all wetness. She craves water now, but not as much as she desires the right words to say. A single tear falls onto the table, spreading out thinly appearing like some unforeseen force was pressing it down. As Agnes stares at it, she is reminded of her own heart, trampled on for many years by the circumstances of life. Her strength comes from the Lord above, Who's been remolding it gently into His own design, which is wonderfully better, but harder. She knows that He is not yet done with her because this last trial is one of the hardest she has ever faced, the life of her granddaughter, whose fate is cruelly uncertain. Agnes is needed. She hopes that she will be able to endure it and come out greater than gold, but she worries too because she is not young anymore. Her body is old and her mind not as sharp as it used to be.

"Alyssa," Agnes says as she glances at her watch. "How about we go see that movie now?"

"That sounds great, Grandma." Alyssa knows her grandmother isn't going to answer her question. Since she arrived, her grandma didn't answer her when she asked about her mom and she thought now she might just stop asking because it hurt worse when she was ignored.

As the two of them move toward the theatre Agnes couldn't tell whose limping, Alyssa or herself, or possibly it is an unexpected bounce in their step as they remember that they are going to see a funny movie. It's a good day.

These are the streets of long ago friendliness, the streets that linked Agnes' past to her present. She walked them when she was a single teenager with her friends as they made their way to the theatre mimicking her steps today. They were a group of giggly girls snacking on sugary sweets trying hard to keep their voices to a whisper during the production, but usually failed miserably. The movie was soon forgotten, but the fun they had, not.

The class size in school was small, about twenty kids. The wonderful part about school was they were all, mostly, friends. They spent time at each others' houses and in town. One looked out for another also. It was a small town, but there were still accidents and temptations. Their moms all stuck together. If they saw one of them walking on the street, sure enough when that girl arrived home their mom knew all about where they were. Her mom never told her who gave out the information, but that didn't matter because she always let her mom know where she was going and with whom she was with, anyway. But still, she wanted to know who was watching her. Her mom knew almost every time Agnes was walking down Main Street which is where she is now. She walked her own children down this street just about every Sunday before.... We would go to church and then go to Ma Ma's Pizza for lunch and follow that with a movie, if it was rated okay for the kids. Charlie and Agnes loved the tradition, especially since they started it before they were married. It has been awhile since their last stroll here which is probably why she was deep in nostalgia.

The town has changed over the years. The store fronts have all been remodeled and most of them are still owned by the same families from when Agnes was young. The library might even have the same green carpet from when she was a little girl. The Country store still carries a bit of everything, including their high prices. That is to be expected since it is the closest one to the ski resort. Most places in this town make their money during the tourist season. The winter months here are difficult. There isn't much to do in town so when the tourists come and enjoy a day on the slopes, they usually celebrate by drinking heavily at night. It did make for some interesting stories to tell at school, recalling this one guy who....

"Grandma, do you have enough money for the tickets?"

"Yes, dear, why would you ask that?"

"Because the man told you how much it cost about a minute ago and you haven't given him the money."

"Oh, I'm sorry. I must have been day dreaming. Can we also have a bag of popcorn too?"

"Sure." He recalculates the total and says, "That will be $19.50."

"Here you go. Thanks."

"Alyssa, where would you like to sit?"

"Up in front. I love seeing everything so big," she says as she grabs Agne's hand and pulls her inside.

As they meander to the front and sit down, Agnes wishes Charlie was here with them. She could almost feel his arm around her shoulders as she remembered, in years past, him sitting in the very seat that now lay vacant.

Neither of them saw the man that was hiding behind the bushes, watching them earlier as they made their way down the street. He followed several cars behind them as they left Agnes's house, and he also waited for them to finish eating their pizza before the movie started. Now, he's sitting a few rows back showing more interest in the two females in the front row then in the film about the cat.

Chapter 4

Anxiety is a close neighbor of mine. It's always near, usually lying outside my door, tempting me like a friend offering a Twix bar. When it knocks, I greet it with open arms, letting it snuggle around my heart and mind. As it races me through tumultuous emotions, my hands begin to perspire. Sometimes, I wonder if without it I could not function well in such conditions, like the one I am about to enter. One day, maybe, I will be able to explore a time of normalcy during intense situations, but it's certainly not working for my present quandary. I wouldn't know how to function without its presence.

I sit in my car in Ryan's driveway. Wait! My driveway! It's 9:50 a.m. and our meeting begins in ten minutes. The time I spent yesterday with Janice is just a dim memory. My muscles start twitching. My future is in Ryan's hands, which is why I am still here struck with mental paralysis, freezing my next step.

Once I go inside, my identity, the core of who I am, will be compromised. Change doesn't come easy to me. Even when it's my choice to change, it may take many months to succeed at it, if I do, in fact, succeed. When I'm told I have to change, a wall surrounds me, and I close up my emotions, locking them into a deep place within me, where they are safe from harm and touch. I'm not sure if the wall is built from bitterness or fear, maybe a combination of the two or something different altogether. To some, I appear emotionally strong being able to continue through times of trials that would have brought others down. This time I feel parts of myself beginning to chip away. Maybe it's from a life lived with too many difficulties.

As the time ticks to 10:00 a.m., my brain's autopilot comes on and I step from the car. I can do this. The elements of this trial are very different from any I have undergone, but the emotions are the same. From anxiety to numbness, this is where I need to be to survive. It's what I know, and I am good at it. I need to focus on my purpose for marrying. Those reasons need to be at the forefront of my mind.

Ryan stands at the front door shifting his weight from one foot to the next. As I reach him, he steps aside. He doesn't offer his usual warm welcome, which is better. Pleasantries would be fake.

"Is there anything you want to do first before we start?" he asks.

"No. I'm ready," I quickly reply.

"Good. Do you want me to read the first letter again?"

"Please don't. I think I have it memorized, anyway." Every word pulsates through my aching brain. It's true, whether I want it there or not. That letter is what changed my life forever. There's no way to go back to the way things were, my old life. I was in control of my old life. I was the boss and I did whatever I wanted to do. All decisions were mine, or so I wanted to believe. Not that I think Ryan will change that; I haven't noticed him make one decision on his own. I don't know what will be more annoying, his indecisiveness or if he ever made up his mind about something and thought I should agree.

"Okay, April, I'm going to pray first. *'God thank You for never leaving us. It's a true comfort to know that You are always near. I thank You for Your word in Jeremiah that says, You have plans to give me "a future and a hope." 'I know You have one for April and me even though we might not see it yet. I know we are both still in shock over our quick marriage and I pray You help us through each day we have together. I pray that You bless our marriage richly, beyond what we could ask or imagine. We are about to read our second letter. We have both honored the wishes not to read it before we got married and we thought it best to wait until after our honeymoon was over. I don't know what to expect at all, as the first letter was a great surprise, but I know You are in this, and that You are in control. I put my trust in You. I give this day to You. Your will be done.'* April, is there anything you would like to add?"

"Um, no. You covered everything."

"Alright," is all he says as he reaches for the letter that sits on the coffee table. Clearing his throat he starts:

> Dear Ryan and April,
>
> I have waited so long to put the two of your names together, but if you are reading this then it means I will not have had the opportunity to see it. Even so, thank you. I don't know how to repay you. Maybe when you get to heaven I will be able to throw you a big party.
>
> I know my last days with you haven't been cheerful because I have been hiding a secret. I haven't had a lot of time to think this through, but I believe that what I'm about to outline is the best course of action for everyone involved.

I'm truly sorry to turn your lives upside down. You have been great friends as well as family to me throughout my life and I love you both. I have never played matchmaker before. I have known that the two of you were meant to be together. I just wish we had more time for both of you to see it too. I have a strong peace that this is right, and maybe even why….

Please don't be angry with me, but I hope you find it in your heart to forgive me. I have written out a plan for the two of you. Read the first step now and when you complete it, then move on to the next and so on. I know what I am asking is lengthy and will, at times, frustrate the two of you, but please think of my smiling face as you do this because that is what I am doing throughout this night as I write these letters. It is about three in the morning and fatigue has not set in and probably won't until I'm done.

Number 1: Start counseling with a marriage counselor from our church. Her name is Helen Frances. (I know that at least one of you, if not both, would read all my requests so Helen has the rest of the list.)

I want you two to have a happy marriage as I know you will when you let down those walls that have grown around each of your hearts. Helen will help you through this as she helped Phil and me many years ago. Please don't blame her for any of this. She had no idea what was written in her envelope. I don't know if she would have approved or not, but you can ask her that yourself if you want. Even in this challenging time, my heart hasn't felt this much happiness in a very long time. Thank you.

Love,
Nancy

I sit here willing my tears not to fall. My sister, Nancy, means everything to me. She's the person I want to be like. We did everything together. She's my best friend. Even when she was dating Phil, I went along. And they didn't mind, or so she said. The only problem came when he started inviting his brother along too. Those times I found other things to do. Nancy knew I wasn't interested, so she didn't push me into joining them at those times. Dating wasn't my thing.

Oh, Nancy, why? Why aren't you sitting here next to me telling me that this is some practical joke and we could just laugh? But the sad reality is that you are gone. In my mind, I can see your body lying lifelessly there in that hospital bed.

Nancy is, I mean, was beautiful. She had golden brown hair that was the envy of every girl in high school, the way her curls cascaded past her shoulders. It was never too curly and never just wavy, like mine. Her eyes changed colors with whatever she wore that day. The best part about her beauty was that she didn't think she was better than anyone else, even though she was the focus of most eyes when she entered a room.

She was kind and she never expected me to do anything I was uncomfortable doing, until now. I don't understand it. We spent our whole lives respecting each other's space and now she's asking for more than I can give. Why Nancy? She knew I would do anything for her, but still she wasn't self-seeking.

Looking at the letter, I can see that it's her handwriting. Knowing that helps me to continue forward through this bizarre series of events that have radically changed me into someone I'm not. I don't see how Nancy would have wanted that.

I wish I could freeze in time. My anxiety has returned. I expect it to be like a sleep depriving robber leaching away my energy for many nights to follow. I'm sure it will pinch me every time I start to drift off, just like it has this past week.

Counseling? What was she talking about? I don't need counseling! I didn't even go to counseling for my past, so why do I need it now? I don't remember Nancy mentioning she went to counseling. Why did she and Phil need to go? They were so happy together. They were the couple that made me start to think that marriage might not be so bad, until she lost him. Her world shattered that day and I'm not sure she ever recovered.

I forgot Ryan was still in the room. As I glance over at him, I can see that it doesn't matter that I ignored him. His eyes are glazed over as he stares out the window deep in thought. His profile isn't giving away any hints to his own emotions. That's a nice quality to have. Most people can tell what I'm thinking by taking one look at my face.

I know my thoughts have been bouncing back and forth and my emotions are moving twice as fast, but ultimately I will do this for Nancy because she was the one that loved me. She was more than a sister, she was my family. She tried her best to give me a normal childhood. She pushed her own wants aside so that mine could be met.

One year when I wanted a birthday party and mom said we couldn't afford one, Nancy, singlehandedly, put one together. I still don't know where she got the money from. I was turning fourteen and mentioned wanting to see this one movie several times. I'm sure I whined and complained about being poor and never being able to go to the theatre like normal people do. I can't remember the name of the movie now, but the actor was so cute, or so I thought at that age. Every girl in my class was talking about how they were going to see it the moment it came out, which happened to be on my birthday. I was really down that I couldn't go. Nancy asked me to go to the mall with her to pick something up for mom and when we walked by the movie theatre, eight of my friends started screaming, "Surprise."

I was indeed that, and very happy of course. After the movie, we ate dinner at a pizza place and then everyone went to Janice's house for the best slumber party ever. Nancy planned it all. She was always particular about the details, and I don't think she missed one! The cake was amazing, chocolate with chocolate icing, which is still my favorite. That was my first and only surprise party. And I don't need another one because it would never be as good without Nancy here to share it. I can't remember one happy memory that she wasn't a part of.

Mom worked three jobs and was rarely home. She did her best, but money still wasn't plentiful. When I was growing up, my new clothes were Nancy's old ones. Nancy knew this bothered me, so about once a year when Nancy received new clothes, she would secretly ask me to pick out one item that I loved the best. And then, she would stash it in the back of her closet, so mom wouldn't find it, and leave it there until it was too small for her, but fit me. She tried to make sure I had one new outfit a year. She also did the same for Ella, the baby of the family. One year, mom asked her about a skirt that she had put aside for me, so she had to wear it a couple of times so mom wouldn't be suspicious. Nancy took care of me. It wasn't that mom didn't, it was that mom wasn't there. Nancy was my best friend, and now she's…, no I will not think about it. I'm good at avoiding painful things.

I remember one day when I was in middle school, and a boy named Carl kept trying to close my locker the moment I opened it. He would succeed half the time and he would try at least twice a day. I was quite frustrated as the weeks went on and there seemed to be no end in sight. I yelled at him most of the time, and he would laugh and point at me as he walked away, sometimes high-fiving a friend. My patience was gone. The next time he slammed my locker door, my head was in it because I was reaching for a folder. I was livid and hurt. I turned and kicked him as hard as I could with my steel toed cow-girl boot. He started howling and as he turned to hobble away, Nancy was standing there with her foot slightly turned out. To this day, I don't know if she intentionally tripped him or not. He went down hard. That was the last time he ever bothered me. I did see him around school limping a couple times. I wasn't happy that I hurt him. I'm not a vengeful person, but I am glad that he stopped pestering me. Nancy knew the whole time how I was feeling. All she had to do was look at my face to know, but we did share a smile too because no matter what, we stuck together. Now that I think about it, it was just the night before the incident that she gave me her boots saying that she outgrew them, giving me a powerful defense.

"How long do you think her list is?" Ryan asks.

"Uhh. What did you say?"

"I was wondering how long you think her list is?"

"I'm really not sure. She did allude to having a lot to write. What did she say? It had to do with staying up all night?"

"I'm afraid so."

"She used to do that when we were growing up. She was one of those people that could stay up all night and be fine the next day. She would only need to go to bed a little earlier the next night. I was always amazed. I tried to stay up with her once. I fell asleep mid-sentence, sitting up, around three-thirty a.m. and I slept there until noon. She loved to remind me of how silly I looked. As the night progressed, I slowly shifted down the wall until around dawn; I managed to hit the floor. I don't think anyone in the family enjoyed staying up either. She was the only one. Ryan, she might not have stopped writing when the sun came up because she probably wouldn't have needed sleep until that night. What are we going to do?"

"We'll just take it one step at a time, even though this is getting harder now that we know she has more planned for us to do."

"Ryan, look, my hands are shaking. This isn't like Nancy. She never pushed her will on anyone. She wouldn't force me to do something I didn't want to do. She would've talked this through with me and explained her reasoning, but instead she insisted it was the only way and that it had to happen right away! Do you think *he* has anything to do with this? Maybe that's why she insisted we go on the honeymoon. She said our elopement had to look real, but maybe *he* is behind this."

"I really don't know." Ryan adds.

Could *he* have altered her thinking? She was acting out of character the past few days before the accident. She would start talking to me and then stop, and when I would question her, she would change the topic to the weather or something mundane like that. I was thinking that she was going through a tough time missing Phil, but maybe that wasn't it. Maybe *he* got to her too.

This couldn't be coincidental. What did she write in her letters? And how many are there? Right after her accident when we both saw her at the hospital, she asked us to get married to each other right away, again, but this time she said all of us just moving in wouldn't work. She insisted marriage was the only way. She told us a couple of reasons that Ryan and I both agreed with, so that was why we rushed off to elope. She also insisted that I take that honeymoon I have always dreamed of. So we did. The elopement felt right then, like I had a direction and some control in fixing the problems. Somehow I thought it might right my fear-led life. These letters don't sound like her. She was extremely considerate of other peoples' feelings and space, but here she doesn't care about either, very unlike Nancy.

"At a time like this, we need to remember why she asked us to marry. The reasons are valid and this does make sense so far, even the counseling. I think it's a good idea that we see Helen. She can help us through this. She can show us how to make our marriage work," Ryan says almost pleading.

"Don't you think we could just get a book, one that specializes on how to have a happy marriage? Counseling sounds a bit too proactive for me, like we have to be perfect at this when we both know that isn't going to happen. Or, maybe it's too pessimistic, like we need help because we fight all the time, or like we are having the usual marital conflicts, but that's not us either. We aren't even friends yet. I don't see how Helen can help us through this marriage of convenience! What we have is too rare of a problem."

"I see your point, April, but we need to give it a try for those we love. Also, we won't know if she can help us or not if we don't go and see what she has to offer," Ryan points out.

"I don't like the idea of counseling at all. I'll go, but please don't expect more from me than I can give?" I ask.

"That's fair. How about if you start to feel uncomfortable, at any time, we let Helen know and we stop the meeting."

"We can do that?"

"Yes, we can, and we will. If you want, I can talk to her about that when I call her to schedule it."

"That sounds okay." I agree.

The queasiness in my stomach is starting to calm down a bit. Ryan does have a soothing tone when he talks. He's also a quick thinker. I like his suggestions. Hopefully the meeting will go smoothly. If I don't do this soon I will talk myself out of it.

"Why don't we go now, the sooner the better, right? I know normally these things are scheduled, but Helen was such a good friend of Nancy's that I know she will try her best to squeeze us in."

"There is no harm in trying, I guess, and if she isn't free, we can just go out to lunch. It's already eleven, so if she is free we can just have a late lunch after. Do you want to drive or do you want me to drive us?" Ryan asks.

He was on a roll, why the indecisiveness at the end?

"I think it's best if you drive. I'm still a little shaky and I might not be the safest driver right now."

Nancy's plans are draining. I'm so tired. I wish God let her live. Life would be so much better. I haven't talked to mom yet. The last time we talked was before Nancy's surgery. Mom seemed confident that it would go well. She said the doctor informed her that it was a routine surgery. What happened? It was supposed to be uncomplicated? It was just a clot in her leg or something like that. Why hasn't mom called yet? Or for that matter anyone else? Nancy was so young, only two years older than me and I am twenty-eight. How can she be gone?

Chapter 5

Helen has been wrestling with taking an extended vacation from counseling. Each step she takes is a struggle. Receiving Nancy's letter was troubling. She said if Helen was reading it, then something went wrong and that she was dead. Helen visited her in the hospital right before her surgery. The doctor said the risks were minimal.

Helen's husband died two years ago from a long battle with diabetes. Grieving the loss of a loved one, sadly, wasn't new to her. She needs to take time for herself without having to help other people through their problems and life crisis's. She knows she isn't emotionally strong enough for both, knowing she wouldn't be helping to the best of her abilities either.

In Nancy's own way, she was the counselor that Helen relied on, and now she was gone or so the letter says. What an unusual way to announce ones' own death. Nancy loves to write letters. It wasn't abnormal to find a letter in Helen's mail box from Nancy once or twice a month, but not this type of letter?

They understood each other, both becoming young widows at about the same time. There was a connection with Nancy that she never had with any of her other female friends. Most women looked at her as if she should have all of life figured out because that's what she did for a living, right? They either sought her out for help or avoided her altogether because they thought she would try to offer advice. Nancy was the only friend she ever had in her adult life that sought her out for friendship alone. Nancy knew Helen was human and made mistakes like everyone else. She also knew that Helen didn't have all the answers.

Helen wished people at church didn't know what her profession was. She thought if that were true, she would have a friend to call right now. Teetering in the denial stage, not wanting to believe what she just read, but longing for some friendly advice, she decided to go to the hospital. It was the only place to go to find out the truth. She focused on what Nancy would say to her in this moment. Whatever your troubles are, life will keep on going on around you. You need to get down on your knees and pray because when times get tough, He is the One that needs to carry you through. And He will; He is just waiting for you to ask. Don't leave Him to be your last friend to talk to, but make Him your first because He is your best friend. He is truly the only one to understand. Also, ask Him who you should talk to next. After all, that is how I became your friend. Her advice rings loud. Helen just wished she could hear it from Nancy's mouth instead of her own mind. She followed God's advice for a friend, and because of that, Helen was blessed for having Nancy a part of her life, even if it was for only two short years.

God, I believe in miracles. I'm not sure why I don't see Nancy's letter as truth. She can't be dead! I don't have a peace about this. Most don't when they just find out a loved one has past but… oh, I don't know, but You do God and I'll rely on that knowledge. God, I believe in miracles and right now as I get down on my knees, I ask You for one. Please bring Nancy back to me.

She cried out loud over and over again, "I don't doubt You God, I believe." She didn't know how long she stayed there, but her legs were asleep and eyes burned, but her heart was at peace.

There was one area that she wished Nancy would have let her help her in, and that was in relation to her sister. Nancy has overcome a lot of her childhood issues, mainly because of her relationship with God, and her ability to obey God, and forgive her parents, but April has not. She's very independent, carrying herself as if she doesn't need anyone. Nancy knew Helen could help her and she had let Nancy know this on many occasions, but Nancy continued to tell her that it wasn't her place to talk to April about it. When Helen looked at April, she saw her hurt reflecting through her eyes. She respected Nancy's wishes. Helen knew April was coming to see her soon to pick up this envelope Nancy sent to her, but Helen is truly perplexed as to why Nancy didn't send it to April herself.

Helen decides that she needs to talk to her boss, today, about a leave of absence. She knows she cannot work, even though she has a full schedule this afternoon. Her brain isn't functioning normally. Her boss will have to figure out what to do because Helen doesn't even know where to begin. She only knows she has to move fast before her next client shows up.

With one intentional fall after another, she feels each step, as much as she feels her age. She pushes on, grabs her purse and heads to Susan's office. Her hand reaches up to knock as the door opens. Susan stands there studying Helen, which creates an uncertainty in Helen's heart in how to explain this situation to her.

"Come in and sit down. I was just going to your office to talk to you. I have spent the morning reorganizing your schedule. I think you need some time off."

As Helen opens her mouth to speak, Susan interrupts.

"Helen, I will not take no for an answer," Susan says as she walks over to Helen taking the seat to Helen's left and puts her hand gently on her shoulder, "You need time off and honestly, you have no choice. As of right now, you have no more clients. Please understand that I'm doing this for your own good." As she says this, Susan stands and walks behind her desk before continuing. "When I feel you are ready to come back, I will make sure you have most, if not all, of your clients again. But for now, the other counselors have each taken a couple of yours. Don't worry about them working too hard. I have that all worked out. All you have to do is go home. I can drive you there if you like."

"Wait, how did you know I was coming in to ask for time off?"

"I didn't know. You haven't been yourself this week and when I saw you in your office this morning while you were reading your mail, I knew you needed time off. I was coming to say hi, but what I saw told me you needed a vacation! If you want to talk about what is bothering you, please call me and let's get together."

Susan is motherly to most of the employees in the office, but now she seems like she wants to pursue a friendship. Only two people in Helen's life could take charge like this without offending her, Susan and her mom.

"Thank you, Susan. I was just coming to let you know that I can't work right now. I'm pleased you took care of everything. You don't need to drive me home, but thank you for offering though. Here is the key to my filing cabinet. All of my client files are alphabetized. I will stop in sometime to finish up on paperwork, but for now, I am going to hang up my counseling apron. Thanks again."

"You're welcome. Call me if you want to talk."

"Okay."

After leaving Susan's office, she remembers the letter Nancy wrote is still on top of her desk. She backtracks to her office to grab it before going out to the car. On the envelope, Nancy had written,

"Please open when April comes to see you. Love, Nancy."

She would love to read Nancy's letter, but would wait until April is with her. Today might be the day that they finally get to know each other a bit.

Taking a quick glance around the office, she's satisfied that there isn't anything else she needs to bring home. Having her clients all taken care of unwrinkled some tension from her mind. Now she could focus on herself. She longs to find out what happened and why no one called her to let her know it happened.

Her hands tremble as she rereads Nancy's first letter to her while she sits in her car trying to work up enough energy to walk into the hospital. Confusion floods her mind. Nancy was in good health when she saw her after the accident. Helen desperately tried to remember what Nancy said to her during that visit, but the only parts she could remember were Nancy saying that her mom was taking care of everything and that she was just happy to feel safe. She smiled after that and said how the doctor was confident that everything should go smoothly.

Did she say safe? Why didn't Helen pick up on that earlier? If she felt safe in the hospital, then what made her feel unsafe before the hospital? Helen needs to find that out, but how? Adrenaline, her natural caffeine boost, jump starts her mind as she rushes out of her car and heads to Nancy's room, thinking someone must have an explanation.

Chapter 6

"**R**yan, do you mind if I wait in the car while you run in and find out if she's here?"

"I don't mind at all. I'll be right back."

There isn't a cloud in the sky. Normally I would enjoy a day like this, the sun beaming down its warmth upon me through the frosted window. I think I'll just rest my head back for a little while. Groggy, I roll on to my side, I open my eyes to find Ryan staring right at me.

"Huh! You startled me. I didn't hear you get back into the car. Did I fall asleep?"

"Yes."

"How long was I asleep for?"

"About an hour."

"What? Why didn't you wake me?"

"You looked like you needed your sleep. You looked so peaceful, like Sleeping Beauty. I just couldn't wake you."

Creepy tingles race up my arm. I hope he wasn't watching me sleep the whole time.

"Is Helen available?"

"Actually, no. She has taken a leave of absence. Do you know what her home address is?"

"No, I don't, but I know where we can go to get it," I answer hesitantly.

* * *

Nancy kept her phone book in her purse. This day is getting more trying by the minute. I wish one part of all this would unfold easily. Having to look through Nancy's purse will be difficult, but to hold the pages of her phone book in my hands will be even harder. To read the names of the people she found important enough to write down, people she loved and communicated with. But the most challenging part is where we have to go to get the phone book.

Fear isolates me. When I think I have a grasp on it, it easily unfolds my hold. Sometimes when thoughts come in, I let my mind focus in on them. I could be thinking about getting into a car accident the next time I get into a car, or that someone close to me will decide I am not worth having around anymore. Once the thought enters, obsession follows, and I start to make up several different scenarios, from worst case to best. Depending on my mood, it might go from bad to worse instead of any form of improvement at all.

I know fear is what traps me from accomplishing things. Like when I started learning how to play the piano in college. There was a hall of small rooms each housing a piano. At first, I enjoyed going there to practice. It was fun. I usually went at night because I knew I had a better chance of being the only one using them. The music was starting to click and I felt such a wonderful thrill playing as my fingers moved, to me, effortlessly across the keys. It was freeing. I felt that I was laying down all my worries and I was living outside of the fear that traps me most of my waking life. My mind wasn't taking hold of any debilitating thoughts, but focusing on the music and I was free to love it, until that one night it all came to an end.

I heard the laughing, echo through my room; I turned to see my roommate and her friend laughing and pointing at me. My stomach churned. My palms became very slippery and my heart longed to jump out of my chest. That was the last time I played the piano. I couldn't take that humiliation again.

I think my most gripping fear started many years ago. I stopped leaving my house. I thought something bad would happen to me, so I stayed home as much as possible. I didn't have many friends, but the ones I did have, came over any time they wanted to. Janice was my housemate then and Nancy and other family members lived close by, stopping over almost every day. It happened naturally. I didn't cook and Janice was particular about brands of food she wanted for the week, so she did the grocery shopping. I was laid off from my job due to downsizing, so I didn't have to leave for work. I wasn't anti-social, just afraid. This went on for about eight months before Janice started asking questions. She was concerned. She would invite me out to the movies. I would tell her to pick one up on her way home and we could order in. She did that a couple of times until she became very insistent that I go out with her. I refused. She practically dragged me to her car one night. When we were both in the car, she drove down the street to the corner coffee shop and waited.

I wanted to run back home and slam the door behind me, but I knew she wouldn't let me get away with that, so I sat there looking through the rearview mirror making sure no one was there. I gripped the door handle 'till my knuckles were white and I left them that way. I was afraid, terrified actually. My breathing was shallow and quick. I knew I was having a panic attack. Janice knew too. She started the car and drove me home. She helped me inside and told me we were going to do that again tomorrow. And we did. I went more willingly the next time, accepting that I had a problem, but after sitting in the car for a few minutes, I started having another panic attack. She continued to take me out every day for the rest of that month. I was able to go out longer each time. By the end of the month, I had a bit of fun when we went out, and a little less fear. I was confused when she didn't suggest it the next day. She said that it was time I took a walk by myself. We argued; something we did often. She said I was ready to go by myself, I said no. She countered with a cluck, clucking sound, and I retaliated by walking to the corner by myself. My pride was what moved my feet.

Why do I go from one extreme to the other? Thinking back to my childhood I can't remember my parents praising me ever for a job well done.

Do I remember them clapping for me when I did well (whether it be a great game on a sports team or a well written poem)? Did anyone ever tell me that I was smart? Pretty? Do I remember them truly believing that I was good at something? Anything? I don't have one single memory of being praised. What do I remember? I remember being yelled at when I dropped the eggs on the floor when I was trying frantically to help put the groceries away, and when I didn't do my chores the right way. I remember being slapped across the face for making too much noise. I remember being told in so many ways that I wasn't good enough and that I would always manage to mess things up. I was called fat, clumsy, dumb, and pig-headed. I had and still have no self-esteem. I also know that I don't know what I'm good at and what I enjoy.

I spent my life worrying about how my actions affected those around me. My fear holds me captive because if I enjoy something, I won't be able to handle the results of being told that I'm not good at it. It has been better not to try, instead of having that knot producing feeling knowing that I am a failure. Someone once told me that failure is not trying at all. So I guess I am good at one thing.

When I make a new friend, I let them down right away. When we have made plans to go somewhere, I'll either show up very late or cancel last minute. I find it easier this way because then they will know that I'm not a reliable person. It is better to let them see the real me instead of trying to be someone I'm not. My logic is skewed, but I also know most peoples' are also. I am stuck, but I don't want Helen's help. It's better to fail Ryan too, instead of thinking that there's any serious hope for us to have a good marriage. I'll let Ryan down, but the question I will be trying to answer now is how?

For the moment, I need to remember that feeling of accomplishment when I walked down that sidewalk. I was able to do it then and I can do this now, for Nancy. I am unsure of what to make of Ryan's presence. He isn't someone I would turn to for comfort. I think it's best if I ignore him when we get there. My plan is to quickly look through her purse, if it's still there, find the address, and leave. I think that's the best course of action, or maybe it's my only one, because I don't have time to formulate another.

Ryan parked the car and is now walking around to the other side to open my door. I do like that he does that. It makes me feel special. I thought it was stupid before when I saw other men open doors for women. It gave the impression that they were too weak to do it themselves. I was wrong; it just makes a woman feel treasured.

As we walk through the doors and up the stairs, I know this is the last place I want to be. How am I going to face…?

"April, this is the room. Do you want me to go in with you or do you want me to wait out here?"

"Please, wait out here," I could hear my voice say as I turn the knob and step into the room. There she is. Lying there with all those tubes connected to her tricking me into thinking they are doing something substantial to keep her alive. It's hard to believe; as I look at her, she looks alive. Her chest rises and falls. Her heart is beating. Her skin has color. She has to be alive.

"Nancy, it's me, April. Can you hear me?" I say as I rush to her side.

Nothing happens. She doesn't turn her head or move her fingers. If only she would open her eyes, then everything would go back to normal.

"Nancy, I need you. You have to open your eyes and talk to me. I can't go on like this anymore. You're supposed to be home living your life, and smiling, and baking your terrific chocolate cookies. Please, wake up."

I don't know when I started crying, but the wetness was soaking through the bed sheets. I can't take this anymore. I can feel the warmth of her hand in mine.

I grab her by the shoulders and gently start shaking her. She has to wake up. She has to.

"Nancy, come on, wake up. Please, Nancy, please. Please, wake up."

I've lost track of my days. Nancy's accident propelled us into a quick elopement. I was afraid that something worse would happen and after receiving her letter now, it did. When Ryan and I received Nancy's letter, I called the hospital. My little sister answered the phone and I asked, "Where's Nancy?"

"She's gone."

"What?" I scream.

"No, she's...." Her voice faded and I dropped the phone. I couldn't believe it. The letter was true. Two short words changed my life just like two other short words that changed where I live.

I hear the door open from the bathroom that was adjoining Nancy's room, but I don't care what anyone thinks. I'm not letting go. She was still here, alive. I didn't want to see her after the surgery because I thought it would have been too hard, so I set my mind to fulfill Nancy's request.

"I miss her too."

I turn to look at who owns the voice while still clinging to Nancy.

"Do I know you?" abruptly spoken, in hopes to cue the intruder that this is my time with my sister.

"Yes, I believe you do. My name is Helen Frances. I'm a good friend of Nancy's."

"Oh, wow! I came here to get your address from Nancy's phone book. She said I needed to go and see you. Umm, I mean we needed to go and see you. What I mean is, before her surgery...."

I can't say anything else as my arm sweeps to Nancy's bed. There she lay sleeping. How could they tell me she was dead? Her chest rises on its own. As I hold her hand, my thoughts continue to jump from one place to the next. Helen put her arm around my shoulders. That's all the encouragement I need. As a child runs and cries to her mother when she's hurt, I embrace Helen and sob. Nothing else matters. This pain is so great and through this hug I know that Helen understands. We don't need words to know how the other is suffering. If I could, I would thank Nancy for sending me to Helen. Already she has helped me, and our words have been few. I'm thankful she didn't send me to some wacko super religious freak.

"Umm, Ryan is waiting in the hallway. I don't know if you are available to help us. Nancy apparently stayed up all night the night before the surgery writing letters." I blow my nose.

"Anyway," I say between sniffles, "she asked us to see you for some form of counseling. I don't think we really need it, because we don't have the usual struggles most married couples have. We aren't even friends yet."

Helen put her hand up.

"Wait. You need to back up a little. Why did you two get married if you aren't even friends?"

"Nancy never mentioned any of this to you?"

"No, Nancy has never mentioned that you married a man you don't like. She actually didn't tell me that you were married."

"Wow. I thought she would have talked to you about her plan. Ok, I'll start from the beginning. Nancy stayed up all night the night before her surgery writing letters."

"I received a thick envelope at work, but my letter inside said not to open it until you came to see me," Helen adds.

"That's one of the letters she wrote that night. The first of the letters asked Ryan and me to marry. She listed her reasons, which are...."

I don't know how much time I spent with Helen, but when we exit the room I see Ryan sitting slumped in a chair, with his feet resting on the table in front of him. His mouth was slightly agape and his hair a bit unruly. Cute. This is the first time I have seen him asleep. At least he isn't drooling, or passing gas in his sleep, or whatever it is that wives complain their husbands do. He looks peacefully cute, not at all what he looks like when he's awake.

I must have been standing there for a bit because when I glance at Helen, she's staring at me with a quizzical smirk.

"Don't you think you should wake him up?"

"Yes, of course." Now how am I supposed to do that? I would prefer to just yell for him to wake up, but that wouldn't be nice. (Not as rude as kicking his chair, right?) Oh, I couldn't do either of those. I'll just sit next to him and hope that the noise I make will wake him. Ok, here I go. I'm walking and he isn't waking. I sit down and he isn't waking, and Helen is still watching. I think I'll just tap him on the shoulder.

"Ryan, I found Helen," I say as I put my hand on his arm. He still isn't moving. I lean forward so that my face is close to his ear and I say, "Ryan." Next thing I know, his arms wrap around me.

"I've been waiting for this for so long. You feel so good in my arms."

The shock of the moment is slow to erase. How did I get in his arms and when did he start to smell so good? Wait, I shouldn't be here. I jerk upward into a standing position.

"What did you say?" I rub my neck as my head tilts to the side. A small part of my light blue skirt is stuck under Ryan. Hoping no one notices, I pull it a couple of times which thankfully frees it.

"Oh, nothing, I was dreaming an amazing dream. Sometimes I take a while to wake up. Sorry about that, it won't happen again," he says as he stands, stretching his arms high into the air.

"Ok, Ryan, I found Helen."

"Helen? Oh, hello, Helen. It's great to see you!" Ryan offers his hand to Helen and she shakes it. Then Ryan leans close to my ear to ask, "How long was I sleeping?" He shifts his weight back and forth then comments to Helen, "We only came here to get your address, not summon you."

"I was here visiting Nancy when you both arrived."

"Oh. Did April fill you in as to why we need to talk to you?"

"Yes, and if it's ok with the two of you, we can reconvene at my house in two hours. I need to do a couple of things first, and then I'll be ready. Why don't you two go get lunch and then meet me at my house?"

"That's a great idea, I'm famished," Ryan says as he runs his fingers through his hair. I do like his hair, it's....

"Helen, do you mind if we meet back here at the hospital? I don't want to be far from Nancy. I know we went to Hawaii because Nancy said that we should go to make our marriage look genuine, but when we agreed, we thought Nancy was just having minor surgery. Then we get her letter and when Ella said she was gone, we thought dead. Now I'm not sure what the truth is. She's still breathing, so I don't want to leave her."

"I like that idea better too, April. Sure, I still need a couple of hours."

"Ok. See you soon Helen."

"Oh, wait, do you mind stopping by my house and picking me up first? I live close to the hospital. My car is acting up again, and I don't want to use it much."

"No, we don't mind," I say as she jots down her address for us. Not sure what Ryan thought, but I can't imagine him being upset about it.

* * *

"Did you enjoy your sandwich?" I ask. I've been trying to talk to her since we arrived at the sub shop, but April seems to be distracted or just uninterested in talking to me. I don't know her well enough to ask what's wrong, so I just continue with the simple questions.

"Yes, it was good." Her monotone barely audible, she reaches for her wallet. How should I respond to this?

"April, you are not going to pay for your meal," I say with gentle authority.

"Why not?" she comments defensively as she reaches into her purse pulling out the check she wrote this morning for rent.

"Because we're married now. I'll pay. Are you ready to go?"

"Not yet. First, I want to give you this check for rent."

"Rent, what do you mean a check for rent? Here, let me have that." I could feel my cheeks grow warm. Is she trying to insult me or is this a test? As I take the check, I rip it in half and stuff it into my pocket. Many words were exchanged, some out of anger, others out of confusion, and some out of despair. She had a lot to say and so did I. I didn't know what was better, first her apathy or then her anger, probably her anger because at least there was some emotion involved. I tried four or five different ways to explain why she wasn't going to pay rent and in her eyes, she shot down each one.

I need some time to think. Our car ride to Helen's house is grippingly chilled as we ignore each other. She's not going to be the first to break the silence and apparently, neither am I.

* * *

The porch creaks from baring our weight. I hope it will hold us just a little longer until Helen answers the door. Paint is peeling off the window sills and the screen door is hanging on by only one hinge. I remember Nancy mentioning that Helen lost her husband a while ago. And now she lost her close friend; she's hurting too.

The icicles hanging down from the gutters are of mammoth length stretching down upon their intruders who long to emerge past the chilling sharpness they exude. I jump as wetness cascades down my neck. The freezing water shocks me; the icicle seems to be declaring its territory. It left its mark; my heart's pounding in my chest. I raise my fist and knock hard hoping that Helen will quickly open the door. If she doesn't, I think I'm going to head back to the car. A hot chocolate would help warm me up, but not calm my pulse.

"Do you think we have the wrong house?"

"I don't think so, but maybe the doorbell is bro…."

The door flies open and before Helen could say a word, I race into the entryway pulling Ryan behind me. I don't know when I grabbed his hand or why it feels natural, but at least we're safe physically. The safety of our emotions is questionable now that we have entered the counselors' house. Before a word could exit Helen's mouth, a two foot icicle comes crashing down right where we were just standing. I was about to apologize for our entrance, but I see that it isn't necessary.

"WWWow, that was close. I'm so sorry about that. I didn't know I was supposed to clean out the gutters until last week when the snow started to melt and then the temperatures dropped. It's one of those house things Fred always did and I never thought about. I'm truly sorry, I had no idea they would crash down like that. Are you ok?"

"No harm done. That might be one of the reasons you have icicles, but most likely there's heat escaping into your attic and that's what's melting the snow. The temperatures outside are freezing it back up into ice. I can come back at a later time and have a look at it," Ryan says as he sweeps his briefcase over his head and starts hitting the icicles down. I should have waited in the car.

"That should be safe until tomorrow if we have another day like today. Do you have a back door you could use until all the ice melts?"

"Yes. I could go through the garage."

"Good."

"Thank you, Ryan. Please, come in and have a seat in the living room. I'll be right back; I just need to get us some hot chocolate. It's exactly what Nancy would ask for on a day like this and after what you two just went through, I insist." She left without waiting for our reply.

I could hear cups clanking together in the kitchen. Glancing around, I try to find something to say to Ryan to ease the tension from our fight earlier. This is crazy that I'm here meeting with a counselor, a marriage counselor. I broke my promise to myself.

When I was 22 years old, I promised myself that I would remain single for the rest of my life. I didn't want a marriage like my parents had. I knew my dad had problems because he was always in a bad mood. They seemed fine, but then he just walked out.

I have always wondered if he has another family out there. Do I have other siblings that I don't know about? Will I ever see him again? Does he care about me? Does he ever regret leaving? I have so many questions that I long to have answered, but I have settled in my mind that they will live on remaining the way they are, certainly unresolved.

THOSE TWO LITTLE WORDS

Marrying someone opens up the possibility to bring this hurt to children. I can't ever trust a man enough to believe that he would stay faithful and remain married to me. My mom was a great woman before he left and if she couldn't make him stay, there's no chance I could. She filled our home with laughter and singing. She comforted and loved us through our, seemingly at the time, end of the world, tough, problems. She was available whenever we needed her and after he left, she was never around. It was as if we lost both parents that year. I understand now that she had to work, but then I was so confused. The loneliness that erupted in my heart took control, sliding me into a deep depression. I was 13 when he left. I stopped eating and avoided my friends. Janice was the only one that I let in, besides my older sister. It took great strength for me to converse with them and our conversations were not as fun- filled as they used to be. That was a time that I might have needed a counselor, not now.

Coming out of my thoughts, I see that I must have missed something between Ryan and Helen because they are both staring at me, with raised eyebrows.

"Helen, this is what I'm talking about. I try to have conversations with her, but it seems that she is so lost in her own thoughts that I end up talking to myself."

"April, what were you just thinking about?" Helen inquires.

"Umm, nothing big, just my past; I was also thinking that counseling might be a waste of time. Nancy has wanted me to see someone for years. Why don't we just go to the hospital so we can start and get this over with?"

"Okay, but first do you want whip cream on your hot chocolate?"

"Oh, I forgot." Groaning inwardly, "Yes, thank you. You're right; this is exactly what Nancy would have done. She was constantly taking care of other peoples' needs." We chatted a little bit, but all of our minds were at the hospital. Quickly, finishing our drinks, we started walking to the car. Helen has a way of making our awkward situation bearable, but the majority of the trip is made in silence. She does live within five minutes of the hospital, fortunately.

* * *

"Ryan, please tell us a little bit about yourself," Helen asks as she adjusts her skirt in her chair. We are back at the hospital sitting in a semi-circle around Nancy's bed, not sure I'm going to pay much attention to this conversation. I'd prefer to hold Nancy's hand.

"Sure. I grew up here in Windham, New York. I went to the same public school as Nancy and April. I was a year ahead of April so we weren't in any classes together. I did the usual guy things, played soccer and basketball, and went to the usual hangouts with friends. Then I went to the University of Albany. After graduating, I started working in the family business."

"What's the family business?"

"Mostly, we run a construction company. My dad and Phil taught Nick and me everything we know. It's great working with Dad. But we all miss Phil. No one could ever replace him."

"He was a great man, just like my Fred. I'm glad they were both strong Christians and I long for the day I can see them again," Helen whispers as she glances up at Nancy.

"Me too. I'm very thankful for that also. Phil encouraged me in my faith daily. He wouldn't let me settle for second best, either. He said God deserved the best."

"I agree. God does deserve our best. Was there something specific you are referring to that he wouldn't let you settle for?"

"Yes, there is. But, uh, I don't think now is the right time for me to share that; maybe when we all feel more comfortable around each other," Ryan replies.

I'm sure he is referring to me. I don't blame him for being uncomfortable around me, sharing deep personal issues, but I wouldn't be truthful if I said I'm not curious. I bet it has to do with the woman in his letter, the one he calls 'his girl.'

"I can respect that, but I do have one more question first. Did you listen to his advice or not?"

"That's a very hard question to answer. I'd like to think so, but I'm not sure. I have spent time trying to imagine what he would say about my choices over the past two years. I hope in some areas I would have made him proud. I am unsure about how he would feel about my most recent choices, and I have longed for just one last conversation with him to find out. I guess I'll never know the answer to that question. He did seek God for answers and I hope that in my seeking, I have heard correctly and not what I just wanted to hear instead."

"I hope so too. April, how do you like married life?"

"I'm not sure how to answer that." She has an interesting strategy, probably switching topics like this to get an honest response from me.

"There is no wrong answer, just tell us the first thing that comes to your mind about your marriage."

"Loneliness." Why did I say that? I shouldn't have answered truthfully. There must be a trick to counseling, one where I could make her think that everything is great and that these meetings are pointless.

"Good."

"It is?"

"Yes. I was expecting you to not respond so honestly. I'm very glad you did. The more you do that, the faster we can get to work on your marriage and make it a marriage you have always dreamed of."

"That would be impossible because I have always dreamed of never getting married." I need to keep my mouth shut, what is going on with me?

"Even before your dad left?" Helen gently inquires.

"I thought counseling was supposed to help me feel better, not worse." Here I go again.

"Sometimes you have to feel, whether it is happy, sad, or another emotion to move past the hurt you have stored deep inside you to experience the joy of forgiveness and freedom."

"What if that is something I don't want? What if I am happier leaving it all alone?"

"Are you happy in your loneliness?"

"No, but it's what I'm used to and that comfort does make me happy." Helen's eyebrows raise. I know she doesn't believe a word I just said, maybe I don't either.

"Okay. Do you know when Ryan's birthday is?"

"No, I don't. But I don't think he knows when mine is either. Am I right Ryan?"

"April, your birthday is May 1st." Ryan puts his hands on his knees as he sits upright.

"How'd you know that?"

"I think everyone that knows you has heard the story of how your mom loves the name April, but your dad said they couldn't name you that because you were supposed to be born in April. He felt that they should name you May instead. Your mom didn't like the name May, and so the story goes that even though she was in labor, she willed it away until April 30th. She managed to wait until 12:01 a.m. May 1st and so your name became April June Peterson. Your dad took one look at you and agreed with your mom that you looked like an April and not a May."

"I didn't know people talked about how I got my name." This is getting too personal. "Wow, look at the time. I think we covered a lot in counseling, so Helen do you think we can look at what the next step is?"

"Alright. I've been eager to open that envelope since I received it, but first we need to discuss homework and scheduling."

"Homework?" we both say in unison.

"What do you mean by homework?" Ryan sits rubbing his hands together until only white is present. I reach out to stop him, but he misinterprets it as a gesture of comfort for he pulls my hand gently in between his and starts massaging it methodically. Goosebumps tingle up my arm and throughout my body. This needs to stop. As I jump up out of my chair, I notice that Helen's eyes are focusing on our hands.

"Helen, are you going to put us through more than we can handle right now? Please don't give us something else to do. My thoughts are all over the place. I'm not sure I can do another thing."

"Your homework is necessary, but also an everyday action and shouldn't be adding extra pressure to your life. I understand how you're grieving, but this will help you. You two need to spend at least thirty minutes a day talking to each other, and because you have so much on your mind April, it should be easy, just say what's on your mind, out loud, to Ryan. It will help the two of you process your feelings, also. With that said, I think we should meet again in a couple of days. Are you free Friday, around seven?"

"That works for me, how about you, April?" Ryan asks, turning to me.

"Yes, that should work fine," I choke out. More counseling? I thought we were going to just meet once and that would be it. This is spiraling me down a long tunnel of superfluous feelings.

"April, here is Nancy's letter to you." My fingers tremble as I break the seal, inside sit three smaller envelopes, numbered 1st, 2nd, and 3rd. I hand the one that said 1st to Ryan and I give the other two back to Helen. I know if I keep them I will tear them into tiny pieces so that no one could read its contents. I guess I should be thankful that was all there was inside, but the dread that has now settled upon my heart is a sign that these three letters would accomplish all that Nancy wants anyway. My life is no longer mine. Decisions are being made for me, and all I have to do is play the character, reading the script that has been written for me. In a way, this feels normal. In past, others have chosen my course through major life events that I had no control over. There usually was someone else narrating for me no matter how hard I tried to do it myself. When I think I finally accomplished taking control over my life, a hand grabs a hold and shakes my world, like one does a snow globe, and I'm left to pick up the pieces. I need to push through this time, until I get to the side where I am left alone with just the pieces. I hope this time that hand doesn't shake too hard.

The letter reads:

My Dearest April and new brother, Ryan,

I have longed for the day when you became a part of the family. If you are reading this, then I must have passed on. I wished to hold your hands as you two went through this, but I am very confident that Helen will see you through to a world of happiness. She's very good at what she does. April, please do not give her a hard time. Remember that she is my closest friend, and I hope over time she will become dear to you too. You have to let her and Ryan, for that matter, into your heart. They will seek your best interest and love you throughout this ordeal. I am proud of you April for going to counseling. I know it's very hard for you. Thank you. I hope one day you will feel thankful too.

I believe the next best step for you two is to learn how to communicate. Spend time talking to each other every day and eat as a family. April, I know cooking isn't your thing, but it's Ryan's. He loves to cook so, please, let him. After you have come to like your conversations together and you long for that connection, move on to envelope two. It's best April, if you give Helen the other two envelopes now because I know you are probably ready to throw them in the fireplace.

I know I have taken control over your life and for that I am truly sorry. I wished it didn't have to happen this way, but I know in the end this will work. Time was running out so we needed to move fast. I am very glad you listened to me and eloped. How was the honeymoon? When this is all over I would like for the two of you to go on a real one, but I will leave that up to you. Again, I wish it didn't have to happen this way, but the control was out of my hands too. I hope you can see that.

I love all three of you and I hope you seek God in this time. Even now, when it seems like I am in control, in actuality He is, in fact, in control, no matter what we think. My prayer is that we all learn to trust Him through this time.

Love,

Nancy

Ryan places the letter back in the envelope and gently puts it on the table. The pin never drops, but the silence does echo. We just stare at the letter. These letters are her last words to us.

"Do you think she can hear us?" I'm not sure who I'm asking, but I hope she can. When I saw her this morning, she looked like she could hear.

"I'm not sure," Helen says.

Ryan rubs his hand over his five o'clock shadow. He shrugs his shoulders and puts his hands in his pocket. He also doesn't know what to say.

"Helen, we'll see you Friday. Thank you for meeting us on such short notice. We will start our homework tonight over dinner. Are you both ready to go?"

"Yes, I am," I say as I squeeze Nancy's warm hand one more time, bending down and kissing her brow I whisper, "I love you Nancy, wake up, ok?"

"Me too," Helen says as she says her own good-bye on the other side of the bed.

Leaving, we walk to the car in silence, but not the awkwardness we've shared so much lately. Maybe I'm tired. Ryan drives us home, first to Helen's house then ours, but as I reach for the door knob, Ryan gently puts his hand on my arm.

"April, I'm sorry about our argument earlier. Can you forgive me?"

"Yes, Ryan, I do, and can you forgive me for yelling at you?"

"Yes. I know we are both worn now, but later can we calmly discuss what we were both upset about? I really want us to figure out a fair solution to that problem."

"That sounds fine." My voice barely audible as I realize the earlier tension has evaporated as his gentleness soothes.

"Okay, good. It's 3 p.m. and I have some work to do at the office. Do you mind if I head there now and we have dinner together tonight at seven? I know it's late, but I need to catch up on a few things. I can make it back home around six to start dinner. Is that okay with you?"

"Yes, that's great. I want to stop at Janice's for a bit." The space he's providing me, I greatly appreciate.

Chapter 7

"Janice, I can't believe he won't let me pay for anything. I tried to give him rent money at lunch today and we had our first major argument. He tore the check in half. He said that this is not the way a marriage works. I told him, maybe a little too loudly, that I agree, we don't have a proper marriage. And guess what? He blew up again. The only words I heard next were 'Phil,' and 'why this way,' and then something about 'trying.' I was really confused because we don't love each other, so I assumed we would try to live as housemates. How else would we live? Then, the most unusual thing happened. We started talking like friends. In general, I have a tough time conversing with the opposite sex and there we were, sitting opposite each other at the table, and I somehow let him know that I was truly perplexed and didn't understand what he meant. He surprised me by leaning over, and gently taking my hand in his, and he started to explain how marriage is based on love, and how he hopes that I could choose to love him someday. And then, I erupted."

"My defenses went right back up. I will not let him trick me into loving him when he has no intention of loving me. I told him it takes two to make that choice, so don't go preaching to me when you haven't made that choice yourself. Janice, isn't he unbelievable!"

Janice's face reveals concern. She opens her mouth, but closes it quickly. And then opens it again saying, "You said that to him? I'm speechless."

"Yes, I did and it felt good too."

"Why?" Janice inquires.

"You will understand when I tell you what he did next. He just stood up and said that I had a point and something else that I couldn't make out. He started walking to the car. We went straight to counseling from there and boy do I have an earful for you."

I went on for a long time. It felt good to talk about this with someone who wasn't immediately involved. Janice is such a good friend to me.

"Oh, I almost forgot. When we arrived back home, he put his hand on my arm and asked me to forgive him for his part in the argument, and I did. I felt compelled to ask for forgiveness also."

"Janice, forgiving someone was really, umm, how would I describe it? It was like I could breath fully again. Weird, huh?"

"No, April that's not weird at all. I'm glad you two resolved your argument, that's great!" The warmth of her smile is refreshing.

"Yeah, it is. Now all I have to do is find a way out of this counseling," I comment.

"Ok, but since there isn't a way out right now, why don't you tell me about what Helen assigned for homework?" Janice asks.

"How do you know we have homework?" I question.

"The whole church knows she loves to give homework. She believes that if a couple doesn't learn how to communicate well, they will endure hardships that could have been easily prevented. So, what is it?"

"Alright, I'll tell you. We have to talk to each other for at least a half hour each day. That's more than I talk to you!" I say crossing my arms.

"Do you have a list of questions for each other?"

"No." My arms are still crossed.

"Great! Then that's what we can do now."

"No thank you. I know enough about Ryan from when I went to high school with him. He was the cute athletic boy that all the girls talked about, all but me."

"I don't understand you April. He is really cute and the few times I've talked to him, he has been very kind. Anyway, let's start.

"Number 1: What do you do for a living?" Janice starts as she eases into her computer chair.

"Number 2: Do you like your job?"

"Number 3: How long have you been working there?

"Number 4: What is your favorite color?

"Number 5: What is your favorite animal?

"Number 6: What is your favorite season and why?

"Number 7: How many serious relationships were you involved in?"

At this point I know Janice's 'first child syndrome' has taken over and there is no stopping her bossy, controlling personality. So, I do what I normally do when she gets this way, I join her. Maybe a little bit of me was curious to know the answers to some of them.

"How many of them did you truly love?"

"I like that one." Janice smiles, glad that I'm finally interested, or maybe that I have put my arms down.

On we went, back and forth for the next twenty minutes or so, until Janice had to start pushing my buttons again.

"April, how about we make a deal? The next time I go out on a date, I ask some of these questions and I will seriously try to get to know the man, as long as you ask Ryan these questions, with the same open mind and try to get to know him." Janice tries earnestly.

I'm not going to tell Janice that I'm already planning on asking these questions because we do have to talk for a long time each day, but I don't want her knowing that.

"Janice," her name hisses out of my mouth. "Why do you have to insist I do something with Ryan every time I see you? Can't we just talk about, oh, anything, but Ryan?"

"Yes, we can. Once you agree to this, I will make a point to only talk about Ryan when you bring him up first. Okay? You ask him these questions, all of them, and when you're finished, I will stop asking you what the two of you are doing or not doing." She folds her hands in front of her with a proud smirk on her face.

"Are you telling me the truth? Do you really mean that if I ask him these questions, you will stop your attempts to force me to do what I don't want to do and our conversations will be normal again?"

"Let me see if I understand you correctly. You mean, no talking about how you spend more time here than you do at your own home, no mention of how you avoid him, or what you two talked about for your homework the night before…." Janice says in between laughs. "I'm just joking with you, April. I understand and yes, I will tone it down, a lot. Ok?"

"Good. Then you have a deal. I would do almost anything to get you to stop."

"Oh, if I knew that, I would have said that you need to kiss him good night tonight also."

Now that is a topic I don't want to discuss.

"Haha. That's enough. You had your fun, but now you're going too far. I think I'm going to leave." Picking up my bag, I close the front door behind me with Janice's irritating laughter following me….

Driving, I realize that I cannot go anywhere anymore without Ryan coming up. Either I am home and see him, or the people I know ask me how he is. When I say, 'he's fine,' that isn't enough and they (mostly Janice) barrage me with more questions. They question me about love and about the quick marriage. I know that in the future everywhere I go in this town, I'm going to be forced to hear his name. That's the problem with living in a small town, everyone knows everything about you and if they don't, they will try to pry it out of you. I can't even escape him at the grocery store. Even now, my own thoughts are betraying me for they are focusing on him too. This is very frustrating. The man all the girls in high school swooned over, except me. My memories of him are of an arrogant and cocky boy who thought he was better than everyone else. He was good at every sport he played, maybe the best on his team, but that didn't give him the right to consider himself above the rest of us. I realize I'm exhausted.

I think when I get home I will take a nap and try not to dream of him. I think Nancy knew what a difficult time I would have over her death, that she created this distraction for me! It's almost working.

Chapter 8

Looking through Nancy's home is necessary. I'm obsessed with her letter and the assumption that she would be dead if we were reading it, than she was, sort of. There was more to it than her attention to detail. I wish I could make sense out of this. Nancy knew something was going to happen to her and that's why she called us both to her house in a panic last week. When April and I were settled on her couch, she began to explain that she needed to provide for Alyssa. She said that since Phil's death she has been struggling to make ends meet, but Nancy didn't tell us the full story. Thinking back, there has to be some details missing.

"Ryan and April," Nancy began, "next week I'm going to declare bankruptcy. I have looked at this from every angle and I know this is my only choice. The reason I asked you both to come over here is because I need your help. Please hear me out fully before you walk out that door. I'm not expecting you to give me an answer today, either. I'd prefer you think about it first and we can talk more tomorrow.

"Alyssa and I need a place to live. Ryan, you have a wonderful relationship with Alyssa. I greatly appreciate all the time you have spent with her since Phil passed away. I know your whole family has welcomed her with open arms and I'm so thankful that she has you and them as part of her family.

"April, Alyssa wants to be with you all the time. She loves you so much and misses you every time you have to leave. She cries when you go and that breaks my heart as well as yours, I know. This idea was actually Alyssa's. She has suggested it many times over the course of the year. Phil and I didn't have a great life insurance plan, and I have no more money, and I'm also single now, trying to raise a six year old girl. Alyssa and I were hoping that April, Alyssa, and I could move in to your guest house. April, before you start yelling please hear me out. Mom can't afford for us to move in with her, and she doesn't have the room. I have been looking for a new job for some time now, but I can't find one. I'll keep searching, but we need a place to live next week and with April and I sharing responsibility, we would be able to pay rent together." She said as her face turned beet red.

April and I didn't say much. In unison we stood up, hugged her and each told her we would call her in the morning and walked out the door. The dazed look in April's eyes mimicked mine. We didn't know at that point, but only a couple of days later we would both make a decision that would change our lives forever. I will continue to trust that God can turn my marriage into good. He will, I know He will.

Nancy kept a very clean house. I hope I find enough clues in her office, so that I don't have to look through her bedroom. A woman needs her personal space, or so my mom says, either way, I'd prefer to avoid her room. Her office seems to be the best place to start. It was the first door down the hallway. Phil and I used to spend a lot of time in this house. It's still hard to picture him gone. He would hate to see what was happening to Nancy and Alyssa now. I vowed that I would do my best to protect them, and I will. I think she's in danger. Finding out from whom could prove exigent, but I have never backed down from a challenge and I don't plan to now.

Searching through the drawers in her desk hasn't revealed a thing. She kept her letters in the bottom drawer. After grabbing a handful, I glanced at the time. It's already 5 p.m. and I need to run to the grocery store before going home to cook dinner. I grab a plastic bag and shove all of them into it; there must be over two hundred notes. Guilt tugs as I take my brother's wife's private mail, but I know there is no other way. I need to know how much danger she was in, and asking her right now isn't an option.

* * *

Resting at home is nice. Home, I like the sound of that. It's strange that I could see myself living here. There isn't one room I don't like. I haven't seen all the rooms yet, but I'm sure I'll like them. I could live here a lifetime before seeing the master bedroom. As a matter of fact, I think I'll make that my goal.

The doorbell ringing startles me.

When I open the door, Helen is standing on the front porch massaging her hands through leather gloves as snow falls on her head. I quickly usher her in.

"What are you doing out in this weather?" I question.

"I didn't know it was going to snow today. It started when I was half way to your house."

"Have you received any news about Nancy? Are they going to pull the… I mean have you talked to a doctor yet?" I ask.

"I don't know. I've been at home since our meeting earlier," Helen states.

"I'm planning to be at the hospital all day tomorrow." I'm not sure why I gave her that information.

"That's good. I'll join you. I was wondering, are you free to talk now for a few minutes?"

"You mean like another counseling session?"

"Yes. I think the more we talk, the faster you'll feel comfortable around Ryan." Internally, I groan.

"We could talk if you want to, but Ryan isn't here right now." I agree, praying she would change her mind.

"That's good. I was hoping just the two of us could talk, anyway." I walk into the living room. She sits on the love seat and I take the one-seater. I want more space than that, I'd prefer emotionally, but I'll take what I can get.

"April, I want to talk about trust today, but first let me tell you some of my thoughts and sum up what I think you said in the previous session. Please correct me if I misspeak. You are married to Ryan, but you do not trust him, you do not love him, and you do not like him, yet. I added yet because I think you were alluding to a possible acceptance of friendship at a later date. Your relationship with him is more like housemates than spouses. You also mentioned that you have never had a friendship with someone of the opposite sex and you have never had a boyfriend prior to your marriage. I want to know, would it be safe for me to say that you don't trust men?"

"Yes, it would."

"Do you know why?"

"Yes."

"Do you want to talk about that now?" Helen asks.

"No," I answer.

"Okay. I respect that. I want to talk about your relationship with Nancy. I know you had a great relationship with her. Would it be accurate to say that you loved her?"

"Yes, she was that person in my life who I turned to whenever I needed help. She was my best friend."

"Okay, good. Would you say that you trusted her?"

"Yes. She deserved trust. She always had my best interest in mind. I think that this arrangement she concocted isn't like her. She wouldn't force her will on me. She wasn't like that, but since she arranged it this time, I would have to say that even though I don't understand it, I still trust her."

"April, that's wonderful. Let's take it a step further. You trust Nancy even though you don't fully understand her reasoning. She has put you into a marriage where she feels you will thrive. Since you trust Nancy and she trusts this situation to be the best thing for you and Ryan, do you believe she was thinking that you two could be able to trust each other?"

"I'm not sure?"

"Do you think Nancy trusts Ryan with you?"

"Again, I'm not sure. I know she thought highly of Ryan, he was Phil's brother. She would tell me about how he was over fixing this for her or that for her. I honestly thought there was something going on between the two of them, with the way she talked about him so much. She would tell me about his time with Alyssa and how it was growing into a beautiful father, daughter relationship. I didn't mind Nancy and Ryan spending time together, but I didn't want Alyssa getting hurt. I guess I resented him for that. I have always thought that he was going to break her heart when he got married and stopped visiting Nancy. I tried to explain it to her, but she wouldn't listen."

"Now that you're married to him do you think you could trust him around Alyssa and know that he isn't going to break her heart by leaving?"

"He could always leave. I don't know if I could ever trust him not to."

"That's great."

"Why is him possibly leaving great?" If she thinks that is great, I need another counselor!

"That isn't what I mean. I mean it's great you know that already. That is what we need to focus on," Helen comments. Darn, I could have used that to get Ryan and me out of the counseling.

"You've lost me. What do we need to focus on?"

"We need to focus on how Ryan and your dad are not the same person."

"I don't know Ryan enough to come to that conclusion. In my mind, they are very much the same person."

"Has Ryan hurt you?"

"No."

"Has Ryan belittled you?"

"No."

"Has Ryan cared about your feelings?"

"Yes."

"Does Ryan want to help your family?"

"Yes, and that doesn't make sense to me. Why is he so willing to give up his future for my family? And why did he marry the wrong sister?" If she is going to give me hard questions, I'll give them right back.

"These are questions you need to ask Ryan. One thing I want you to remind yourself when you talk with Ryan tonight is this; he is not your dad."

And with that, she put on her coat and went back out into the storm. I hope she doesn't have car problems on her way home.

* * *

I quickly move through the store locating all the groceries I need for tonight. I wish I was able to think ahead and write out a weekly list. I usually don't cook much for myself, but now that I have a wife, I need to be more prepared. Maybe she and I could come to an agreement and she could go to the store sometimes too. There are so many components to marriage that I never thought about before. I think there are even more for us because she doesn't love me or even like me yet. But I'm not one to cower from a challenge.

Turning the corner, I push my cart a little too fast, bumping into an oncoming cart.

"I'm sorry about that." I say pulling my cart back. The cart's owner comes into view.

"Oh Ryan, how are you doing? I haven't seen you around town much. I need you to come over to my house soon to fix my kitchen cabinets. It doesn't have to be all business though, if you know what I mean. Heehee." Her fake chuckle makes its way to my eardrums. Kelly and I had a very short dating relationship when we were in high school, which I regret. I succumbed to the peer pressure that jocks needed to date cheer leaders and it cost me the love of my life. One day I hope to win her back.

"Kelly, I'm very busy now that April and I got married. I can let Nick know tomorrow and he can call you to schedule it with him or my dad." Her hot pink purse falls off her shoulder to the floor. I bend to pick it up and notice that her toenails match her purse perfectly.

She begins with her whiney shouting which grates like a knife scraping a stoneware plate, "You married April? Why would you do that? You two never got along, much less associated with each other." Bringing her voice down a little she adds, "Honey, I wish you called me. I would have married you in a heartbeat. Well…," she starts to say as she runs her long fingernails down my arm, "when this thing fizzles out, give me a call, my cabinets can wait until then, so don't bother your daddy. Call me when it's over," she says as she taps her 4 inch high heel shoe on the tiled floor.

"Kelly, it isn't going to be over. Marriage is for a life time," I explain taking a step back.

"Hey, guys, what are you two talking about or should I say flirting about?"

"Hey Dan, how're you doing?" I say offering my hand.

"Well…tax season has started, so I've been busy with that, now that it's the end of January. I haven't had much time for anything else. You?" Dan wants to know.

"I have been busy myself, which is what I was just telling Kelly."

"Dan, he married April," Kelly whines.

Why did I ever date her?

"Can you believe that? They weren't even friends. There's no way that they're in love," she says as she twirls a piece of her over-bleached blond hair.

"Yeah, why would you marry April? She never liked you. I can't see that changing. How did you get her to marry you?" Dan inquires.

"She said 'I do,' and that is all you two need to know. I hope you both have a great evening. Dan, I'll bring over all of my tax information as soon as I have time. You've done a great job with my taxes in the past and I appreciate it, but right now I have to go. I need to get home to my wife. See you around," I say as I wave over my shoulder.

In a small town everyone knows your business, whether you want them to or not. I'm surprised they didn't know I was married yet. I should have kept my mouth shut. The sad truth that everyone knows she doesn't love me will never be easy to hear. A loveless marriage is not what a man would ever desire. I know they knew about Nancy, but I'm thankful they didn't bring her up. It hurts too much. And the hot gossip I just gave them will minimize the talk of Nancy.

As I wait in line, I decide to use my time well. God please change our hearts. Show us how to love You more. I know April has a relationship with You. Otherwise, I wouldn't have married her, but I also know trusting is an obstacle for her. Please help her want to trust me, and that in time we can develop a strong friendship that blossoms into a rich love.

Checking out, I travel home, more at peace after talking to God. I hope our homework assignment goes well tonight.

Chapter 9

Dinner is a quiet affair. My stomach has been all twisted knowing we have to spend time talking to each other. I need to remind myself that he is not my dad. I have avoided him, and most males for that matter, most of my life. In sixth grade, Ryan and I spent a good amount of time together when the school combined the sixth and seventh grade gym classes. We played tennis together; I wasn't very good, but he didn't seem to care. He would serve the ball and I would swing and miss, and then run after the ball. I would attempt to serve the ball back, and after a couple of tries, I would throw it over the net to him. Then, he would serve the ball and I would miss it again - and on we went until he suggested badminton, which I was marginally better at.

"What are you thinking about, April?" Ryan has a soothing voice.

"Honestly, I was thinking about those few times we played tennis together in the sixth grade."

"You remember that?" Shock registered on his face.

"Yes. I must have frustrated you so much! I could never hit the ball. I'll never know why our gym teacher thought it was a good idea to pair us up. You were very good, even then, and I didn't have an athletic bone in my body, but strangely, I had fun."

"I had fun also. We should try it again sometime."

"Maybe when our lives settle down a bit. Ryan, I never asked you when your birthday is."

"My birthday is January 23rd."

"What? That was the day after we got married. Why didn't you tell me?"

"We were both a little shocked by our sudden marriage and I forgot about my birthday until we got back. It's no big deal anyway." He shrugs his shoulders.

"I disagree with you completely! It is a big deal. Janice just gave me this terrific cake recipe. Do you like chocolate?"

"Yes, but you don't have to make me a cake. I know you hate to cook."

"So, you already know that. I do hate to cook, but I like to bake, a little. I haven't told anyone that yet though. I discovered it when we had that bad snow storm last month, before Christmas, and no places would come out in the storm to deliver food. I went to bed hungry that night and when I woke up the next morning to all that snow, I knew I needed to cook something or I was going to starve. I do own a cookbook, surprisingly, but I had to tear apart my apartment to find it. When I did, I silently thanked Nancy for the gift and opened to the dessert section. I made a variation of oatmeal raisin cookies. I didn't have all the ingredients, but that didn't stop me. They tasted pretty good. I ventured through the dessert section, trying every recipe in the book. So now I am going to make you a birthday cake."

"Okay, I'll help you then," Ryan states.

"You can't make your own birthday cake," I protest.

"But you need me. You don't know where anything is." He motioned with his hands.

"That's true. You can help, but next year I'll make it on my own."

"Deal." There's a twinkle in his eye as he looks at me. He must love cake.

"Can you get out a couple of mixing bowls for me while I get the recipe?"

"Sure."

As I turn to leave the room I had a strange feeling that this night was going to end up like one of our tennis games. I'm not sure if it will end with me ruining the cake or having fun with Ryan, but I hope that it's the latter. I left the recipe on my dresser so it wasn't hard to find. On my way back to the kitchen I hear Ryan singing. Boy! He must really like cake.

"Here it is," I sing to his tune. He turns and takes my hand in his and waltzes me around the kitchen island while singing this song about dreams coming true. He spins me out and back in. I come back in a little too hard and my head bumps into his chest. To balance myself, I put my hands on his biceps only to feel them tighten around me, pushing my hands up around his neck. I pause a moment, reflecting on how I made it into his arms, not sure if I like this new feeling or not. Gulping, I look up into his eyes. I've never looked into a man's eyes before or at least from this close proximity. The room was getting hot, maybe he already started preheating the oven.

"We can't bake a cake from this angle." I need to get out of his arms. They are electric, sending chills down my spine. As he releases me from his hold I walk over to the refrigerator. The cool air sets my heart back to a normal rhythm.

"Ryan, please, help me find the eggs." Did I just ask him to come near me again, what am I thinking? I step back, but not quick enough. His hand brushes my shoulder as he reaches in, pulling out the eggs.

"Thank you." This is going to be a long night if I have to ask him where everything is.

"Ryan, do you mind taking the list and getting out all the ingredients?" The amusement on his face is apparent. He is having too much fun teasing me. I think I'm having fun too. As we get to work mixing the ingredients, our hands occasionally graze each others. We work well together.

"Do you like your job, April?"

"Yes, I do. I'm an assistant teacher in Alyssa's first grade class. The woman that was the assistant went on maternity leave for the year and I was grateful for the opening. I've been working with younger ages previously. It's fun seeing all of the different little personalities in the room. I have enjoyed getting to know all of the kids. How about you? Tell me more about your job."

"You know I worked with Nick, Phil, and Dad. It was very hard for us when Phil passed away. We had to rearrange who does what in the construction business, but that was easy compared to missing his presence every day. But anyway, we build mostly new construction. It's fun to see a building through its stages. Sometimes I think about Jesus being a carpenter, and I wonder what he enjoyed building."

"Hmm, I wonder too. What's your favorite part of the job?"'

"Hands down, it's the people. I love working with my dad and close friends. They challenge me daily and lift me up when I am down."

"Down? You? Come on, I don't buy that! You were forced into a marriage that you had no personal ties to and you're still not down. That's something I don't understand. Didn't you have dreams of getting married to the love of your life?"

"Yes, I did." His face is hard to read. He is definitely deep in thought.

"I also have dreams for Alyssa. I promised Phil years ago that I would take care of her and now I feel like I'm a step closer to fulfilling that promise. She needs security and a father figure. I plan on providing that for her, as well as a loving home for you."

"You perplex me. You would sacrifice your life for a promise? Please don't take that the wrong way. I am very thankful that you would want to do all of this for Alyssa. She is the most precious child I know and she deserves only the best, but I still don't understand why you would give up your chance of having a love life." He opens his mouth as the buzzing of the timer sounds.

"Let me check that." I jump up, entering the kitchen. Searching for a pot holder, Ryan leans around me opening the drawer to my immediate left. We both reach to grab it and our fingers brush each others'.

I jump back falling into his arms. I slowly turn to see if there is a way to escape, but find his eyes calling me closer. His lips are slightly parted and I hope he kisses me. What am I thinking, no I don't. He might be a nice guy, but that doesn't mean we should start anything, besides his heart belongs to another. Reminding myself of this, I break eye contact, looking down. He steps back and I look in the oven to find that the cake was, indeed, done. Pulling it out of the oven, my hand grazes the side of the pan. My gasp causes Ryan to rush back over.

"Are you okay?" he asks, as I put the cake on the stove top.

"Yes, I'm fine, just a little klutzy." I usually am not this accident prone.

"Let me see," he says gently taking my hand in his. "You need to run this under cold water. Let me help." All I want is for him to stop touching me. These new feelings are too much to handle right now. My sister is in the hospital and Alyssa needs to come home. I wish Nancy hadn't arranged for her to take a vacation this week with my mom. My thoughts need to be focusing on making an amazing home for Alyssa.

"How does that feel?"

"How do you think? Cold."

"Ha-ha. Yes, cold. But does it burn anymore?"

"No, it's much better now. Thank you," I say taking my hand out of his.

"Now for the icing. I should have made it while the cake was in the oven, but we were talking and, huh."

"Huh, what?"

"I was just thinking that we did our homework without thinking about doing our homework. That was so much easier than I thought it was going to be." Things are moving too fast. I think my heart went from friendship to something a little more, way too quickly. I need to guard my heart. We only had one evening together, things need to slow down.

"It's not at all what you thought?"

"No, I was expecting a cocky jock attitude that oozed an 'I'm better than everyone else's persona."

"Ouch. Where did you get that idea from?"

"You!"

"Me, what do you mean me?" he calmly asks.

"Never mind, I said too much."

"Please explain. If I did something to make you think that I am better than you, I need to know," he pleads.

"When we were in high school you acted that way. You didn't say anything to me, you didn't have to. You hung out with the jocks and the cheerleaders. You fit in with them and that whole crowd overlooked everyone else in the school, except when they were making fun of an outsider."

"I know when I was in high school I did try to 'act' cool, but I didn't make fun of people that weren't athletic, I don't think. I never meant to if I did. I'm sorry if I ever treated you that way. Can you forgive me?"

"Sure. Now you said you wanted chocolate icing right?" I cannot let this conversation go on. I'm not ready to tell him what I overheard him say to a bunch of his friends. He truly does seem sorry though, even if he doesn't remember what happened years ago. I planned on never being around him again, once we graduated, and I succeeded for many years.

"I would love chocolate, but first are you sure that was all that happened? I really meant it when I said I'm sorry. I never meant to hurt your feelings."

I busy myself making the icing, hoping he doesn't see me wipe away the tear that escaped onto my cheek. Why did he have to go and apologize? He doesn't even remember what happened. I was fine disliking him forever. I said I forgive him, but do I really? I know that I can't trust him, but forgiveness is a command. I have to forgive him, but how?

"Taste this," I say, handing him the spoon.

"It's delicious."

"Good. Let me finish up icing the cake, and then we can have some."

After we ate our cake, I insisted on cleaning up. He said he had some reading to catch up on, so we went our separate ways. Overall, I have enjoyed his company today.

Chapter 10

No one notices the creaking sound as the intruder creeps up the stairs. The house is quiet and the nightlights make his job easier as they illuminate the floor. Without it, he might have tripped over the small stack of books that occupy the middle of the living room floor. He already did a thorough search of the first floor and found no one in any of the rooms. He knows he will find what he needs upstairs. He wishes she would have just listened to his advice, then none of this would be happening. He didn't want it to go this far. He never imagined it would, but now that it has, he has to take care of things. It's his responsibility. Reaching to the top floor, he hears someone walking around in one of the bedrooms. He doesn't want to hurt anyone, but he would if the need arose. He isn't in a hurry, so he can wait a little bit in hopes that she'll fall asleep again, but he won't wait too long.

Chapter 11

Invading someone's privacy can be challenging when you need to watch your back to make sure you don't get caught. Your pulse quickens and depending on your skill, the rush either makes you work better or you get sloppy and make mistakes. I don't have to consider getting caught because the owner of these letters is in the hospital. My heart isn't beating faster and there is no rush, just sadness. How could Nancy have known something was going to happen to her?

I have read over twenty letters so far and none of them gave me the slightest clue as to what happened. She and Phil shared a lot of their hearts in these letters and I feel guilty reading them. I think the best approach is to find the most recent ones and read those. I'm lost in this pile. Tediously, I sort by year. The earliest is in 2004, seven years old. Phil and Nancy got married in 2001, so there must be more letters somewhere else. I hope I find what I'm looking for here.

A half hour later I can see that there are only a few letters from 2007 'till now. This is a more manageable bunch.

The clock ticks, but none of the letters from the past three years gives me a clue. I know more than I should about Nancy now, even that my best friend Nick has been writing to her, but nothing helpful in solving this crime. I'm sure a crime has been committed, even if I don't have a shred of evidence. Maybe I should talk to Nick since he knows Nancy more than I thought he did. Why has he been writing to Nancy? I know there's more to this that I need to figure out, but right now I don't have time to think about it.

Stacking some of the letters together, I put them back in the bag. As I finish putting all the dated ones in, I scan my bed to see if I left any. I forgot that I put a letter on my nightstand that didn't have a date on it. As I pick it up, there's a knock on my door. Turning to go and open the door, I find Nick standing in the doorway.

"Man, you look awful. Have you slept lately?"

"No, as a matter of fact, I haven't. My plane landed two hours ago. I saw your dad and he briefly told me that you and April eloped, which I'll yell at you about later, and that Nancy is in the hospital. I'm in shock and I'm worried sick about Nancy. Ryan, I was thinking on the drive over here that someone did this to her. She was really spooked before I left for the business trip. She wouldn't let Alyssa out of her sight and she was babbling about needing to figure things out. What happened?" He runs his hand through his hair as he paces back and forth.

"It's a long story. Nancy called both of us over to her house the day before her accident and convinced us that she, April, and Alyssa should move in with me. We left her house that night and after a long night in prayer, I went over to April's to see if she wanted to go ahead with the plans. She said yes, and we called Nancy. Nancy said she needed a week to get everything in order and that we could all move in then. But Nancy didn't get a week. The brakes on her car stopped working while she was running errands.

"Nancy was fine from the accident, except for her leg. She needed a couple of surgeries. It wasn't fatal, that's what the doctor said. Two days after her accident, April and I received a letter from Nancy insisting we elope instead of just having everyone move in together. April was afraid and I was too. We thought it was an accident but since then I have questioned that. We went on a quick honeymoon because Nancy insisted in her letter to make it look real, and her mom was going to watch Alyssa. It was a poor choice to go, but I'll tell you more about that later. Do you want to see it?" We scan my room, eyeing piles of letters stacked haphazardly across my bed, but that wasn't where this letter is. It's in my night stand. I keep it there because I like to read it every night, the single sheet that changed my life forever.

His eyebrows rose and fell several times, "She didn't write this. It isn't Nancy, she wouldn't write, 'Since you are holding this letter it must mean that I have gone to heaven. It's urgent that the two of you elope and learn how to love each other, so that you can be a great couple for Alyssa. Make it look real and go on a honeymoon. Mom is watching Alyssa.' Why would she write this? It makes no sense. There has to be something else going on. I know she went on to explain why, but even that doesn't add up. Ryan what is going on here?" His voice is growing louder. If I didn't know him better, I would think that his fist above his head was about to make contact with something. It was natural to take a step away from him. He slowly brings his arm down and gives me back the letter and I put it away.

"Nick, April and I have discussed it and we haven't figured it out. Anyway, we only stayed for a couple of days on our honeymoon and decided it was better to come home. I tried to get April to talk to me, but she wouldn't. It was frustrating. Nancy left us more letters with instructions and steps we need to take to make life better for Alyssa and each other. Mostly good stuff, but the timing is all wrong. We need to be focusing on Nancy, but she has us in counseling and doing homework instead. I agree with you that Nancy wasn't in an accident. Someone intentionally hurt her, maybe even wanted her dead, but why?"

"Ryan, I don't know. I thought you might know something since you and April both saw her after me. Does April know anything?"

"No, she doesn't. She thinks Nancy was in an accident. Nick, please close the door." He gets off the bed and clicks the door shut. "I went to the house earlier and found over two hundred letters. I went through all the ones dated in the past three years. None of them gave me a clue as to what spooked Nancy, even though there were some interesting ones from you."

"That, we can talk more about later. Not even one of them?"

"No, oh wait. I forgot about the one that I put aside. I was about to read it when you walked in. It was the only one that wasn't sent through the postal service. It's right here." Nick is right next to me, looking over my shoulder as I open it. It reads:

You didn't heed my advice and now I'm going to take Alyssa.

"What? Why wouldn't she talk to us about this? Now we know it wasn't an accident. Ryan you have more experience. What do we do next?"

"We need to find Alyssa. Let me get my keys."

"Should we tell April?" Nick inquires.

"I don't want to, but I think I should. Once we see that Alyssa is fine we can bring her here and protect her."

"Alright. Let's go."

As I grab my keys, I start yelling for April. The look on her face shows me that I woke her up.

"April, quickly get dressed. We need to go to Alyssa."

"Is she okay?" The panic on her face breaks my heart.

"She's probably fine, but I want to go over there to make sure."

Within one minute we were all in the car. April doesn't care about getting dressed, she only wants to see that Alyssa is safe. I know I'm breaking the law as I drive, but it doesn't seem to register with my foot. We make it to Agnes' house in record time.

April unlocks the door and we all spread out. I tell Nick to check the bottom rooms as I follow April up the stairs. She runs straight to Alyssa's room so I turn left to her moms' room. Agnes is face down sprawled out on the floor. There's a pool of blood by her head.

"Nick call an...."

April's shrill voice alerts Nick.

"Alyssa isn't here. Where is she? Has someone...." I don't want her to see her mom on the floor, but it's too late. April stares at her and then takes one step forward and starts to fall to the ground. Racing to her side, I catch her on her way down.

"Nick, call an ambulance," I shout as I check for Agnes' pulse. He reaches over the bed and grabs the phone. Fortunately, we're in a district where 911 is available.

"Tell them she has a head wound and has lost a lot of blood, but she has a pulse." I'm not a trained EMT, but I have had some experience. I know that April will be fine, but her mom might not be.

"They said they'll be here any minute. An ambulance is close by. In the meantime they want us to put pressure on the wound. We need to support her spine as we turn her. Ryan, why couldn't we have figured this out sooner? You and I usually do, why not this time when it involves a family that is close to us?" Nick fumbles over his feet as he rushes over to help.

"I don't know the answer to that Nick, but I do know that this isn't over yet and you and I are going to figure it out. We need to find Alyssa. She's so little and in the hands of a sick person. Who would do something like this? That is what we need to focus on. Once we get Agnes and April to the hospital, we are going to search Nancy's house again. There has to be something else there."

"You're right. We're going to find him. I will not let him hurt another person, first Nancy and now her mom. If he harms Alyssa, I'm going to kill him!" A vein bulges as his cheeks turn crimson, mine mimicking his.

"Nick, I'm with you there. We're going to get him," I say with a firm set jaw.

The ambulance arrives, as April starts coming to. Once they stabilized Agnes, I ask them to give April something to calm her down. April and Agnes are rushed to the hospital while Nick and I wait for the police to arrive.

"Nick, I think it's best if you wait for the police and I go over to Nancy's again."

"That's a good idea. No use wasting time. Call my cell if you find anything. I'll call you as soon as I'm done here," Nick states.

Chapter 12

"Mom, Mom, can you hear me? Why won't she answer me? Please tell me why? She's going to be okay, right?" My head turns frantically searching the eyes of the two EMTs, knowing that if it is bad news their eyes would reveal it.

"Ma'am we need you to be quiet while we work on your mom. I know this is hard for you, but we need it silent." The taller of the two demands.

"But will she be all right?" They won't make eye contact with me.

"You don't quit do you? We are doing everything we can for her and I can do a lot more for her if I wasn't talking to you, so if you want the best care for your mother than be quiet."

God, why won't she open her eyes? I have lost almost everyone important to me, Nancy, my mom, and now Alyssa is missing. They are my heart and now there is something wrong with each one of them. Please God, I'm begging You, help all three of them. I know I don't open my heart up to many people. There are only four or five people in my life that I do and three of them are in danger of death. I know I don't trust well or at all, really, but You leave me with no choice but to trust You now. I trust You God. I trust You, God. Each time I say it to You, I know it's true a little more. You tell me to lean not on my own understanding. I have made a mess of my life. I don't have close friendships. My mom has been trying to rebuild our relationship for many years and I haven't given her that chance. I'm afraid. I don't want to hurt anymore, but I trust You. Please bring her through this so that I can be the daughter she needs. Please bring Nancy through this, so that I can be the sister she needs, and please bring Alyssa home, so I can love her the way I've wanted to love her since that first day I held her after she was born. I see now that whoever is doing this is not in control, but You are in control. Please help. I know my prayers are selfish and for that I am sorry, but please....

I don't know how many times I repeated my last thoughts before the lights dimmed around me.

Chapter 13

Iknow the police would want me to wait before I enter Nancy's house, but Alyssa's sweet little face keeps popping into my head. I need to do everything I can to find her. As I climb the front steps, I notice a light on in the kitchen. I didn't leave a light on when I left, but I'm not the only one with a key. As I open the door and scan the living room I know someone else was here, or is still here. The furniture was left turned over and papers were scattered across the floor. I hope he didn't find what he was looking for.

I thought best to start in Nancy's bedroom this time, but first I better call the police. As I dial the number, I head toward her night stand. Opening the drawer, I see her Bible. I know she would want to have this with her the moment she wakes up. I know Helen would tell me I'm in denial about her waking up, since two different people from April's immediate family have informed us that she is gone, but after seeing her I still think there is life left to live. As I lift it up, I notice a small stack of letters lying underneath. The sirens grow louder and I know I don't have much time, so I stuff them into my jacket pocket and zip it up. Quickly, I scan her bedroom.

"Ryan, you know better than to touch evidence," Officer Smith reprimands. He's my least favorite among the police department. He has very few friends and doesn't care to make any either. His attitude of authority slams you in the face before his body enters the room. He has a need to make sure everyone around him knows he's a powerful man.

"I was just getting Nancy's Bible for her. I thought she would like it if, when, she wakes up."

"Did she wake up yet?" Smith demands.

"No, but we're hopeful that she will soon," I add.

"Has the doctor said when she'll wake up?"

"I haven't talked to a doctor." I reply as my eyes scan the room looking for more evidence.

"Did you touch anything else?"

"I came into the house earlier today. Then, the house was just the way Nancy left it. I went into the office and sat at the desk. When we found Agnes and discovered that Alyssa was kidnapped, I came back here to see if there were any clues as to who did it. I only touched the nightstand though. I called you guys first. I'd still like to help and look around." I almost beg.

"Ryan, you overstepped a line this time. You knew we were going to come here right after we left Agnes'. You should have left it to us. No, you cannot help. You can wait outside until we're ready to question you." He really is a jerk. He treats his colleagues the same way. He almost got himself fired last year 'cause of his mouth. Now he only belittles those who aren't his boss.

As I walk out the front door, I know waiting outside is going to be a waste of time. I need to get moving. Maybe I can find someone else to take my statement so I can go.

"Ryan, what are you doing here?"

"Blake, boy, am I glad to see you. I came here straight from Agnes'. I thought I could find something that might help us locate Alyssa. Smith sent me outside to wait to be questioned. Do you think you could do it? I'm in a hurry."

"Sure. Did you see anyone?"

"No. I came here earlier and…." I tell him almost everything I know. He jots down my comments and informs me that they will do everything they can to bring Alyssa home. Blake and I went to high school together. We were on the same basketball team. I feel bad for him since he has to put up with Smith all the time.

"I need to get to the hospital and check on Agnes and April." I say impatiently, letting him know we need to wrap up this conversation.

"I heard you and April tied the knot. What's that all about? I've never seen you two together?" he questions.

"Blake, April is a wonderful woman. How about we get together when this is all over and I'll tell you the whole story."

"Alright. See ya around."

As I race to my car, I call Nick to give him an update.

* * *

Ten steps to the wall, turn, and ten steps back the other way. My thoughts are spiraling me into outlandish behavior and I don't care. Who has Alyssa? Is she hurt? Is she afraid? Alone? Hungry? How's my mom? Is she going to make it? When will the doctor come out to tell me something? The nurses' station is thirty-five feet away.

Every ten minutes I walk there. I should call Janice to wait with me, but I don't want to leave this area to use my phone. Has anything changed with Nancy? I'm so torn, who should I think about? Ten steps to the wall, turn, and ten steps to the other wall.

Ryan comes in and hugs me. I let my weight rest in his arms as he moves us into the two chairs closest to the nurses' station. Strangely, I feel safe with his arms around me which causes a wave of panic knowing Alyssa was anything but.

"April, I'm going to talk to the nurse about finding us in Nancy's room when they have news about your mom, okay?"

"Please," comes out of my mouth, but barely audible. Ryan's back at my side before his seat grows cold.

"April, it's all arranged, we can wait in Nancy's room." We walk in silence, neither wanting to voice our fears. Numbly, we go through the corn maze of the hospital. As we enter the hospital room, we find Helen sitting beside Nancy.

"There hasn't been a change in Nancy since I arrived, but I haven't been here long. She seems like she's just sleeping. Have any of you noticed that the hospital staff doesn't seem to care much about her? Every time I've been here, I haven't once bumped into anyone employed… uh, here. What's wrong with you two?" Helen inquires.

I have no desire to carry on a conversation. Helen looks to Ryan and he fills her in.

"I'll be right back, I need to get a drink. Do either of you want one?" Ryan adds.

"Yes, please, something caffeinated. Thanks Ryan," Helen says.

I shake my head not trusting my voice to work.

As Ryan reaches for the doorknob I hear a moan.

"Helen, are you okay?" I ask.

"I'm fine, but Nancy just moaned." We all rush to her side. She moans again.

"I'll get the nurse." He runs from the room. Helen and I watch Nancy very closely. She starts to stretch a little. The nurse comes in all smiles.

"I see Nancy is waking up."

"Yes, but why aren't you paging the doctor?" I inquire.

"There's no need. This is normal. She should be opening her eyes shortly."

"What?" we all practically shout!

"Why are you all so surprised? She had surgery two hours ago and we needed to take her off the anesthesia slowly so now is about the right time for her to be waking up. After her other surgeries, she had a rough time coming to. She would rant and scream, so we decided that we would take her off slower this time and hope she had a better time adjusting. We put her on some other medications at the same time for anxiety."

"We thought she was dead," I shout.

"No, she is anything but dead. She had a rough time coming to after her first surgery so we tried something different for her second and third surgeries. That's all."

"Wait a minute; please back up to the beginning."

"Alright, Nancy came in to the hospital a week ago. Her brakes stopped working as she was driving and she hit another car. She suffered a head injury, which over the course of this week has healed nicely. Her leg was pinned in the car and that is where we've been focusing. She had surgery five days ago. She has needed two other surgeries since then. This last surgery, which was today, went very well and we hope that she will have full mobility when she heals.

"So, when was there talk of her being dead?" Helen asks.

"Uhh. There never was. Now I'm confused," the nurse says as her forehead wrinkles.

"You mean to tell me that she was never told she might die during her surgery?" Ryan wonders.

"These surgeries are low risk. She wasn't given the impression that she would die."

"What?" My vocal cords were back in full swing. "She tricked me. My own sister tricked me. I can't believe it. I need to get out of here. I'm going home."

"April, why don't you wait a little bit? Let Nancy wake up and explain," Helen gently asks.

"I can't, I need to go." I'm afraid of what she will say when she wakes up, so I do what I'm good at and avoid the tense situation, by leaving. I start to walk out the door and down the hall when I remember that my car isn't here. I don't want to go back in there, so I stop and stand still. I'm feeling betrayed by the only relative that has seemingly loved me unconditionally my whole life. She accepted me for who I was and never tried to change me.

She wanted what was best for me, but never pushed me to become someone I wasn't. Now I'm married to a man she chose because she was dead. I'm glad she isn't dead. Wait, she isn't dead.

I rush back down the hall and into the room. I stare at her. She really is alive. For that I'm grateful, but I can still be mad at her. Now it makes sense as to why my mom and other family members haven't been calling me. I still need a little time alone.

"Ryan, can you take me home?"

"Yes, I can. Helen, do you mind calling me the moment this starts to make sense to you?"

"Definitely!" They exchange numbers and I continue to watch Nancy's chest rise and fall.

We turn to leave as Nancy starts ranting.

"This is what she does every time she comes to. She starts yelling about someone named Alyssa needing protection, but each time we've questioned her when she's fully alert she would say that everything was fine," the nurse explains.

We watch Nancy, who seems to be stuck in a nightmare, one that starts to flood her reality as she throws her arms back and forth.

"April, do you know where Alyssa and mom are? I tried calling there and no one answered. It's 1:30 a.m. Mom should answer the phone." She still isn't making sense.

"Nancy, I'm so glad you're okay. I've been so worried about you. How do you feel?" I say.

"I feel fine. April, where are they?"

I give the nurse a pleading look. How can I not tell her? I have to tell her because she might know something crucial.

"Nancy, tonight we went over to mom's to check on them and…." Taking a deep breath, "…we found mom injured on the floor. Someone hit her on the head and Alyssa wasn't there. I don't know what to do? Mom's here in the hospital and I'm waiting for the doctor to tell me how she's doing. Ryan told me he would call the police and make sure they were doing everything possible to find her. Then, they put me in the ambulance with Mom. I'm so glad you're awake. Now please tell me why when you first woke up you knew Alyssa was in trouble."

"I knew she was in trouble because he told me he would take her if I didn't listen to him. That's why I panicked and called you both over. After I talked to you and Ryan that day, I arranged for mom to watch Alyssa for a couple of weeks or so, but you knew that already. I didn't explain myself to Mom. I knew she would object to all of us moving into Ryan's guest house and I didn't want to spook her by emphasizing her need to keep an eye on Alyssa either. Also, I didn't know how long I would need to get everything arranged, so all I asked her was to watch Alyssa for a while and informed her that I was moving out of the house. I thought moving would throw him off and I could wipe out all my debt at once. I also figured she would be safe at moms. I was stupid to keep all of this from the two of you."

With her left hand she wipes her eyes. "Then, I spent the next couple of days packing up the back rooms and running errands. I was driving to a store and as I approached a sharp turn, my brakes stopped working. I just had the brake pads changed the week before, so I knew they were fine. As I pumped my brakes, trying to stop, I knew it was him who caused this, making it so I couldn't stop. All I could think about was, 'I hope he doesn't find her at Mom's house.' I don't know who he is.

"I got a letter in my mail box. It threatened that if I didn't change my ways, he would have to take Alyssa away. The letter was very vague. I didn't understand it, but I was afraid. That's why I thought it best for all of us to live with Ryan. I felt safer. I'm sorry I didn't tell you all of this before suggesting it, but I didn't know of any other way. He said he'd hurt her if I told anyone."

"Nancy, it's him again!" My lips tremble as the words come out.

She nods her head while wiping more tears away. After all these years, it couldn't be him. I don't want it to be him. I stand up from the bed and for the second time in one night, my world blacks out.

Chapter 14

We decide to meet in the hospital parking lot. Nick is waiting for me as I walk to his car. Sliding into the passenger seat, I know that we don't need to exchange any words; we have an understanding in times like these. Alyssa is too important to waste time on useless communication.

I pull out the letters. There are three. The first one reads:

> *"You know how I feel about single moms."*

There is no signature and no date. The second one reads:

> *"If you don't change your ways, I will have to take Alyssa away. And if you tell anyone about this, I will have to hurt her."*

Again there is no signature or date. The third letter says:

> *"This is your final warning."*

The handwriting resembles the previous two, along with the one I found in the office. Pulling open the glove compartment, I grab a plastic bag to put the letters in. Fortunately, I didn't take my time at Nancy's house to remove my gloves. I hope I didn't smudge any prints.

I inform Nick of Nancy's waking up and the bizarre, but nonfatal situation. His eyes reveal his eagerness to go inside, but we both know we have a job to do and that his visit will have to wait until later.

"Ryan, I'll take these to the department and you go in and find out how all the women are doing, including Nancy. When you know, give me a call." I pull the handle and walk out into the chilly night air, heading back to the hospital.

I ask about Agnes at the information desk, but there still isn't any new information. I walk toward Nancy's room, hoping she is able to handle a little questioning because I have a bunch that need answers. She must have some information about who wrote the letters.

Entering her room, I see April and Nancy in an embrace. They're crying and rocking each other back and forth. My weight shifts from one foot to the other, resembling my torn emotions. They need time together to reconnect, but impatience emanates through my mind as well, because every second counts.

I sit on the edge of the bed longing to move forward in my search.

"How are you doing, April," I interrupt, whispering into her hair.

"Truthfully, not good. I'm happy Nancy's awake and back to normal." She starts to pull away from me. "I still haven't heard anything about my mom. Have you heard anything about Alyssa?"

"No, not yet, but they're out there looking for her. I want to talk to Nancy to see what she knows and, of course, to find out how you are." April sits back on Nancy's bed, so I give her more space and take the only chair in the room.

"Where's Nick? Is he out looking for Alyssa?" Nancy inquires.

April and I exchange a quick glance. We both know there's more to that question. We just aren't sure how we both missed it until now.

Nick doesn't usually talk to me about his love interests until he's in a dating relationship. By that time, he talks to dad. He has always said that there was no point in talking to me about love because I'm not experienced in that area. He called me a coward once because I didn't have the guts to ask out the woman I love. He was right too. I never had the gumption.

"Yes, he's bringing the letters we found from this guy over to the police station." The women both pale. "Nancy, do you have any idea who this guy is?" in

"No, I don't know who he is. It probably is the same man from years ago that the police didn't catch." Somehow my hand makes its way into April's and she twists it like someone would ring out a wash cloth, making sure not a single drop of water is left. The pain doesn't compare to the heartache we all feel by the choices made by this man. Someone we don't know is controlling our emotions.

April has had a lot of trials in her life and she has made it no secret that she has an issue with trust. Not verbally, but through her actions. If she is praying to God during this hard time, then she is seeing that He really is trustworthy.

My phone vibrates; stepping into the hallway I answer it.

"Okay. What did she say?" Nick wants to know.

"She confirms receiving the letters. She doesn't know the name of the person who sent them. She thinks it's the same guy from years ago, you know who, the one the police didn't catch. You?"

"The police are checking the prints as we speak, but besides that, there's no other evidence. They didn't find anything in either place, and no one has seen Alyssa." Nick informs.

"Maybe we can go back and search the houses. We could double check. There has to be something." What's my next step?

"Ryan, you know as well as I do that they aren't going to let us in. They're both considered crime scenes. They're off limits to us."

"Yeah, I know. Nick, then what do you suggest we do?"

"I'm coming to the hospital to guard Nancy, and I think you should take April home before the kidnapper calls."

"You're right, I didn't think of that. Maybe he wants money. Okay, I'll take her home, but can you please call us when there's news about her mom?"

"Yes. I'll call as soon as I know."

"Thanks."

"No prob."

* * *

It's hard leaving the hospital without word on how my mom is doing, but Ryan is right about needing to be home to wait for a call. I didn't think of that. Ryan somehow knows I'm struggling. He reaches over and holds my hand, gently rubbing his thumb back and forth along the backside of my palm. Sitting in the car makes the situation worse. Here, I'm not doing anything.

Pray.

That's true. I could pray. I lean back and close my eyes. I trust You, God.

"April, it's time to wake up. We're home." Ryan gently shakes my shoulder.

"Oh, sorry, I didn't mean to fall asleep. What time is it anyway?" I question, as my weak body moves through the front door.

"It's 3:30 a.m.," Ryan responds.

We both sit on the couch and stare at the phone. I could hear the coo-coo clock tick. Each second lasts longer than the last. Why wouldn't the phone ring? Ryan checks the empty machine and I only have a cell phone, so I don't need to worry about my apartment. We don't talk; we just will it to make noise. Questioning, in my mind, several times if we're waiting in the right house, but then I think about how he knows what happened to Nancy, because he did that to her. He knows what happened to my mom because he was there also, so I'm the one who's left. I don't fear him anymore. He has devastated my family's and my life long enough. I'm going to catch him this time. I hoped he disappeared, for good, years ago. He will not get away this time. I remember a lot about him, and with that knowledge I can find him. This town is small and I have lived here my whole life. I can find Alyssa.

"What are you thinking about?" Ryan asks.

"Alyssa, and also about how I have to find her," I answer.

"Me too and we will find her. How are you feeling?"

"I'm feeling angry at the man who is doing this."

"Me too."

"It's him. You know the man who ruined my life and my family's life years ago. I thought he wouldn't come back, but I've lived in fear, thinking he lurked around each corner. I can't believe he's back. I'm different this time around. I'm not afraid of him. I want justice. I want him behind bars. For a long time I've wanted him dead, but I don't anymore."

"I'm glad you don't want him dead, but it's okay if you're afraid."

"I'm not afraid. I'm very angry. It's my turn, again. He already hurt everyone else in my family. He's waiting for me, but I'm okay with that. I want Alyssa home, and any way that I can help her get here, I will."

"April, he isn't going to get you. I'm here to protect you. All you have to do is stay with me and nothing bad will happen."

"Ryan, I do feel safe around you. That's hard for me to admit because I have never felt safe around any man before. I've lived in fear of him for so many years, but I don't anymore. I'm starting to trust God and I do believe that He is in control. God surprised me today by bringing Nancy back to us. I'm amazed and now I believe that He will protect me also, but Alyssa is just a girl. What if that guy hurts her?"

"I'm praying God sends angels to protect her because if he lays a finger on her, he will be answering to me."

"So we're both angry. That's good." I can't hold in my yawn anymore. Ryan is now saying something I can't make out.

The ringing of the phone jolts my head up off of Ryan's shoulder. I grab it and say, "Hello."

"April, it's Nancy. Any news about Alyssa?"

"No, I thought you were the kidnapper."

"Mom is going to be okay. She's stable. She lost a lot of blood, but they said her color is much better then when she came in. She's awake and asking about Alyssa. They're going to put her in my room tomorrow."

"That's great. God is really answering my prayers. I told him I would trust Him and now He has already brought you and mom back to me. He will bring Alyssa back too. I just know it. I'll call you if we hear anything about Alyssa. Oh, is Nick still there?"

"Actually, yes, he thinks I need protection. He's sweet, looking out for me and all," Nancy comments.

"Yes, he is and when things settle down you need to tell me more of what's going on."

"When all four of us are living in Ryan's house we can sit down with our hot chocolates and you can talk for as long as your heart wants."

The fatigue is wearing on my thought process, "Wait, what, do you mean by all four of us?"

"April, I'm the one that was in the car accident, not you. Remember, Ryan and you agreed that the four of us could live at Ryan's house. I know it has been delayed but…."

"Nancy, what about your other plan? The one where you demand that Ryan and I get married? You know the one you wrote?"

"April, how do you know about that?" Nancy questions.

"Ryan and I received it in the mail."

"WHAT?"

"What do you mean, WHAT?"

"You weren't supposed to read that!"

"What do you mean we weren't supposed to read it? WE FOLLOWED IT."

"WHAT, NO!" she groans.

"I thought you tricked us into getting married because you weren't really dying. I thought you just wanted your way. I thought you were really dead. Nancy, I don't ever want to think you're dead again," as my voice whines, my thoughts tumble out, in random order.

"April, I wrote those letters just in case he came after me again and killed me. Those letters had nothing to do with my surgery. I knew the surgeries would go fine."

"I'm confused."

"So am I, because I never mailed them."

"Then how did we get them?"

"I really don't know, I didn't even tell anyone about them. April, did you and Ryan, really, get…ummm… married?" she asks timidly.

"Yes, we did."

"April, I'm sooo sorry. I only wrote them as a precaution, this guy threatened me. I should have told you and Ryan everything that day I asked us to move in with him. Please, forgive me, April. Please, you weren't supposed to get them."

"Yes, I forgive you. But what am I supposed to do now?"

"Honestly, I don't know. I don't know."

"We're going to focus on getting Alyssa home and leave the rest for later."

"Okay. Call me if you hear anything."

"Okay. Bye." As I hang up the phone, Ryan inches closer.

"How's your Mom?"

"She's stable. They said her color has improved greatly and tomorrow they're moving her into Nancy's room."

"That's great news."

"Yes, it is. Ryan, you aren't going to believe this, but Nancy didn't mail those letters and she only wrote them in case this crazy man killed her." I have no idea how he's going to react, but I brace myself for the worst.

"Really? Then who did?"

"We have no idea," I whisper.

"How do you feel about that?" Ryan wants to know.

"Honestly, I'm confused and my thoughts are centered on Alyssa. When we get her back, we can figure things out then." I could hear my voice fading as my head slips down. My last thoughts are about Ryan taking care of me as I drift off, thinking comforting thoughts about him bringing Alyssa home safely.

Chapter 15

He said my mom would be here soon. He told me to be patient a little bit longer and she would be here to take care of me. I don't like any of the food he brings me. It all tastes bad. He makes me stay in this room all the time. At first I really liked it. There are a lot of toys and video games. I really like the ones about princesses. But now, I just want to go home. He keeps telling me I will soon, once mommy gets here.

He seemed like a nice man yesterday, but I don't understand why he won't take me home, and because he won't I don't like him. I won't tell him that though because he might make me drink more of that yucky stuff he made me drink before. It was really bad. And it made my head feel weird too.

My Mommy always said, never go with a stranger. Sometimes she would get down on one knee and gently hold my shoulders and she'd say, "Alyssa, whatever you do, never go anywhere with a stranger. If a stranger tries to take you with him, yell at the top of your lungs 'help, he's not my dad'." I don't know how I got here. I would have yelled that, but I didn't get a chance to. I just woke up here. I was in my bed, and then I woke up here on this ugly, dirty couch. I hope Mommy isn't mad at me. I would have yelled, I really would have, if I had the chance.

I want to see outside. I'd yell if I did go out. I've been waiting for a really big snow storm to come, and he won't let me go to a room with a window in it. Ryan said the next snow storm that comes we're going to build the biggest snowman ever. He said maybe we could get mommy to help too. I really liked that idea and that's why I want to see outside. I'm thirsty and last night I was very cold. I didn't brush my teeth or get dressed today. I told him I needed to, but he said that we would get my clothes today. I asked him to take me home and then it wouldn't matter. He told me grandma had an emergency and that's why I needed to stay with him. I asked what happened and he said that there was a little accident, but Grandma was going to be okay. She just needed to rest and that's why we were going to get mommy soon. I can't wait to see mommy. She knows what food I like and she'll brush my hair. When I put my hand through my hair, it gets stuck in a big knot and it hurts to get my fingers out. My Mommy will take care of me. Where is she? Why isn't she here yet? Maybe I should tell him to call Ryan too, and then Ryan can bring my Mommy. He'd do that for me. Ryan loves me.

Chapter 16

The doorbell rings. I try to jump up off the couch, but the blanket is wrapped around me so tightly I roll, and instead of my feet landing on the floor, my whole body does instead. My shoulder hits the ground hard and my feet are still trapped. I'm struggling to free them when the doorbell rings again. Somehow, I manage to right myself into a sitting position, but the blanket still won't release its hold from my feet. I need coffee. The doorbell rings again and I yell that I'm coming, but I'm really not sure how.

"This blanket must be taped together," I mumble as I try again to escape its strong hold.

"Here, let me help you. And, no I didn't tape you into your blanket last night. You must have been tossing and turning a lot in your sleep." Ryan takes the blanket and gently unwraps my body from it. Just as he finishes, the doorbell rings again. This time I can reach it.

I can't find a peep hole to see who it is, so I fling the door open knowing Ryan is right by my side.

"Did you find Alyssa?" I plead.

"No, but we have decided that we are going to set up camp in your living room. We need to be here when he calls." The police officer standing on the front step motions toward the house with his hands, as if I don't know where the living room is. "Can we come in now? It's cold out here."

"Yes, of course." Stepping aside, four men rush in. Within minutes, the living room is unrecognizable. They each take two trips to the car carrying equipment which they spread across the coffee table and the floor.

"Do you think you can find her today?" I ask timidly.

"We are doing everything we can," he says with a wave of his hand.

Another officer steps forward to explain that Sergeant Smith is in charge, but if I have any questions I need to talk to him.

"Hi, April, you probably don't remember me. My name is Carl and I was in Ryan's graduating class. I want you to know that we are doing everything we possibly can to find Alyssa and we aren't leaving until we rescue her. We want her safe at home and I'm personally not going to rest until that happens. What we need you to do, April, is to stay here with us

89

and wait for him to call." Not the news I was hoping for, but if that's what I need to do, I'll wait. I thought I would be out there searching the streets, but I guess that's just what they do in movies.

"Thank you very much, umm, Carl, right?" I'm normally bad with names, so without much sleep I know I'll forget everyone's name shortly after they introduce themselves. But that fact I won't lose sleep over.

"Yes, that's right. So, remember any questions you have, please ask me. Smith over there," he points to the shortest man of the bunch and whispers, "isn't very good at talking to the human race."

"I'll remember that. Thanks."

Carl then walks over to Ryan. They begin talking in hushed tones. This can't really be happening. She can't be missing. I miss her so much. I have to be able to do more than just sit. I reach for the phone, but Sergeant Smith scowls at me as he swats my hand away from where he's sitting. What am I, a two year old? He didn't say anything either, just furrowed his brow. He better be a whole lot better at his job than he is at communication, because if this jerk messes up and Alyssa isn't found I'll, I'll, I'll something. Stomping my feet, I storm into my room.

I reach for my cell and call Nancy. I need to hear her voice right now. Maybe she has heard something. The phone keeps ringing and ringing. Maybe she's in the bathroom. Or maybe he's trying to hurt her again. I race back to the living room to find Ryan.

"We need to go to the hospital."

"Why, what's happened?" He grabs his coat as he waits for me to answer. I'm causing him to panic.

"Nancy isn't answering her phone." He pauses as he searches my eyes.

"Okay. How many times did you try to call her?"

"Once."

"Why don't we go into the kitchen and try again, first, before I go. Maybe she's sleeping." He puts his hand under my arm and gently leads me out of the room which is now filled with staring men. Maybe I'm overreacting, but then again, maybe I'm not. Too much has happened lately to think that I am.

"I'm calling Nick. He was there last night."

"Okay. I'll try the hospital again."

As we both wait for our phones to have voices speaking through them, I lean my head into Ryan's shoulder. He puts his hand on my back and soothingly rubs it.

"Hello." We both say at the same time. As I talk to Nancy and he talks to Nick, we both relax.

"Nancy, I just called you, why didn't you answer?"

"I'm being discharged and so is mom. We were a little busy filling out paper work. Is there any news on Alyssa?"

"No. I was hoping you've heard something."

"No, nothing here. Mom and I are going back to her place. We're hoping he might call there. The police think it's possible, so we'll be there in about an hour."

"Wait, I thought Mom needed to stay longer."

"The doctor said she's doing very well and that what she needs is rest. So I'm going to take care of her at home. She'll sleep better there, anyway. The cops are already there and we'll have Nick stay with us until they catch this guy."

"I want to see you. I was going to go to the hospital today, but they told me I needed to stay home and wait for a call. It's hard just sitting here. Isn't there more we can do?"

"We can pray."

"I have been Nancy. Really, I have," I say, hoping she believes me.

"I know you have. Oh, mom wants me to tell you that she loves you."

"Let her know I love her too." My voice cracks a little on the word love. After seeing her on the floor last night, I never thought I would have the chance to say those words again.

"Okay, call me if you hear anything."

"I will. You do the same. I love you."

"Love you too. Bye."

"Bye."

* * *

"Nick, what's going on?"

"Nothing happened in the night. The guard at the hospital fell asleep, so he's useless. I'll be ready for him. I'm taking Nancy and Agnes home now. We're going to Agnes's house. I won't leave them. How are things on your end?"

"Nothing's changed except the police have moved in. We called because we wanted to make sure you're all okay."

"We are as good as can be expected, under the circumstances."

"Same here. Alright then, talk to you soon."

"Oh Ryan, your mom and dad stopped by the hospital this morning and they said they were coming over to your house soon. Today, I mean. They said they were leaving to go to your house shortly after I saw them."

"What? I told them I would let them know when there was a good time to visit."

"They want to help, after all, this is about their family now too."

"That's true. I didn't really think of that. Thanks. Talk to you later."

"Yeah. Bye."

"Bye."

* * *

"April, my parents are coming over today. I don't know if you remember them or not, but they want to help. I know the timing is pretty lousy for you to meet your in-laws. If you want to lie down and take a nap instead, I'm sure they would understand. I would too. I don't want to add any more stress to your day. You have enough to think about without the added pressure of meeting them now, too."

"That's kind of you, Ryan. You think about others more often than yourself. I really like that about you, but I'm fine meeting your parents. I remember them from a long time ago. They were very kind to me then and I think they would be a comfort to have around today. I don't know how talkative I'll be, but like you said, I'm sure they'll understand."

Ryan reaches over and pulls me into his arms. As he holds me, I can't help but think about how honest I've been about my feelings, as of late. I grew up learning how not to express my feelings. My sister didn't know how to handle my tears, so she told me to stop crying even though sometimes I caught her crying too. I have noticed that since getting married, I've slowly started to let my feelings come back up to the surface. In the past if I had a sad feeling, I would do something to distract myself away from that feeling. Sometimes I would eat, other times I would call a friend, or watch a movie. I can't recall sitting down with anyone and talking through the problem. Helen and Ryan are the 'sit down and talk through issues' type of people. This is really different for me. They, in a way, are showing me how to process my feelings. I can see by his reaction that he actually cares about my feelings. I'm not used to that kind of attention. I can understand Helen caring because she gets paid to do that, but Ryan?

There was a buzz of excitement coming from the next room. As we turn the corner, we see the cops racing back and forth, getting their coats on, as they all seem to be in different conversations at the same time, pandemonium at its finest.

"Did you find her?" Not a single conversation pauses.

"Did you find her?" This time Ryan taps a man I haven't met yet on the shoulder. He addresses him as Bruce.

"Uh, Ryan, we didn't find her, but Nick caught a guy poking around Agnes's house. He was looking in the window. We think we have our man. One of our guys is bringing him in now. We're going to the station to find out more. We'll leave all the equipment just in case it's not him, but we're hopeful. Douglas will stay here for now. Gotta go."

Sergeant Smith, Carl, and Bruce leave. Douglas, who looks like a child whom has just discovered that there are no more cookies left in the cookie jar, remains sitting on Ryan's couch.

"Wait." Ryan pulls open the door. "What about us? We want to go too," he shouts after Carl and the rest of them.

"Sorry. You both need to stay in case we have the wrong guy, same plan as before. And, besides, right now we have to be cautious. He has it out for your family. We don't want him to see you and make matters worse. We'll let you know and maybe change the plan later, but right now you two stay put. Douglas, can you please answer anymore of their questions for them, I need to go. Ryan and April, we'll keep you informed," he says as he turns and races to his patrol car.

"Ryan, do you think that we'll have her back today?" I ask him as I grab his hand.

"I hope so. Let's call Nick. I'll put him on speaker."

Seconds later, the recording came on, informing us that he'll get back to us later. We try Nancy's next, same thing. It's hard to sit and wait. I like to have my list of things to do. I like to focus on how I'll get them all done in a day, and I spend time thinking about the best and most time efficient ways to do them. This sitting and waiting doesn't compute with my personality. It's not who I am. I can't plan how to do it, or what order to do it in, or feel like I'm making any progress. All I want is Alyssa home safely, but there's no plan for that.

"Ryan, when was the last time we ate? I'm feeling hungry all of a sudden. I think I'll eat some birthday cake. Do you want some?" I realize that I'm still holding his hand. I squeeze it before letting it go.

"Sure, cake sounds good."

I'm sure the police have him, finally!

"Douglas, do you want some cake?"

"Cake for lunch? Sounds great!" That's the closest he's been to happy since he found out he was being left out of the action.

I didn't realize it was lunch time when I suggested cake. Time melts together when you haven't slept much the night before. Coffee for breakfast and cake for lunch, I wonder what dinner will be, and if Alyssa will be here for it? Maybe I should cook. I don't think I should try without help. Maybe I'll ask Ryan to teach me how to make an easy dish.

Chapter 17

Phones remained soundless when I want them to ring and doorbells ring when I want them to be noiseless. I hear Ryan walk to the door. He'll call me if it's anything important. Busying myself with pouring milk and slicing cake, I miss the click of the front door closing.

"Mom, Dad, you remember April. April, my mom and dad are here, along with Nick. They all pulled up at the same time. Nick was telling us about the man he captured." That grabs my full attention.

"He was quite stupid in his approach. I was sitting in the living room watching him meander across the street. He was walking out in full view, seemingly, not caring who saw him. I didn't think much about him until he crept around the side of the house. He peeked through the office window and continued looking into each window that he passed. I told Nancy to call the police and I went out and tackled him to the ground. When I asked him what he was doing, he said he was just looking and that was it. I asked him where Alyssa was and he said he didn't know who that was. He was playing dumb. They'll break him any minute now. I know they will. He didn't have any ID on him so they're taking his prints and running them through the system." As Nick finishes talking, I reach for Ryan's hand. I hope he tells us where Alyssa is soon. She's so little and she shouldn't be left alone. She's probably very afraid, but it's a relief to know that he isn't with her now.

"I hope for good news soon. We went and saw Alyssa just a couple of days ago and she was happy and healthy. I can't believe someone would take her." Ellen wipes her eyes, sighs, and says, "Sorry. Umm, did you already eat lunch?" Ryan's mom wants to know.

"Actually, we lost track of time. I was cutting up cake for a snack not realizing it was lunch time," I say.

"Good, April, if you don't mind, we brought lunch over." Ryan's mom holds up a huge bag. "We stopped at that Italian restaurant down the street. We didn't know what anyone wanted, so we bought a few different appetizers and entrees. We expected a bunch of cops here, so we picked up a lot, but that's alright you can just reheat what's left over for dinner tonight, if you want. You shouldn't have to think about food preparation at a time like this."

"Thank you, Ellen. That was very thoughtful of you and it smells delicious. I haven't been to that restaurant yet." We start chatting as we set the table. She knows where everything is, while I'm still forced to pull open and shut drawers with nothing to add to the table.

Lunch was anything but quiet. The Nolsen's are a social bunch. I half listen as they joke with each other, longing for news about Alyssa. As we finish, Ellen shoos the males out of the kitchen. She and I work side by side cleaning up. We don't say much. What should I say to a woman I just met, after I eloped with her son? Do I say, sorry we didn't invite you? Or do I ask, what has Ryan told you about us? I try to think this through as my hands begin to sweat. Better to be in the situation without spending time worrying about it earlier. I think for now I'll continue to dry the dishes and hope she talks first.

"You know Ryan is a very special man," she starts.

"Yes, I'm seeing that. I'm so sorry we eloped. I honestly never would've wanted you to miss your son's wedding."

"I was shocked when I read his email. That was an unusual way to find out, but I respect his decision."

"You do?" I say as my eyelids hold high.

"Yes, I do. Ryan has an intense respect for those he loves. He wouldn't intentionally hurt his dad or me ever. We know he prayed long and hard about marrying you. Don't get me wrong. He has wanted to marry you since the sixth grade, but he wanted to marry you when you were ready. He always knew you were the one. He pined over you all through high school and when you went away to college, he was planning to switch to your school. I probably shouldn't have said any of that to you, but seeing you around him has warmed my heart. I have thought of you as my daughter for a very long time and I'm very happy to finally have it official."

She reaches for a napkin to wipe her eyes. When she finishes she pulls me into a hug. Did she really just say that? Me? I'm the one he has wanted to marry all along? Wait! Why am I not upset about this? I need to think this through. It was okay being married to Ryan when we both didn't love each other. It's completely different and scary being married to a man that loves me. The fluttering of my heart keeps informing me that my emotions are out of control. Am I having another panic attack? Am I going to black out again? I need to sit down. What does this mean? The chair supports my body's weight, but not my hearts.

"Are you sure you have the right girl? He always hung out with the cheer leaders."

"It might have appeared that way, but they hung out with him. Whenever he turned around, someone was talking to him or asking him for help. He has always had a tough time saying no when someone needed help, but I'm sure I don't have the wrong girl. He always wondered what happened between you two. He said that one day you just stopped talking to him. He couldn't figure it out. He dated a couple of girls in high school and he thought maybe that had something to do with your not liking him. I think that was his biggest regret. But that doesn't matter now that you're here, where you belong. Do you know that he built this house for you? He would ask Nancy and Alyssa what your favorite colors were and what you liked in a house. He wouldn't settle for anyone else either, it was you or no one, and for a very long time it's been no one. So no, I'm not upset about how you two married, but if you want to have another wedding at some point or even just a reception, we would be happy to put it together with you."

"That's very kind of you. I'm a little overwhelmed right now. I had no idea that he liked me. No idea at all." My hands begin to get sticky.

"Uh-oh. I've said too much. I should have let him tell you. I just assumed you knew."

"Really, it's okay. When we have Alyssa home, maybe then we can talk about a reception or another wedding. I haven't thought of having a wedding day for many years. I didn't want to get married or I thought I didn't want to get married. Now that I am, I'll have to think about it."

"Take your time...."

"Mom, are you giving April an earful, where I have to come in and save her?" Ryan's strained voice asks.

"Absolutely not. We were just having a great chat about you."

"Uh-oh, just what I thought." He sits down next to me at the kitchen table.

"My mom has a way of talking too much, sometimes. We tease her, saying she couldn't have raised a daughter because they would have overrun each other's sentences all the time."

"Ha-ha, Ryan, but true. I do talk too much, sometimes." She winks at me, but says nothing else about the matter.

"Why do I have this feeling that now is one of those times? Mom, what did you say?" She shrugs but doesn't even let her lips part.

"It must be bad, you're not saying a word." He turns to me.

"April?" I could tell that he's nervous about what his mom said. Truthfully, so am I. How can I reassure him when I need time to process what she just told me? I want to ask him if I'm the other girl, the one he has loved for years! I smile at him, hoping that's enough for him. It seems to be, since he puts his hands on his legs and pushes himself up.

"I guess I'll leave you two to your conversation," his head lower than when he entered the room.

* * *

I need some fresh air. My thoughts are suffocating. I know my mom told her everything. How am I going to explain to her that I have loved her since the sixth grade without sounding like a stalker? Oh, wait, I don't have to now. My mother already did. Arghh. Now what do I say to her? We were just starting to be friends and I felt a spark between us. I was hoping we could move past friendship soon, but now I might be a stranger to her again. She might panic and think that I am some sort of crazy person.

God, I'm desperate here. I was going to let April know when the time was right, but now that she knows I'm not sure how to act around her. I feel like a school kid with a huge crush. God, please make this work. I can't lose her again! I thought she was starting to like me, really like me.

Why did I have to leave the kitchen with Dad and Nick? I could talk to them any time, and our conversation wasn't exactly wholesome.

Thinking back, Nick was really trying to push my buttons.

"Ryan, please tell us what the most challenging part is for you in your marriage," Nick inquires.

"Why would you be asking questions about marriage, Nick? Or should I ask; why Nancy isn't here with us?"

"Nick, you've been spending time with Nancy?" My dad questions, while leaning forward.

"Actually, yes I have and I'm not saying anymore than that. I haven't run off and married her without telling you. So that brings us back to Ryan. Please tell me, have you struggled with gas yet?"

"Excuse me?"

"You know exactly what I mean. Are you two able to fart around each other yet?"

Punching him in the arm, "Nick, you really know how to pick a winning conversational piece."

"I'm serious. Do you hold it in as much as you can, until you have to leave the room before you let it loose?"

"No, I'm not comfortable with that. Can we talk about something else?" I say as I shift my weight to my left side.

They're both enjoying watching me squirm. When we were growing up, this was one of the topics that came up. We weren't sure if we could make a marriage work, because of gas. It was a puzzle to us.

"How about slowly letting one out? Have you done that, yet?" Nick pushes.

"Nick, have you ever done that around Nancy?" I question. "Or are you asking because you want an expert's opinion?"

"Alright boys, that was pretty funny. But seriously, Ryan, about eloping. Your mother and I understand why you did what you did and we respect your decision. We're hoping to have a reception for you if you would let us throw you one."

"That would be great Dad, but I'll have to talk to April first. We're hoping the police call any minute to tell us where Alyssa is. After she's home and safe, we'll talk about it. The waiting has been hard."

"Sorry, son. I'm not trying to be insensitive, I miss Alyssa too. If you were taken from me, I don't know what I would have done? You're doing everything you can, Ryan. I know you're praying non-stop and so have your mom and I. Nick has kept us informed about everything that has taken place, and we can see how God was in control yesterday, and how He is in control today, and the control is His tomorrow too. Keep on trusting Him to bring her home."

"I will Dad, I will."

* * *

The breeze is bitter as the sun barely peeks through the clouds.

"Ryan, we've been looking for you. We found the ladies talking, but didn't know where you went. You okay, son?"

I'm not sure, Dad. Mom told April everything before I've mentioned a thing to her. I'm not sure where that leave's April and me. I don't know if she's going to run. She must think that I've been stalking her all these years. And it does seem that way. I've been over at her sister's house often. I have a great relationship with Alyssa. I do almost all of Agnes's house repairs and as I'm saying all this, I'm convincing myself, that is exactly what I've been."

"You have loved her a very long time and you have kept your distance for so many years. You have respected her and loved her from far away. I have admired you for your dedication to your heart and have respected the lines that you have drawn. You have done nothing wrong and now she's your wife. God has blessed you. Now you have a great opportunity to go to her and talk to her about these feelings of yours. I know your mom didn't mean to make your situation harder for you. And if I can guess correctly, when she saw April grab your hand, she made an assumption. She probably thought you two already talked. She didn't mean harm, but if my guess is correct than your mom already thinks that April is in love with you. She wouldn't have opened her mouth otherwise. Son, your mother is rarely wrong when it comes to matters of the heart."

"You're right, Dad." We walk inside, finding Mom and Nick waiting with their coats on. Stalling would just make things harder. I've longed to tell April that I've loved her for over fifteen years. My sweaty palms are an indication that today is the day. After we hug everyone good-bye, April immediately excuses herself to go and take a shower. I'm not sure if I should wait here for her or busy myself with something else. Admitting love when you're not sure how it's going to be received is pace-worthy.

Chapter 18

I'm not sure what I should do. The shower didn't take nearly as long as I would have liked. Maybe I'll clean my room before I go back downstairs. My heart is pounding as if I just ran a quick mile. This is ridiculous! We have been around each other so much lately and I felt relaxed with him. Now, I'm not sure how to act around him. I'm not sure how I feel, either. I need more time to think this through. I could call Janice, no, she wouldn't get it. She'd call me an idiot and tell me to act like I'm married. I could call Nancy, no, she's taking care of mom and right now mom needs care and so does Nancy. I could call Helen but, I don't want a phone counseling session. Sara is probably still out of town because she hasn't called yet. What I want is a friend. I want someone that I can open up to and share my feelings with or at least work through my feelings with. Two hours ago I would have sought out Ryan, but now that's not possible. Maybe I should seek him out anyway. I have to talk to him sometime, right?

As I walk down the hallway, I hear Ryan talking to someone. It's not Douglas, so I think I'll sit on the steps and wait for whoever it is to leave. Today has been a madhouse with the amount of people showing up. They must have moved closer to the steps because their voices become clearer.

"Frank and Dan, how'd you know I was here and not at the office?" Ryan asks as he extends his hand first to Frank, then to Dan.

"We saw Nick earlier and he told us you were home. We just had to come and see for ourselves that you married April."

That voice sounds familiar, is that Dan or is it Frank?

"He's just kidding man," Dan says as he jabs him in the ribs with his elbow. "I came over to see if you wanted me to get your tax information. I was driving by and remembered you said you would bring it by my office. I just thought I'd save you a trip. Frank works with me now at the office and we were out grabbing a late lunch at that Italian place around the corner, so we decided to stop by."

"Thanks Dan. I did say that, but I don't have it all ready yet. I've been too busy."

"I did hear about Nancy and then Alyssa. How are they doing? Did they find Alyssa?" Dan asks.

"Nancy and Agnes are healing well, but Alyssa is still missing. I don't get why anyone would take her. She's so little and has such a strong bond with her mom and aunt. Alyssa must miss them terribly. I pray that somehow she has comfort in this time," Ryan replies.

"It's really sad," Frank puts in.

"Yes, it is. I'm not sure when I'll get around to taxes. I'll have to get back to you next week or the week after. Thanks for stopping by. I appreciate it," Ryan says.

"No problem. See ya, Ryan," Dan adds.

Now I remember Dan and Frank. They were on the basketball team with Ryan. They were a part of the group of guys that were talking about me all those years ago. Now that I think about it, so was the cop that was here today. Actually, Carl was the one who started that conversation and Frank and a few others were just listening and laughing at me while Ryan added his own comments. That day I declared that I would never talk to any of them again. I think it's time I settled this with Ryan once and for all.

As I was getting up from the top step, Ryan starts to walk up them. Our eyes lock and I'm ready to do battle.

"Ryan, I'm ready to talk."

"Good, so am I." We walk to the family room so we can have some privacy from Douglas. We each take the center cushion on the couches that face one another. I cross my arms, as I sit rigidly.

"I want to talk about that conversation I overheard many years ago between you and the guys."

"I'm not sure what conversation you're talking about. Can you be a little more specific?" His tone is calm.

"Yes, as a matter of fact, I can. And just to clear things up, I'm not a tramp and I'm not loose," I spit out.

"April, I need a little bit more information than that."

"Those were your words." Ryan leans back and stares at me. That look of confusion on his face is making my blood boil.

"Don't act like you don't know. Practically the whole basketball team was there. Even Carl the cop and Frank and Dan, who were just at the door, were involved. You were all there laughing at me like I was some sort of object. The way you were all talking about…." This is harder than I thought it would be. What they said about me was so hurtful. I reach for a tissue from the coffee table. I couldn't act angry anymore because, in truth, I was and still am deeply wounded.

"You were all talking about my dad and that since he left, someone had to take over the role. You were saying how I would go out with any man now that I didn't have a dad to keep me under control."

"Ohhh, April, I remember that conversation now and it's not what you think. There was a group of guys, mostly from the basketball team. They were talking about dumb teenage boy stuff and yes, they were talking about you. They were saying awful things about you and I lost it. I started yelling at them. I was being sarcastic though, not literal. I was saying what did they think, that just because your dad left, you lost your values too? Did they really believe that you would turn into a loose tramp just because of that? Did you hear anything after that?"

"No, that's when I ran to the girls' bathroom and cried the rest of the school day. I vowed never to talk to any of you again. And I didn't until this week."

"I wish you waited a little bit longer. I went on to say that you weren't anything like they were saying. Yes, you were gorgeous, and still are by the way, and you had a strong love for God and a respect for His Word, that you would never do something like that. I continued by telling them that you were a rare find among girls and that none of them could take that away from you ever, and that you were kind and sweet. I wish you heard that part. I wish I knew you were there. I would have taken you in my arms and held you until you stopped crying. I always wondered what I did to make you stop talking to me. I thought you just didn't like who I was. I...." Ryan stands up and comes over to my couch and embraces me. I hug him back, letting the pain drift away, as I absorb the truth that happened on that day long past.

"Guys, someone named Helen is here to see you," Douglas comments as he peaks his head around the corner.

"It's never quiet around here, is it?" I say.

"April, we need to talk more. Can't we cancel with Helen?"

"What do we do? She's already here."

"Yes, she is, but...."

"Hi, Ryan and April. Isn't it great that we don't have to meet at the hospital?"

"Yes, it is," Ryan answers Helen, but his eyes never leave mine. I can't believe after all these years he was the one defending me. I was a complete snob to him every time he came over to talk to me. I ignored him when he addressed me and I avoided places where I knew he would be. I spent so much energy hating him, when he was the one sticking up for me. Why didn't I learn how to communicate properly growing up? All I had to do was ask him about it. I'm such a jerk. One minute is all it would have taken to clear up years of hurt and anger and that sour tasting bitterness that entered my mouth, mind, and heart every time he was around. I didn't focus much on the other boys involved because they weren't the ones I liked. The day before that conversation, I decorated my folder with my and Ryan's name together in little hearts that said true love. But all that changed after that day. I was determined to make him my biggest enemy. I hated him with a passion. I majorly messed this up. He's never going to forgive me.

"April?"

"Yes."

"Are you alright?" Helen asks.

"I'm, just, uh, deep in thought," April responds.

"Do you want to share? Maybe we could help you sort through it?" Helen asks.

"Yes, April we could help." His expression longs for a response. Is he serious, he wants to talk this out in front of Helen?

"No, that's alright. I'll work it out in my mind first. Helen what are we talking about today?"

"I have good news. Nancy and I have been talking about her lists of events for you two to follow and she was letting me know that she put them into place because she thought she would be dead." We already know that, but I want Helen to be quick, so I don't interrupt. "She wanted to make sure that you were both the best parents you could be for Alyssa. She didn't want to leave her in a household where her two main parental figures were fighting all the time or ignoring each other or…. Anyway, she had one more 'or' but I can't remember it. Let me see, I took notes from our meeting. Ah, here it is 'or stuck in a home where there was no love between the two of you.' She said she knows that love in a marriage will provide a happy home for Alyssa and that a home without love between the married couple will cause hurt and heartache for everyone, hence the very long 'to do' list. She heard about you two holding hands and she thought you would figure it out on your own. She has left it up to you if you want to continue counseling after today, and she also said that I could rip up the list." Helen ends as she takes the letters from her bag.

"No, don't do that. I'll take them." I jump at the idea of retrieving them. Partly wondering about what she would have put us through and partly sentimental.

"Are you sure?" Helen asks.

"Yes, I'm sure. I'll put them in my purse." Ryan leans forward as Helen hands me the list. I know he wants them too. I don't want either of them to rip it up. For a while, they were the last thing I had that Nancy wrote. I wasn't sure if we would ever talk again. These papers are surprisingly special to me.

"Nancy also wants to talk to you at length about all that has happened. She feels really guilty about forcing you two to marry even though she has wished it for years. I know I'm speaking for her, but she said when we're all able to get together, she wants a chance to say it again, but for now she wanted me to tell you in person. She wanted to come over herself, but you know no one is permitted to leave their house in hopes that Alyssa is found, and that she is busy caring for your mom, and Nick is taking care of Nancy. I know the police think they found the man, but my opinion is different. I spoke to him today."

"What? They let you talk to him?" Ryan questions.

"Yes. They wanted someone with a psychological background to evaluate. I'm not supposed to say anything. Actually, I could lose my license, but finding Alyssa is more important than my career."

"I thought that we'd be holding her any minute. Why do you think he's not the one?"

"He seemed to be telling the truth. I saw the footage from when they first talked to him about Alyssa. He was surprised, truly surprised. He had no idea what they were talking about. The way he carried his body showed me that he wasn't hiding anything about her either. He was hiding something though. I couldn't get it out of him, but I doubt its' Alyssa's whereabouts."

"You've got to be kidding! The police have practically closed the door on this case when Nick assaulted the guy. Are you sure, Helen?" Ryan's voice is anything but quiet. He's pacing back and forth, running his hand through his hair repeatedly.

"Why didn't you mention this when you first walked through the door, or for that matter right after you talked to him?" Ryan questions.

"Ryan, I already told the police all of this. I hope they listen to me and that they get back out there to find the real guy. I did come here right after I met with them. I wanted to tell you the good news first because I wanted to give you a little more time of relative comfort. I was wrong. I also don't want either of you to do something stupid, but that's not my decision, it's yours."

"You're right about that," Ryan says as his nostrils grew.

"I'm sorry," Helen replies.

"It's alright. I have to go get Nick. I know I'm not supposed to leave, but April you're here. Helen, are you free to stay here for another hour or so?"

"Yes, I can," she quietly answers.

"April, you and I will talk later," he calls as he quickly moves to the door. Abruptly, he turns back, picks me up and kisses me long on the mouth. He steps back looking intensely into my eyes, then swiftly grabs his coat and goes out the side door. I have never been kissed by someone I like, but I have no time to think about my kiss and my feelings toward it. Alyssa wasn't coming home. I stupidly let my mind move on to other thoughts since I figured the police were bringing her home. Is she safe? Has she eaten anything? Is she freezing somewhere? Where is she?

Oh, God, please bring her home. I'm desperate. We can't do this without You. We can't find her. The world is too big, but You know where she is. You can see her right now and You can keep her safe. Please keep her safe.

I sit with my head in my arms for a long time. Helen knows I need it quiet as I plead with God. My guess is Helen was doing the same. I don't know what Ryan thinks he can do, but I hope it works.

Sapped, exhausted, dysfunctional, and bleary-eyed, my thoughts are randomly playing, one over the other, but not one producing fully as they incompletely surround me. Pacing back and forth, I try hard to think of something productive that I could do in this situation. How can I find her? Nothing, not a single idea comes to mind. I haven't helped her one bit sitting here in this house, her house, but she might not ever get to live here. I should go out and look for her. How can I get rid of Helen long enough to leave? I have to do something. And on I go back and forth, back and forth.

"April, please sit down."

"I don't want to."

"Okay, but what you're doing isn't helping."

"What do you want me to do? Tell me what I can do right now that will help?" I shout as she sits there silently. "I didn't think you had a better idea for me; please only talk if you think of one." I say slightly softer.

I'm letting fatigue and worry engulf my tongue. I can't get over how I'm losing control, I should just walk out. Usually, when I don't agree with the person I am talking to, I let them talk and try to politely finish the conversation. If I'm in a place where I can't leave I try to change the subject, and if those two fail me, I excuse myself and go to the bathroom. It's rare for a person to continue the same conversation once I've returned, so I have had great success with this method, but now there isn't time or patience.

Pacing seems to work best for me when I'm in this state.

"Ladies, we finally got him to talk. He didn't do it. Some man approached him on the street and gave him money to go and look in the windows. He didn't think he would get arrested, but the guy told him if anyone asked him what he was doing not to tell them. He said the man was about five-eleven, medium build. He had brown hair and was wearing jeans. That's all that he remembers. We are patrolling the streets. A couple of men are coming back here, but most will be out combing the streets." Douglas informs us.

"What can I do? Can I go with one of them to help look?" I plead.

"No, we need you here in case he calls. We have to keep you by the phone because if one of us answers, he might get spooked. For Alyssa's safety, you have to stay and Nancy has to stay by her phone too. It's the only way."

"We've stayed off the phone this whole time. Why hasn't he called?" I frustratingly whine.

"I don't know the answer to that, but when he does call we'll be ready," Douglas states.

"Does Nancy know this?" Helen asks.

"Yes, the men over there have told her."

Douglas goes back to his station in the living room as Helen and I sit in the family room. If Nancy has this information, then I have to think that Nick will find out also. Hopefully this news will make its way to Ryan. There has to be a way to bring her home. This man has harmed everyone else so maybe I need to make myself visible so he can get to me too. Then I can bring Alyssa home myself. The plan was formulating in my mind. I can do this.

Chapter 19

What is taking so long? This man is a liar. He said to trust him and that my mom would be here soon. She isn't here and I'm not sure she's coming. I know he could just pick up a phone and call her. If he did, then she would come right away. She always comes when I call her. She leaves her job too, sometimes, just to come and see me at school. Sometimes she brings me my lunch and sometimes she takes me home, so I don't have to ride the school bus. She knows how I don't like the bus. She hugs me and tells me she loves me. She feeds me food I like, not like this man. He buys these gross tasting sandwiches that have hard bread and hard cheese in them. I don't eat them. He told me if I didn't eat dinner, he would force me to eat it. He also made me drink this bad tasting drink. He won't bring me water until I drink it. He told me he won't leave the room either, so I drink it every time.

I want my Mommy. She would hold me right now and rub her fingers through my hair until I fall asleep. She would keep me warm too. I'm so cold here. I asked him to turn up the heat, but he must not know how because it's still really cold. He gave me a sweatshirt that's way too big, but that's okay because it helps a little.

I've seen this man before, but where? He told me he was a friend of mommy's, but I don't remember seeing her talking to him, but I have seen him before.

"Alyssa, here's a drink for you."

"Who are you?"

"I told you, I'm a friend of your mother's."

"I never saw you talk to her before."

"Maybe not, but you saw me talk to your aunt, right?" he questions.

"I don't remember?"

"It doesn't matter. Drink this."

"No."

"If you don't, I won't bring your mommy here."

I reach for the cup because I want my Mommy. I drink it fast because it tastes very bad.

"I want my Mommy now."

"She will be here very soon, sooner than you think."

"Really? I'm not feeling very good." My stomach hurts. That stuff must be poison. My Mommy told me I could die if I drink poison. Am I going to die? I need to tell someone. I need to go to the hospital, but there is no one here but this man who is trying to kill me.

"Why are you trying to kill me?"

"I'm not trying to kill you."

"I don't feel good and it's because of the stuff you just gave me to drink. You gave me poison." I feel funny. I feel dizzy.

"Put your head down on this pillow."

I need my Mommy. The loud click tells me that I'm alone again. If my Mommy doesn't come by tonight, I don't know what I'll do.

Chapter 20

Driving around isn't helping any.
"Nick, we need a better plan."
"I was thinking the same thing. He's not going to have Alyssa parading the streets. He's hidden her well. Maybe we should talk to the community. Perhaps someone has seen something unusual, or even seen her."

"We need to get her picture out everywhere. Let's call Carl at the station and find out what we can do from here. After that, I'm going to call the church and have as many people as we can praying and looking for her. I'll call him now." I punch in his number and wait.

"Carl, we want to know what you guys are doing about finding Alyssa."

Nick taps me on the shoulder and motions for me to put it on speaker phone.

"We have been working non-stop. We have every extra person looking for them."

"Them, what do you mean them? You have him in custody already."

"No, he's the wrong guy. He confessed to taking money from a man. All he had to do was peek in a couple of Agnes' windows."

"Helen was right then," I mumble under my breath.

"What did you say? Oh, I don't have time, so don't answer that. Anyway Helen was right, she talked to the suspect earlier and we were listening to her about him too. That's actually how we got him to talk," Carl states.

"What did the man say he looks like?" Nick was writing it down.

"What about the media?" I ask.

"Her picture has been on the news every half hour. We have her on the local stations and we have guys going around town asking if anyone has seen her."

"How can we help?" I want to know.

"You can get people together to start asking around also."

"Okay, if there's anything else we can do, let us know."

"I'll talk to you soon. Bye, Ryan."

"Yeah, bye." Click.

"That didn't get us very far."

"No, it didn't. Nick, call the church and have them run this through the prayer chain, and also if people are interested in helping, tell them that we're going to have a prayer meeting tonight at the church, let's make it for 7 o'clock. We need all the help we can get. Maybe someone there can help us figure out a better way to find her."

"Okay, why don't you swing by Nancy's and I'll make all the calls. We should go back home and protect our women too."

Chapter 21

"April, how are you feeling?" Helen asks.

"I'm feeling angry."

"At?"

"At the man who has Alyssa. He tricked us."

"Are you feeling anything else?"

"Yes, I'm really worried about Alyssa. What if he's hurt her? She's so little." I slump down onto the couch reaching for the box of tissues that are on the end table next to the lamp. This is unbearable.

"Why her? Why my family? Why won't he leave us alone? He has ruined my life repeatedly. I want him locked up for life. He must be caught." If Helen wants feelings, I don't mind sharing them.

"I agree. He must be caught. When you think of Alyssa what do you feel?"

After a long nose blowing, "I feel worried and fearful. I wish I could take her place."

"Do you think she's still alive?" Helen asks timidly.

"Honestly, yes." My voice holds surprising strength. "I don't think she's dead."

"Do you feel at peace about her being alive?"

"I didn't think of it that way. But yes, I think that's the calmness that I feel. I don't feel anxious about her mortality, just about her well-being, if that makes sense. I want her home. I don't want her in that creepy man's hands." I say shuttering from head to toe.

"I don't either."

The doorbell's ring causes both of us to jump up and race to the door. Douglas beats us. A woman with very windblown hair stands on the front step bundled from head to toe.

"I don't know who you are, but let me in. I need to see April."

"Douglas, you can let her in. That's my friend Janice," I voice.

As Douglas steps aside, Janice rushes in, bumping him along the way. She isn't fazed, nor does she care enough to apologize.

"April, what happened? Ryan said it was an emergency and to come over here at once." She's still in her bathrobe and her hair is up in rollers, some of it anyway.

"It's…." I fall into her arms as a cry escapes my mouth. We embrace for a long time.

"Alyssa," I say as I pull away and sit on the couch. "She's been kidnapped."

"What?"

"You know about Nancy getting into a car accident. She's fine but we found out that it wasn't an accident. The same person that messed with her brakes took Alyssa from my mother's house last night. He hit my mom on the head. She lost a lot of blood and we weren't sure if she was going to be alright, but she's doing fine now also.

We haven't heard anything from the kidnapper. I've been sitting here by the phone waiting for it to ring and it hasn't. They tell me I can't leave or do anything else in case he calls. It's been horrible, Janice. I just sit here waiting, longing to cradle my Alyssa in my arms. I've been praying, more than ever, too. I hope God answers soon. She's so little."

"I can't believe it, not Alyssa."

"I can't believe it, either," forgetting that Helen is in the room.

"I wish Nancy could be here. They want her to stay over there by her phone too. We need to keep our cell phones free also, so we can't even talk to each other. There has to be something else I can do besides sitting here," hoping Janice can think of it.

"I can see why they have you staying here. If anyone else answers, he might hang up and that could be very bad for Alyssa."

"You're right. I know that in my heart, but my mind wants to go do something more."

"Why don't we plan Alyssa's favorite meal? That way when they find her, all we have to do is warm it up."

"I guess. I really don't feel like cooking right now, but if you want to, I'll sit in the kitchen with you."

"Okay. What shall I make her? Oh, wait, first have you eaten dinner yet?" Janice wonders.

"No, but I'm not very hungry."

"You still need to eat," she insists.

"I'm not hungry," I mumble.

"That doesn't matter. I'll cook you all dinner and then you can decide if you're not hungry after you smell it."

"Fine, whatever you want to do, Janice."

113

"Good."

"Why are you in your bathrobe?"

"Isn't this the latest style?"

"Ha-ha. Really," I wonder.

"Ryan said it was an emergency."

"Yes, I remember you saying that, but you didn't answer why you were in your PJ's and bathrobe at 5 p.m."

"Oh, I was just lazing around the house."

"Spill it, Janice."

"You know me too well. I went out on a blind date last night. We talked on the phone a few times before the date and I thought we really had a connection. Turns out that when he saw me last night, there was nothing resembling the man I talked to on the phone. He barely said five words the whole night and when I ordered dessert, I could see the judgment on his face. I actually only ordered it to make sure I was right about him. I mostly pushed it around my plate while I made nonsensical small talk. I wasn't about to tell him that I've already lost twenty pounds in the past five months. If he couldn't like me for who I am right now, then the loss is his. I was sulking today. That's why I'm still in my bathrobe, but I didn't run to food like I usually do."

"I had no idea you were going on a date. He sounds like a real loser to me. You're right. If he can't like you for who you are, than good riddance to him. Janice, you are one of a kind and someday soon, some great guy is going to come along and see that."

"Thanks," Janice shrugs.

Janice is a whiz in the kitchen. Within no time, she has a meal made for all of us. It smells great too. Even Douglas comes in to sit with us.

"Janice, you're a great cook. I haven't had a meal this good since, well, I can't remember. Please, don't let my mom know I said that," Douglas confides as he leans his shoulder into Janice's arm.

"You don't have to worry about me saying anything; I'm very good at keeping secrets." I'm the only one in the room who knows Janice well, but I just didn't have the heart to laugh at the outrageous lie she just told. As we clean up the dishes and put away the food, my mind keeps trying to formulate a plan to get Alyssa home.

"Janice and Helen, I know it's only a little bit after six, but I need to get some rest. I'm going to lie down. You're both welcome to stay."

"Janice, if you're willing to stay here, I think I'll make my way over to Nancy's. I can't believe she's home when only a couple of days ago we thought she was dead. I would like to spend more time with her."

"I'm fine staying here. I think I'll just watch some television. If you want, April, I can spend the night."

"It's up to you. I need to stay by the phone, so I'll nap down here in the family room. Janice, you can watch television in the room with Douglas. Good night, ladies." I didn't think another day would go by without seeing Alyssa. The couch was fairly comfortable for sleeping. I'll just rest for a couple of hours, then….

Chapter 22

My cell phone chimes once. What time is it? It's dark out, but that doesn't mean much because it's in the middle of the winter, and it gets dark very early now. My phone is, unfortunately, stuck in my pants pocket. No matter how hard I twist, I can't manage to get my hand around it and back out of my pocket. I need more sleep.

What day is it? Standing upright seems to be the only way I could retrieve it. It's from an unavailable number, a text message. It says, "Don't tell anyone or I'll hurt Alyssa. Go into the kitchen, grab the garbage and walk out the back door." My phone chimes again. "If anyone asks, just tell them you're taking out the garbage." My hands tremble as I put the phone back in my pocket. Douglas is in the living room and Janice is sitting next to him, talking. They don't hear me walk by. I don't know where Ryan is, but my phone says it is 6:30 p.m. so it's not very late.

As I walk to the kitchen, I grab the garbage and look for a coat to wear. The only one available was on the back of a chair. It looks like a man's coat, but I don't have time to be picky. I have to think fast. He's outside waiting for me, and I cannot put Alyssa in danger. I glance around the countertops and notice a piece of paper, but no pen. I'm running out of time. I pull open the first drawer closest to the paper and luckily find a pencil. I scribble, 'Help, he told me not to tell or he'd hurt Alyssa. April.' I don't know if that makes sense, but I have no time to change it. He might hurt her.

I lift the garbage and walk out the back door. I don't see anyone. What am I supposed to do now? As if sensing my indecision, my cell goes off again. Flipping it open, it reads, "Drop the garbage and walk to the side of the house."

I know this is crazy. I should have told someone, but I can't risk Alyssa's well-being. I should be terrified, but I'm not. I ought to be shaking. I know that this is what I have to do. This is what I've been trying to think of earlier, a way to get him to come to me. Now I can protect her. This man doesn't scare me anymore. He no longer has control of me, like he has for the past several years. As I walk my confidence grows. I can do this, one foot in front of the other.

A hand forcefully covers my mouth while another wraps around my stomach. There's no turning back now. I don't put up a struggle, there's no point. I want to go where he's taking me. I can't see his face, but I don't want to either. His smell is all too familiar. It's one I'll never forget, but it's alright. Alyssa will be home soon, even if I don't get to return. He pulls me toward the front of the house, but stops abruptly as headlights shine on us. He throws me up against the side of the house, bruising my shoulder. I start to slide down the wall, but he yanks me up by my strawberry blond hair. He leans close to my ear and whispers that if I make one wrong move, Alyssa's blood would be on my hands. I stand perfectly still, even though my head and shoulder are throbbing.

He waits about ten seconds and then pulls me back toward the neighbors' yard. The snow is deep and it's hard to keep up with him, but I try my best. Slipping on a rock, I lose my footing and twist my ankle as I fall down. I let out a yelp and find a gun pushing into the side of my head. He pushes it hard while he grunts orders for me to get up. I slowly stand and start to run with him again as pain shoots from my foot on up my leg; my ankle is either sprained or broken. I know that if I don't move, I will be risking Alyssa's life. We continue through two more backyards which lead us into a wooded area. A car sits parked on the deserted road. As he shoves me into the passenger seat, he puts the gun away. Relief should be flooding in, but I'm still not afraid.

I quickly look in the back seat hoping to see Alyssa there, but find only empty space. Where is she? There are no keys in the ignition. He slides into his seat, "Give me your cell phone."

I reach into my pocket and hand it to him. I was hoping to send a message first, but he beat me to it. I didn't think I would get injured or lose my phone.

"Try anything stupid and you'll get hurt. Do you understand?"

"Yes," I choke out as apprehension creeps in. I didn't think his voice would send chills down my spine, but now it does and now I'm afraid. This battle between fear and peace rage on. *God, how do I trust You, now? I know You are in control, but I'm afraid. What's he going to do to me? Help me.*

Chapter 23

"Janice, I'm glad you're here, but where's April?" Ryan demands. "She's taking a nap in the family room."

"No, she isn't."

"What do you mean, 'she isn't'?" Janice shrieks as she jumps up and starts calling April's name. We search the whole upstairs and find no sign of her. Her bed is made and her clothes are neatly put away. Her car is still in the garage. We continue through the first floor.

"She wouldn't have left. April would do anything to get Alyssa back and she knew staying by the phone was the most important task for her to do. She wouldn't even sleep upstairs for fear of missing the call," Janice says as we sit down at the kitchen table.

"You're right Janice, April would do anything for Alyssa. What if the kidnapper contacted her and she…?" My eyes scan the counter and that's when I see her note.

"Janice, look at this, it says, 'Help, he told me not to tell or he'd hurt Alyssa.'"

"She went with him," Janice says as her face loses all color and she grabs the nearest chair.

Now Douglas was in the room reaching for the note and his phone at the same time.

"How could she have left without letting me know? I would have taken him down." Douglas starts turning red.

"Maybe they're still out there." I stand up and run out the back door, not wasting time finding my coat. I draw my gun, which I only carry when necessary, and hold it pointing down. In front of me is a bag of garbage. I creep along the side of the house and follow the tracks recently made in the snow, by what appears to be two adults. Alyssa wasn't with them. The tracks lead along the side of the house. They must have been standing on the side of the house for a little while. There are an abundance of footprints as they approach the front of the house. Someone fell by the wall and was dragged about two feet.

"Did you find anything?" Douglas shouts as he makes his way around the front of the house.

"Yes. There are two sets of prints. There seems to have been a struggle here. It leads to the neighbor's yard. Let's go." After only a few steps we notice a big indentation, like someone fell hard to the ground. As I bend down I see a red tinge in the snow.

"There's a handprint here. It looks too small to be a man's. It must be April's; along with a little bit of blood." My stomach rocks back and forth at this realization. She's hurt, my wife is out there and some man has hurt her. My hand clenches into a tight fist, wishing to make contact. I will not let anyone hurt April. She's too precious to be treated like this. We proceed quickly through two backyards and come to a wooded area.

That's where we lost the trail and all that's left are tire tracks leading down a snow covered dirt road, the road that took April out of my life. I have waited all my adult life to make April my wife and now that she is, I will not let someone take her away from me. She needs me more than ever, and I will bring her home. April, please trust that I will bring you home. But what if it's not God's will? Not a thought I'm going to dwell on.

We turn and run back to the house. I need to get in my truck and see what direction they're heading. Douglas is panting behind me trying to keep up. When we make it back to the house, three police cars are in the driveway.

"What happened, Doug you were supposed to be watching her?" Captain Smith yells.

"I, I, I was watching her. She was taking a nap on the couch in the family room. I didn't think I needed to stand over her and watch her sleep. I don't know how this happened," he yells back.

"One more screw up and you're fired," Smith sneers.

"I'd fire me too." They're wasting my time; I need to interrupt this claptrap.

"Smith, there are tracks that lead to some dirt road I've never seen before. I'm not sure where it exits, but I'm going to check it out." By this time, Captain Smith and a few others are listening.

"Wait one minute, Ryan. You're not going to interfere again in a police investigation, are you?" Smith snorts.

"There is no interfering when the victim," through my tight jaw, I finish with, "is my wife."

"That's where you're greatly mistaken, Ryan." He steps closer to me, but I'm not going to let him bully me. I stand up straight to my 6' 2" height and look down at him.

"I'm not here to argue, Smith. I'm going and that's final. If you want to send a man with me, tell him now." I move passed him to my truck. As I reach for the door handle, Carl grabs the passenger side one.

"Wow, Ryan, you really know how to piss Smith off. I love it." He chuckles as he slides into the vehicle. The humor's lost on me. All I can think about is bringing Alyssa and April home. Peeling out of my driveway, I long to hear their voices.

When we approach the second house, I slow the truck down to a crawl. We scan the right side of the road looking for a dirt road outlet. The street comes to an end and so does my hope. We've lost them by now and we still can't find where they came out. We circle the surrounding roads, but still have no luck. We back track and seem to find more of the same thing, nothing.

"How about we do this from the other direction? Let's park in front of your neighbors' house and I'll get out. I'll run the track and when I get to the other end, I'll wait until you circle around. I'll call you when I get there," Carl persuades.

"Alright." His plan sounds good since we know they're not here. He gets out and starts running through the backyard. I'm not sure where I should drive. Maybe I should have gone with him? What if he finds something and doesn't tell me about it because I'm not with the force? Hitting the steering wheel, I should have thought of that before agreeing to this.

"Nick, it's Ryan. April's missing! She left a note. He took her! He said he would harm Alyssa if she didn't go without saying a word." I choke on the last two words. *God, I thought waiting so long to marry her was going to be my biggest trial, but I was sorely mistaken. Please help me get her back.*

"What? How did that happen? There are supposed to be cops watching her!" Nick shouts.

"I know. I'm not sure, either. Looks like Douglas might get fired. Can't say I'm sorry for him either. He really messed this up. But I should be pointing the finger at myself. I should have been there right beside her. I should have been there protecting her, not Douglas."

"Ryan, you were out looking for Alyssa. You can't blame yourself. You were doing everything you could do to help."

I let out a heavy sigh as a single tear runs away from my left eye.

"Nick, I don't know what to do."

"Pray, and wait for me. I'll be right over."

"No, don't come over. You need to be there protecting Nancy and Agnes. I can't let anything happen to them again. And I need to get to the prayer meeting. More than anything right now, that's where I need to be."

"You're right. We need to stay in touch at least. Call me when you know anything or if you need to talk through any clues or scenarios."

"Okay. Bye."

"Bye."

Chapter 24

"Where are you taking me?" I question.
"I'm taking you to Alyssa." he replies.
"Is she okay?" I ask in a timid voice.

"She's fine, a little sleepy, but fine. I told Alyssa I'd bring her, her mother, I mean. She needs some clothes, but I don't trust you, yet, to buy them in the store. I'll think of something."

Before I could come up with a plan to make him think he could trust me, something causes him to slam on the brakes. I fly off the seat and my head smacks into, what I think is, the glove compartment. The sharp pain spreads from my temple down my back. I'm stuck between the seat and the dashboard. I'm confused as to which way I'm facing. My hands are tied behind my back and I have a blindfold around my eyes, making it so I can't see which way to turn. He steps hard on the gas and my nose hits something hard. I struggle to get back on the seat. I can hear him chuckling under his breath. The blood starts to trickle down into my mouth. Tears prick my eyes. The pain throughout my body is almost unbearable and I'm close to blacking out from it, but I know I'm not quite there yet.

I hope Alyssa hasn't suffered like I am now. For her I will gladly die, just as long as he keeps his hands off her. When he placed the blindfold over my eyes, I could smell his stale breath. He leaned close to my ear as he tied the knot, and my stomach churned remembering the last time he was that close. To repeat those events from a long time ago might lead me into a state of insanity. I don't know if I can emotionally survive another.

I give up trying to get back on the seat. It's evident that he doesn't care where I'm sitting. I might be safer on the floor anyway. I find a spot to brace my body against. The next time he decides to stop short, I'll be able to hold myself up.

"Where is Alyssa now? Is she all alone?"

"Nice try. I'm not going to tell you where she is, and as for her well-being, let's just say I've taken very good care of her." His voice oozes with perversion.

"You better not have touched her." I try to hit him with my shoulder, but only come up hitting air.

His elbow crashes into my check. "Try something like that again and you will, truly, regret it. Alyssa might get hurt too."

"I'm sorry." I'll say anything as long as Alyssa stays out of this. "Alyssa has nothing to do with this, please leave her alone."

"Now, that is where you are greatly mistaken, April, Alyssa has everything to do with this."

Chapter 25

"April, tell me where Alyssa's father is?" His voice drips with chilling sarcasm.

"He died."

"Don't lie to me, April," he growls as his hand rushes across the seat and grips my neck. His grip tightens as he leans over to my ear.

"April, where is Alyssa's father?" His lips are pressed against my ear, saliva sprays down my earlobe as he emphasizes each word. Green repulsion rises up in my throat as his fingers squeeze the last bits of light from my eyes.

"He's dead," comes sputtering out of my mouth as my life fades into bleakness. *God please keep Alyssa and Ryan safe. I love them both, so much. I just wish I was able to tell them myself.*

Chapter 26

All three hundred and twenty of us hold hands. We circle the church building, each standing in six inches of snow, but no one seems to care. The frigid air doesn't interrupt anyone's thoughts. Our mitted hands link, along with our hearts, we believe God is in control and that's what is keeping our eyes focusing on Him and Him alone. We pray that He would keep Alyssa safe.

Many of us are burdened to pray for April's safety as well. We know she is in great danger, probably even as we speak. We cannot hear beyond ten people away as the fierce wind whips through our sphere, but it also brings phrases with it. *Protect April, I can feel that she is in great danger. She is in the presence of the enemy, but You are still in control. You are a Mighty God. You are the Alpha and the Omega, beginning and the end and this man has no hold on her, release his physical hold on her. You are with her right now. You will never leave her. Give her peace. Keep her alive please. Help them escape. Please continue to carry her.... and on the wind tosses our prayers to the ears of the ones that need to hear, to encourage others to pray.*

At some point during the prayers, the nights' coldness lifts replacing itself with a spring like-breeze. Gloves are shoved into pockets and scarves flung aside. The warmth brings renewed spirits. Some leave the circle while others enter it, never leaving a gap. A sweet small voice starts to sing Amazing Grace and after the first verse and chorus, the rest join in. Chills run up my arms and down my back, confirming that no matter what happens, my faith is standing firmly on solid ground. I haven't heard a chorus this large and passionate. The uplifting hands and the powerful voices praising God fill the community. Maybe April and Alyssa can hear our voices and know that we are praying for them.

I surrender my wife to You. I trust her in Your hands alone. Please bring my love back to me. Thank You for the peace that You are giving me. I know that no matter what the outcome, You will never leave me or them and I thank You for that.

Chapter 27

A hand reaches out and grips my shoulder.
"Ryan, we might have a lead. Come with me." I barely release
the hand of the person next to me as I push Carl toward his car. We break
into a run. My heart pounds hard, but not from exertion. Are they all right?
Are we going to find them alive? Am I going to be able to hold April and tell
her I love her? Will the one kiss we shared be our only? The questions were
too tough to handle. I slide into the passenger seat knowing that I'm not in
charge of this any more than the enemy that holds her hostage, but my best
friend JC is.

"Did you see her?"

"No, we just got a call from an anonymous tip saying they saw a light
blue mini-cooper leaving your house right after April was taken. We spotted
one on…wait there it is. What is he doing at the church?" He was pointing
across the street from the church at the car he was just talking about. It's
cruising by at a very slow pace, but we're quite a distance from him.

"Carl speed up, you are going way too slow."

"I don't want him to see us. After all, I'm driving in a marked police
car."

"But at this rate, we'll lose him."

"I know how to follow someone, Ryan," he spits out.

He isn't doing a good enough job. I wish I had my truck. We creep
closer to the mini-cooper, but he steps heavily on his gas pedal and flies down
the road. Carl finally follows suit and takes some action, but we're losing
him. He reaches for his walkie-talkie and puts out a call.

"I've spotted the suspect in the mini-cooper. He's going westbound on
23, repeat going westbound on Route 23. He just passed the church, Ryan
what's the name of your church?"

"The Windham Community Church."

"Just passed the Windham Community Church, I repeat the Windham
Community Church." We race through town, but no matter how fast we go,
there was no sign of the Mini. Gritting my teeth, I find it hard not to strangle
Carl. He really messed this up, strike two for the police force. If I were
driving I would have April and Alyssa sitting next to me by now.

Chapter 28

"Now, this is fun. The church family outside holding hands, singing a song to some God they believe created this world. Ha-ha. April, do you hear them? They're outside singing to your God," he mocks.

Silence.

"I'll show them who has power. Look at them, the sight of them holding hands in the cold. If only they could see how their prayers are being answered right now, if they could see you on the floor, motionless. They would see that I have the power." He grips the steering wheel as he chuckles under his breath. "I'm in control over you now, April. I have waited several years for the right time to have you and now I do. You'll learn, over time, to obey and talk nicely to me. You'll learn how to respect me. If not, I'll continue to beat you until you do. Once you learn that, then we can be a happy family. You'll love me, too."

It's time to go, he thinks as he watches those idiots for far too long. There they stand praying for April when she's within walking distance from them, and they have no idea. Why doesn't their God tell them that? They have no clue. He's tempted to roll down his window and shout, 'I found her.' But he'll wait just a little bit longer before he lets them know that he's the one with the real power. He prides himself on how perfect his timing and planning are.

April hasn't made a sound. Flipping on the overhead light reveals a pool of blood on the floor, next to her head. He doesn't want her to die, yet. He hurries home to fix her up. It's good for her to suffer though, like she made him suffer all these years.

Pushing hard on the gas, he turns around the bend and down a dirt road that only he knows about. It leads straight to nowhere in everyone's mind, but his. His second home is two miles into this deep forest of land, his land.

Stopping the car, he turns off the ignition and pulls open the passenger side door. He nudges her, but she doesn't stir. He pushes a little harder and still nothing. He isn't a medic by any means, but he knows the next step was to see if she has a pulse. Bending over, he places his slimy fingers on her neck and waits, nothing. Maybe he has the wrong spot. He tries different places, but only winds up with the same results. His fists clench, as his nostrils start to flare. Kicking the car hard with his boot, than slamming the door, he's unsure of what to do next. He feels his perfect planning falling apart. She messes up everything. He cannot drop her off at the hospital and he doesn't want her dead. He goes back to the side door and opens it. She still hasn't moved. He reaches over and picks her up. Maybe trying the mouth to mouth stuff he's seen on House might work.

As he enters the living room, he sees yesterday's leftovers lying on the coffee table, or is that what he ate two nights ago. Days tend to blend together after a while. Shoving garbage off the couch and onto the floor, he puts April down. Her cut is still bleeding. That must mean she isn't dead, right? Can dead people bleed? He thinks about googling that later. He needs to think. What should he do? Oh, the mouth to mouth thing. As he bends down to start, April's eyes fly open and she lets out this horrific scream. She starts scratching at his face and kicking her feet.

* * *

"Get away from me. Don't touch me," I continue to scream, and kick, and scratch. I'm fighting for my life, but he doesn't fall. He keeps on coming back and blocking me. He has my wrist now. He pulls it too hard behind my back.

"Aghhh."

The pain is shooting through my entire body. I must have broken part of my arm and now he's breaking my wrist. I have to calm down. I'll never make it out of here this way. He'll overpower me every time.

"Please stop." Black spots enter my line of sight.

"Who's in charge?"

"You are." The agonizing pain rips through my body and creates a sheet of blackness through my line of vision. My knees buckle, no longer willing to hold my weight. I don't know if I fell or if he dropped me, but I'm now on the cold, filthy floor. My vision surges back as the pain abates.

"There's a bathroom over there." Pain shoots through my neck as I turn my head to see him pointing to a door three feet away. "Get up and put yourself together before I show you to Alyssa. She can't see you like that."

"She's here?"

"Yes, and she wants to see you. I'm tired of her whining about the food not tasting good."

As I push myself up with my hands, my left hand warns me of my limited mobility. Somehow, I managed to get to a sitting position, but have to lean over and lose my dinner along the way. I waver as I force my body to stand. I don't want to waste another minute without Alyssa. I give more than I ever thought I had to give. I hope she's okay. Stumbling forward, I find the bathroom. The mirror reveals a strange woman who looks in need of medical assistance. I don't recognize the face that's staring back at me. My left eye is nearly swollen shut and my cheek is the size of a plum. My teeth are, thankfully, all in place. Blood coats my temple and trails all the way down to my hair line, then proceeds to my neck. A quick bleary glance reveals nothing sanitary, leaving me no other choice. I rip off the end of my already torn shirt. Somehow I manage to fasten it around my head. I'm not sure how to put pressure on it, but I'll think of that later. I need to get to Alyssa.

"You look horrible. Maybe I'll lock the two of you up until you're better to look at. Come this way."

My eye is focused on the closed door a few steps in front of me. "Yea, though I walk through the valley of the shadow of death, I will fear no evil; For You are with me; Your rod and Your staff, they comfort me."

He opens the locked door and shoves me in. As I stumble forward, he slams the door shut, locking it.

* * *

Our search has been called off so we make our way back to the jail. There hasn't been another lead either. Carl and I drove up and down every street in this town. I even called Fred, the sanitation man, to see if we missed any spots that he could think of. He led us down a couple of roads that I didn't know exist, but we still turned up with nothing.

"Now that we know the type of car he drives, we can narrow down our search."

This is the information I can't get without the police force. I want to ditch Carl and pick up Nick, but not before I find out about that car.

"Carl, there can't be that many Mini-Coopers registered up here. This has to be it. How long until you have the list of names?"

"Not sure, it might take a little bit."

Great, a noncommittal reply, that's common around here.

"I'm going outside to make a phone call. Please let me know right away if you find out anything."

"I will, Ryan, I will. Now go and let me work."

I grab my phone from my pocket and punch in Nick's number as I walk through the precinct, if you could call it that. There's a holding cell and a small office, along with a tiny waiting room. It only takes a few small steps to reach the door that brings me outside.

"Nick, we lost him. Or, rather Carl lost him. I can't believe it. I told him to go faster and he just moseyed along the street like we were out sight-seeing. I'm so mad right now. Nick what if..., what if Carl was a part of her disappearance? After all, he was one of the guys talking badly about her years ago," I whisper into my cell phone.

"Ryan, slow down. Start from the beginning. All I know is that Carl came and said something to you and off you ran. That's all anyone knows."

"Carl told me that there was an anonymous tip about a light blue Mini-Cooper by my house around the time of April's disappearance. He said someone spotted it close to where I was, so he stopped to pick me up. When we got into the car, he pointed across the street and there it was. Doesn't that sound too coincidental to you? That had to be a set-up."

"Maybe, what happened next?"

"We were really far away from the mini. I told him to step on it so we could catch up to him. He insisted that he has done this before and to leave the tail-gaiting to him. But right as he said that, the Cooper took off. I'm not sure why. Maybe he saw us or maybe Carl set the whole thing up. He finally went faster, but by that time we already lost sight of him. We searched every street we could think of. Nick, do you know of anyone with a light blue Mini-Cooper? There can't be more than one or two of them up here on the mountain."

"I can't think of even seeing one, but I'll ask around."

"Thanks. How are Agnes and Nancy doing?"

"They're a mess. I left them with Bill at Nancy's house. I'm still at the church. Do you want me to come to you?"

"No, not yet. Bill's a good guy, but do you trust him to keep them safe?"

"I did, but now that you put it that way, I think I'll go back over there," Nick replies.

"Good. I'll call you when I know more."

In front of me sits a frozen metal bench, a small parking lot, and mountains surrounding me on all sides. They could be anywhere out there. What if they're freezing in a cold shack that was hand built by this crazy man? *God, how am I going to find them? Your world is so big. I remember the time I disobeyed my mom and hid in the clothing racks when we were out shopping for school clothes. I couldn't have been more than six. When I came out and yelled boo, my mom wasn't there anymore. I was so confused because she was standing right there when I went between the clothes. Why wasn't she there when I came back out? It didn't make sense to me as a little boy. I didn't understand that just because I couldn't see it happening doesn't mean it couldn't happen. I remember that scared feeling of not knowing what to do, so I sat down and started to cry. I cried out, 'mommy, mommy,' but she didn't hear me. Then, I remembered something my Mom and Dad told me. That no matter where I am in this great big world, whether I'm with a group of people or all alone, You know right where I am. And You know right where all my loved ones are too. I remember asking You to bring me to my mom and to my little hearts delight, that is exactly what You did. I stood up and turned the corner and there she was, franticly looking for me. God, I'm lost again. I'm lost without April and Alyssa. They are my family. I love them beyond what I could ever express and You know right where they are. Please guide me or someone else to them. Please bring them back home.*

Chapter 29

"**A**lyssa?"
Silence.

God, please help me to my feet. I wasn't sure what to expect, but I hoped that Alyssa would be running to me by this point.

The room's murky glow conceals its dimensions. Rolling to my right side, I pull my knees to my chest. Panting, I twist my shoulder into the floor. My left hand is stabilizing my right shoulder, but unfortunately my only choice is letting go. Resulting in a sharp stabbing pain shooting down my left side. Grunting, I push my hand into the floor and lift part of my upper body off the ground. Not wanting to lose momentum, I propel the rest of myself to my feet. There must be a light switch here, somewhere. Stumbling forward, I eventually bump into a wall. Perspiration drips down my face, or is that blood?

"Alyssa?"

A faint chuckle echoes through the wall. What has he done to her? Is she dead? *Please God, no.*

My feet move as if only my mind is in control. Quickly, my hand searches the wall for a switch. I reach a corner and begin down a second wall, then a third, and back to the wall where I entered. I wish my head would stop throbbing, so I could think logically. Of course, it would make the most sense to be by the doorway. As I make my way to it, my hand flips up the switch.

The illuminated room divulges a couch, television, and a bunch of toys. On the couch was a pile of blankets with blond hair sticking out. My heart plummets, Alyssa's blond hair. Moving as fast as my body would allow, I pull the blanket off. She looks fine, like she's sleeping. But if she's sleeping she would have answered me when I called her. I reach out and gently shake her shoulder.

"Alyssa, wake up honey?"

Nothing, shaking her again still concludes with no response, which stirs a panic deep in my heart. She needs to be okay.

Clenching my fists I yell, "What did you do to her?" No sound from anywhere. Is she breathing? Turning her gently, I lean my cheek close to her nose to feel for her breath. One second, nothing, two seconds, nothing, three seconds, nothing, four seconds, maybe something. One second, nothing, two seconds, nothing, three seconds, nothing, four seconds, air. That's definitely air coming from her nose.

Thank You, God that she's still alive. I know You will get us out of here. I trust You with our lives.

Somehow, I manage to fit myself next to Alyssa on the couch. I tuck her head around my right arm. My eyelids grow heavy as my thoughts attempt to plan an escape. Having Alyssa in my arms brought a happiness that no pain can erase.

Chapter 30

Returning to the county jail, Carl was nowhere in sight. After asking around, I learn that no one knows where he went either. What should I do now? He's the only top guy in charge that'll let me near this investigation. Smith won't even give me the time of day.

There's no point in staying here. Who could I call to give me a lift home?

Chapter 31

"Aghhh..." The scream pierces through my ears. Where am I?

"Alyssa, it's okay. It's me, Mommy."

"Mommy, it doesn't look like you," she sobs, "but it sounds like you, and this is your hair and your eye. Why is your face so big?"

She's starting to breathe normal and her cry is quieting as I hold her in my arms, slowly rocking her back and forth.

"Alyssa, before I answer that, please tell me, did that man hurt you at all?"

"No, but he's a terrible cook. I'm so glad you're here. He kept telling me he would bring you, but then he didn't. So I thought he was lying to me. He made me drink this stuff that tastes yucky. Do I have to drink it again, Mommy?"

"I'll do my best to keep you safe, Alyssa. My face is big because he hurt me, but I'll be better soon," I say as I scan her face and body for signs of abuse.

"He's a mean man, Mommy. He wouldn't take me home. I want to go home now. Can you take me home?"

"Sweetie, I wish it were that easy," I say as I brush the hair out of her eyes and the tears from her cheeks. My whole body hurts and any movement sends sharp pain throughout. I know I have some wounds that need medical attention. Maybe he will take us to see a doctor and we can escape then.

A scraping sound grows louder with each second. My intake of breath causes Alyssa to dig her head into my stomach. I hold her tight with my right arm. God answered my cries and now, I'm here to help keep her safe. Even though I'm injured and weak, God is my strength and He will be our Protector.

He must've put something against the door and by the sound of it, it seems big and heavy. He planned this well. There are no windows in this room and no escape exit in the bathroom either. The only way out was through the door that now has a large barricade on the other side. This was the moment God has been preparing me for. In my past, when a situation seemed hopeless, I would believe it to be. When someone would ask me to trust them, I would run the other way, but now I'm ready to fight.

The door opens and before I could make out the face of our captor, the lights go out. Alyssa squeezes me tight. I didn't know how strong she was, or maybe I'm just that weak.

"I see you two have had a happy reunion." I'm facing the door, but his voice is coming from my left. His movements are silent. I'm not sure if he's planning to attack me again so I need to keep him talking so I know where he is.

"Yes, who are you?"

"You don't remember me, April?"

"No."

"That's a shame. Don't you remember me from, how old are you Alyssa?"

"I…I'm six," she stammers.

"And when is your birthday?"

"My birthday is January 3rd."

"So, April let's do the math." His voice is closer now.

"Do you remember me from seven years ago? Let's refresh your memory a little. We met in the month of April. I thought that was a fitting first meeting."

I hoped it wasn't him, but now there's no doubt.

"Answer me, April."

"Yes, I remember that, but who are you?" My throat chokes out the words.

"You'll have to wait for that answer. Don't you like how we keep meeting in dark places?"

"What do you want from me and my family?"

"Family? That's an interesting word. Looks like we'll have to make it official." He grabs my hair and pulls me close to him. He leans down to kiss me as I throw my forehead into his nose. He releases my hair and curses under his breath.

"You'll regret that, April. I'll make you pay, and if you don't start respecting me real soon, I'll leave with Alyssa and you will never see her again," he growls at me as he closes the door. The scrapping starts again right after he exited. My head throbs as I start to fall to my knees.

"Alyssa, Mommy needs to sleep. Please keep your hands on this clothe around my head. The blood will stop soon, if you do that. Honey, can you do that for me?"

"Yes, Mommy, you're really sick aren't you?"

"Yes, Sweetie. But God will keep us well. Trust Him."

Chapter 32

As my vision fades, my thoughts bring me back to that April many years ago when I was a happy college student. I ventured three hours away from home to go to school. My life had meaning. I made friends with a great group of girls. It was the six of us together, as usual.

"Hey, gals how about we all go out dancing, tonight?" Kelly asks.

"I have a major test in two days," I groan.

"And you have been studying for it for three weeks. You need a break."

"Maybe, you're right, Kelly," I sigh.

"Come on, it'll be fun and besides we need you to be the designated driver," Kelly informs.

"I knew it! You are all using me for my car."

"No way!" three girls shout in unison.

"We know that's the only way you'll come with us. And we love having you there," Melissa adds.

"Yes, and you also attract the best guys too," Janelle chimes in.

"Like I said, you're all using me," I chuckle. I need a break and we usually have a great time dancing. I really don't mind driving and they are right about me attracting interesting fellows.

"Alright, I'll go. What time?"

"I'm thinking that we go to the cafeteria for dinner at 6 p.m., and then we come back here to get ready. Then off we go around eight." Kelly is the scheduler. Rarely do we argue with her. It's just easier to go along. We have a blast anyway.

"Great. You can pick me up some food right before you leave the café, and then I'll eat it while all of you get ready." I hope they let me study longer.

"April, come on." Janelle put her hands on her hips.

"Really, guys I need a little longer to get this information in order. And you all know it only takes me a few minutes to get ready. It's the rest of you that need an hour or more."

"Well, April we all don't have your beautiful looks. Some of us need to work at it," Liz says pointedly.

"We're all beautiful. I just don't care to use makeup and hair primping is not my style, but that doesn't matter, you all go and I'll get to do my studying. It's a fair compromise."

"Alright, we'll go. But you better not change your mind. We are counting on you now," Melissa reminds me.

"I might change my mind, but I'm not going to change my actions. I'll still drive. Now, please, go so I can study."

"Testy, testy. Let's go ladies. The clock is ticking and I can't wait to go dancing." Kelly moves them all out the door of our dorm suite and into the hallway. I can hear their giggles all the way down the stairs and out of the building. We're a loud bunch, but I love every one of those girls. We all met my freshman year. It amazes me how we've all lived together for the past three and a half years and we never wanted to change roommates. I have heard some horror stories about roommates. I'm very glad I didn't have to experience any of them. These girls will probably be my best friends for the rest of my life.

Back to the books for me. I finished most of my GenEd classes long ago, but had discovered that I was short three credits and needed one more class which explains why I am here, studying Italian. I'm horrible at learning languages. I thought Italian 101 would be easy and help me keep my 3.8 GPA, but now I see my error. I might have to find a tutor. But before I can think further about that, my phone rings.

"Hello April."

"Hi Nancy."

"April, I'm glad I caught you. How are you doing?"

"Good, but I'm struggling with my Italian class."

"I'm not surprised, I would be too. Why did you pick that one?"

"I picked it because I thought it would be easy. It's a beginning course, the only one I could find this semester. Now, I'm stuck in the class and it's going to ruin my GPA."

"April, it can't be that bad."

"Really, it is. How are you and Phil doing?"

"We're doing well. Our marriage is great! We're adjusting to the different ways we do things. The challenge comes in when one or both of us turns selfish and doesn't want to compromise, but we are working it out with lots of forgiveness. We're trying to have a baby, but I told you that last time we talked."

"Yes, I can't wait for that exciting news and I'm glad you're working it out. After all, remember I'm moving in this summer and I plan to add to the selfishness." I love teasing her.

"Ha ha. Are you still undecided where you're going after you graduate?"

"I'm going where I can find a job. All the girls and I are planning to find jobs close to each other, so we can keep up the girls' dorm life."

"I hope it works out for all of you, but please know that our door is always open. You are more than welcome here and at Mom's too."

"I know. I just want to try and make it on my own first. You both live in the middle of nowhere, and I want to experience life with people all around me."

"I understand that. I hope you all pick a great city to live in," Nancy comments.

"Me too. Kelly has been trying like crazy to organize the whole thing. She has even applied for at least one job for each of us. No wonder she isn't doing well in some of her classes. She spends too much time controlling our lives, but she does keep us having fun. She's really big on scheduling that."

"She sounds a bit domineering!"

"She does push when she has her mind set on something, but she has learned over the years when to back down too. You should see her crazy lists and time charts. She has one of those calendars that's as big as her desk top and it's all filled up. I should take a picture of it and send it to you."

"She sounds like quite the character."

"They all are. I wish you could come to visit so you could get to know them. You would love them too."

"I'm sure I would."

"Nan, they're coming in from dinner now, so I have to go. We're going out dancing."

"Okay. Be safe and have fun."

"I will, Nan. I love you."

"Love you too. Bye."

Chapter 33

"Mommy, Mommy, why won't you answer me?"

"How long has she been like this?" The mean man with no name is back.

"Ss…ss…since I woke up. What time is it?"

"It's five in the morning? I heard you screaming, so I came in to see why your Mom wasn't taking care of you."

"She told me to hold this clothe on her head. I did and then I fell asleep. Did I hurt my Mommy?" I didn't mean to hurt my Mommy. The water in my eyes was making it hard to see what the mean man was doing. I wipe it away quickly, so I could protect my Mommy from him.

"What are you doing to her?"

"I'm feeling her forehead to see if she has a fever and she does. She stopped bleeding though, so I'm thinking she just needs to rest. You stay right here with her. I'll be back with some water and a clean cloth."

"I'll stay with her."

He left the room.

"Mommy, he's gone. You can wake up now. Come on, Mommy, wake up."

She doesn't move. I can see her tummy rise and fall. She looks really bad, almost not like Mommy at all. I wish Aunt Nancy were here to help. She would know what to do. She would fix Mommy.

Chapter 34

As the girls dress and re-dress, I enjoy my hamburger from the cafeteria. Not really, it tasted like cardboard with ketchup, but I'm glad I didn't have to go over there to get it.

Not knowing it, these women have helped me feel like I have a family here. My sister has always been there for me, but my mom was working all the time, which, unfortunately, made it so I never saw her. I do long for a relationship with my mom, but I think I'll have to wait until she retires. Maybe I'll graduate and get a job that makes a lot of money, so I can help her out. She has done so much for me. I really do appreciate her. I miss spending time with her. I wish we were able to talk on the phone.

My mom has tried, but it felt forced. I didn't make it easy for her. I think she woke up one day when I was in high school and she realized that all her children were growing up and she didn't know much about them. She started making an effort to find out how our day was going and stuff like that, but at that point it was too late in my mind. I thought, why bother, she was going to vanish again, anyway. I didn't want to get hurt again.

Maybe I should try a little. I don't want to go through this life and not know my mom because I chose not to try. Tomorrow I'll give her a call and see how she's doing. She would like that, I think. Nancy keeps on trying to get me to call. She has told me how mom has regretted losing touch with us. She also told me that Mom cries over not knowing my younger sister and me. I'm going to call her. I can't call my dad because he left and didn't care about us. But knowing my mom does care gives me a desire to reach out. Maybe I should skip going out tonight and talk to her on the phone instead.

"April, come on. You have to get ready now. We're all almost done."

"I'm already ready."

"No, you're not," Melissa said pointing at my shirt. I look down and see a glob of ketchup on the front of my blouse.

"April, why don't you wear this dress?" asks Kelly. I groan. Her asking really means, wear this or else. She was holding up this below the knee, but not as conservative as I like, A framed red dress. It has spaghetti straps and the fabric flows perfectly when I walk in it. She's always trying to get me to dress up.

"Kelly, we're going dancing, not out to the theatre," I try.

"I know, but you look so great in it, and look at the rest of us. We're all wearing dresses. Come on."

As I look around the room, each girl gives me that look.

"Alright, I'll wear it!"

A chorus of cheers echo throughout the suite. Turning, I walk to my room and lock myself in. Each time I get dressed up, I meet some interesting guy I don't care to meet. The girls will be happy though. They will each pick them off my hands throughout the night. I'm not trying to sound conceited. I truly don't want the attention. I would prefer to just turn up the music in the dorm room and dance here. We have done that many times before and have had a blast. I know they won't change their plans now. Who knows, maybe I'll have a great time too.

Quickly, I throw the dress over my head, then grab the first pair of sandals I could find. Opening the door, "Okay, I'm ready. Oh, wait, I forgot something." I took both of my hands and run my fingers through my hair. "Okay, now I'm ready."

"You make me sick, April. Seriously, how are you able to do that? We spent over an hour getting ready and you take two minutes to get dressed and then you rub your fingers through your hair and you're ready. I hate you." Melissa flings her hair at me as she grabs her purse and stomps out the door.

"Melissa, you have gorgeous hair."

"Yes, I do. But it took me half an hour to get it to look like this. You take ten seconds and you're all made up."

"I love you, Melissa."

"Ugh. You make me so mad sometimes, but I love you too." I know that would calm her down. She walks over to me and we link arms as we go out to the parking lot to find my car.

I thought the excited chatter would die down when all six people squeezed into my five passenger vehicle, but my ears hear otherwise.

Chapter 35

"Has she opened her eyes?"

"No."

"Has she said anything?" the mean man asked me.

"No."

"Urgh. That's not good. Alyssa, has she made any movement? "

"No, she hasn't. She needs to go to the hospital."

"That's not an option."

"Why not? You have a car."

"Because I can't risk it."

"Risk what? I don't understand," I whimper.

"Don't worry about it. It just isn't an option."

"Are you a doctor?"

"No."

"She needs a doctor. Do you know one?"

"No. Now stop with your questions." He growls at me. He bends over my mom. I wasn't sure if I should let him. He put the back of his hand to her forehead then pulls it away as he says a word I've never heard before. He seems very angry. He grabs a bottle, shakes it, then opens my mom's mouth and pours it in. She starts to cough and choke. He lifts the bottle up and lets go of my mom. She falls back with a thud and groans. I'm scared. He's scary. He gets up and storms out of the room.

"Mommy, I'm here." I take my sleeve and wipe her mouth. I put my hand to her forehead just like the man did and pull my hand back quickly. Mommy is really hot. My hand hurts, she must have a fever. Mommy always says I need plenty of rest when I'm sick so maybe it's a good thing she's sleeping. What else did she and Aunt Nancy say I needed when I was sick? I can't remember. I need to remember because I need to help mommy. Mommy would put a blanket on me, so I can do that. They sang to me sometimes.

"Jesus loves me this I know
For the Bible tells me so.
Little ones to Him belong,
They are weak, but He is strong.

Yes, Jesus loves me.
Yes, Jesus loves me.
Yes, Jesus loves me.
The Bible tells me so."

As I place the blanket around Mommy, I change from singing to humming. I am weak, the song is right. Humming starts to get hard to do. My throat is tight. I might be weak, but the song goes on to say that He is strong and He loves my Mommy, so Jesus will get her to the hospital even though this man won't.

Jesus, please come and take my Mommy to the hospital. Please.

Chapter 36

Jesus loves me. Not sure why I'm thinking about that as I drive us all to the club, but I know it's true.

A magnificent time to me would be getting all A's this semester, or going out to eat with my family and seeing my mom smile the whole time, or having my dad come home. Those dreams are all far from reach for now, but my hope is still strong. Maybe one of them will come true. I can make two of them happen, maybe. I would be a step closer if I was home studying.

"April, why are you pouting? Smile, you know you are going to have a great time! You always say you won't and that you should be home studying, but when the night is over you do admit to having a good time, right?" replies Janice.

"I don't remember that."

A chorus of protests come my way.

"Alright, alright. Sometimes I do have fun. I'll admit that, but not every time. Oh, look, here we are."

Driving around the block, I spot a place to park. Great!

The club is noisy, but no smoke. The guy to girl ratio was 4:1, which is good for my friends, but not for me. I've tried to explain to them that this really isn't a place to meet a guy you want to spend the rest of your life with, but they come back with, "We are only looking to have a good time, nothing serious." I don't understand it. Why waste the time on someone you have no interest in seeing again? Their logic is mind-numbing.

Somehow, we manage to find an empty table with two chairs. Almost perfect, one chair less would have been ideal. I grab a chair and put my purse in the other one to deter everyone from the male population. Luckily, my friends all take off for the dance floor. Usually, they would try to drag me out there with them. I lean over and grab my text book out of my bag. This isn't an ideal location to study, but at least I can try to get some work done.

Occasionally, I would spot one of my friends dancing with a guy. They're having fun and I'm glad, because next time it's my turn to decide what we should do. We're going to have an all night girls' night with several chick flicks, lots of chocolate, and plenty of delirious laughing.

"Hey, April, this is Jake," Kelly gushes as she links arms with her new beau.

"Hi, Jake, nice to meet you."

"Yeah, you too," Jake comments with his resounding bass voice.

"April, Jake and I are going to go out to dinner so you don't need to give me a lift home."

"Sure, have a great time." Lifting my chin a quarter of an inch, I give her the, are you sure look. She gives me 'a thumbs up' and off they go. I expect this from her, but as the night progresses every one of my friends leave with someone else.

"Bye, April. Thanks for waiting around for me. I'm sorry you have to go home alone. We'll hang out tomorrow, okay?"

"Sure, it's fine, Janice. I'm just going to study tonight anyway."

"See you tomorrow." And she rushes off to the tall football player waiting at the door. Shaking my head, I gather my belongings and start walking out the front door. It isn't that late. Maybe I'll stop at the store on the corner and pick up some snacks for studying tonight. The car was within sight, but the street lights were all out. I should've asked Janice and her new football stud to walk me to my car. I increase my speed and hold my keys tight. The cool breeze blows my hair into my face. As I brush it away, I drop my keys. Leaning down to retrieve them, gravity brings my bag down off my shoulder, with a thud to the ground. Now my papers scatter about and my books lay bent.

"Here, let me help you with that," comes a voice from behind me. My heart starts beating triple its normal speed as the man approaches. I move faster to gather all my papers, but so does the man.

"It's okay. I'm just trying to help," he says as he hands back three books and most of my papers. I shove them into my bag, but as I take them, his hand brushes against mine. I jump and look up into his eyes. They look kind.

"Thanks, I appreciate the help," I say with a gulp. I need to get out of here.

"No problem, just trying to help out a pretty lady."

"Thank you. Bye." I quickly put my bag on my shoulder and start to walk away.

"Wait, what's your name? My name's Chris."

"I'm April. Thanks for the help, but I really need to go."

"I saw you in the club and I found it rather interesting that you picked a club to study."

"It wasn't my pick, my housemates dragged me."

"Ah, that explains it, but where are they now?" I'm tempted to lie and say that they're waiting for me in the car. This man was getting too personal for my liking.

"They're around, but I really need to go now. Thanks for your help."

As I turn to leave, he says, "Wait, I just want to give you my number, you know if you ever want a study partner."

He hands me his number. I don't want to say thanks again, so I just turn, again, and walk to my car. It's nice of him to help me and for that I'm grateful. I could have lost part of my paper if he didn't come along then. As I open the car, I look around, but I can't see much with the street lights out and the clouds covering the moon.

I dash into my front seat and slam my door quickly behind me. I can't tell if the loud thumping sound is my heart beating hard or footsteps on the pavement. Fumbling, I lock my door as fast as I can. The wind continues to blow leaves and such around. I find it fitting for this night. All I want is to get home and study. As I turn my key, the car makes a roaring sound and that's it. I turn it off and decide to wait a minute.

I've had this happen many times before. My car is a 10 year old Volvo with 175,000 miles on it. It was all I could afford. Normally, I would have just joined the rest of the college population and taken the bus, but my waitressing job wasn't in route of the bus. I would have had to walk about ten minutes even after taking a 35 minute bus ride. It made more sense to buy the clunker and only have a 15 minute commute. I like my job. The fast pace suits me. I have an excellent memory, so I also don't need to write down orders. It's fun. There is always one couple whom question my ability to remember their order, and it's worth the look on their faces when their order comes out right. I usually get the biggest tip of the night from that table. I could work somewhere closer to campus, but the restaurant I work at is more classy then the ones near where I live. I need the money to pay for school and clothes. My mom can't help financially and I really don't want to be paying off my loans into my thirties. This job was the best solution.

I reach for my keys again and turn. This time it sputters, but starts. Smiling, I'm aware that at this rate, everyone else is going to beat me home. Wouldn't that be something? I pull out and made a quick U turn. There must be a storm coming because the wind is pushing and pulling me all over the road. I hope a cop doesn't see me, he'll think I've had something to drink! Yikes!

I start humming a tune. I'm not sure why that childhood song is stuck in my head. As I drive along, I have an intense craving for a chocolate milkshake. Fortunately, I have to pass by the best ice cream shop in the state. As I pull in, I notice that there's no line. I might get a good night of studying in after all. What were the odds of all my friends finding someone to go out with after the club? Most of them will regret their choices come morning, or maybe they'll all have a wonderful time that they keep going out with their men, and then I won't have to do this club thing again. It's hard not to be frustrated with them. They all drag me out for a night of "fun," and then take off. I need to focus on retaining a lot of information tonight hence my extra large, sugar boost, milk shake.

I'm so thankful I'm not focusing on having a relationship. I need my space and my independence. Growing up with being in charge of my days might have helped. I think of my independence as a great asset to my success that will soon follow my degree. I'm determined. Some might call me stubborn, but I think of myself as making my own path and then setting proper goals to achieve it. I want to own my own house by the time I turn 25. I want to have a new car within my first year of graduating and I want to be debt free by 24. I know that sounds odd wanting to get rid of all my debt just to take on more with a house, but that will be different. I want my own place. I want to be my own boss too, but I haven't formulated a plan for that, presently.

I'm not planning to do all of this with my waitressing job. As soon as I land a big job, I'm going to quit the restaurant and maybe only go there to eat. I'm a planner, but I'm also driven to see my plans finished. After paying for my shake I have a renewed burst of energy to put into my night, which is good, because exams are just around the corner.

As I turn the key, the engine roars. Maybe I don't need to take it into the shop again. It would be great to save some money.

A light rain begins to fall as I make my way around the enormous circle of the campus. Parking here can be tricky sometimes because there aren't enough parking spots for every person. I sometimes have to park in the freshman lot and walk fifteen minutes to my dorm, but at least I have a car. Tonight, I'm thinking shouldn't be a problem because it's still early on a Saturday night, early for college students anyway. Every space was used on this campus. I thought for a while the school would get rid of the jogging trail that goes through a thin line of trees by my dorm, but the sports department vetoed that thought. They insisted the athletes need it for training. As I turn the corner, I can see a few parking spots toward the end of the lot. I hope I can get something closer, I don't like getting wet. Driving up and down each lane pushes me to believe that I'm not getting anything closer.

Fortunately, there are campus lights everywhere. After pulling in to a spot at the end of the lot, I turn off my car. Putting my bag over my shoulder, I reach for my umbrella. It's right in its place. I love being organized.

Closing my door, I lock my car and start toward my building. If I can get through Unit 5 in my business book, then I should be all set for the exam on Monday. After church tomorrow I can focus on my paper and after dinner I can review again. A big gust of wind lifted the front of my umbrella. I have to pull hard on it to get it back down. I don't want that to happen again, so I pull it even lower this time and pick up my pace. With the way the umbrella is positioned, it makes it hard to see a couple of feet in front of me, but at least now I'm not getting wet.

One minute I'm walking and the next I'm being pushed along. The voice talking into my ear tells me that if I yell, I will be shot right there on the spot. He also tells me that no one can hear me scream over the rain, so that if the bullet didn't kill me right away, I would be left alive and alone until I lost too much blood.

"That would be a pity for someone as pretty as you." I can't see his face, but I feel his hand gripping my arm tightly. I try to pull myself free but he tightens his grip and jams his gun into my ribs so hard that I have to hunch over to catch my breath. He doesn't give me a chance. He pulls me along with such force there is no way I can fight back. I'm confused. Why is this happening? Why won't he just let me go? Maybe he wants money.

My breathing is labored.

"I…have some…cash. Please take it. You…can have my…car…too." Nothing changes. He's still pulling me along.

"Hold the umbrella in front of us," he grunts. His voice is raspy. Panicking, I'm not sure what to do. He says he would kill me if I scream. I don't think I should do that. Maybe I can reach my cell phone. Wait that won't work. He has one arm in a tight grip and my other hand is holding the umbrella.

Where is he taking me? We aren't heading toward the dorm building. I'm too afraid to ask and I don't want to look up. I don't want to see who's threatening me like this. Is this it? Am I going to die tonight? I have so many plans left. I don't know where the courage came from to ask.

"What is it you want from me?" my voice squeaks out.

"You'll find out soon enough." As he speaks, he tightens his hold. That is when we enter the woods by my dorm, the jogging trail. A few feet into the wooded area, he throws me to the ground. I hit my head. I'm not quick enough to cushion my fall with my hands. My face is half squished in mud. He flips me over and that is when I see part of his face.

"The whole night could have been better for the two of us if you weren't so snobbish to me earlier tonight." It's the man who sat next to me at the club. He said 'hi' once, but I didn't even look up from my book. I wasn't interested.

"You were too stuck on yourself with that nose of yours in a book. But you really are pretty. I wish we didn't have to do it this way, but you left me no choice. I thought maybe you have changed over the years, but when I saw that you are still the same old snob as you were years ago I had to step in and set you straight."

What is this man talking about? I was studying; I didn't do anything wrong now or years ago. Who is he? "Please let me go. I'll say 'hi' next time, just please let me....go," I beg.

He didn't say anything else for a while. I squeeze my eyes tight and hope that when he's done, I would still be alive. The pain is so great! At some point I black out. Pain shot through my jaw.

"You stay awake. I have something to tell you that you better remember. Do you hear me?"

"Yes," I barely whisper.

"If you get pregnant, you better have an abortion or give the baby away to a family with a mom and a dad. I won't be having any child of mine out there without a father. You better listen to me because I know a lot about you, and I know where you live." I'm shaking. With that, he raises his fist and comes down hard on my eye. He gets up and starts to jog off into the distance. I can't tell where I begin and the mud ends. My body doesn't work. I'm telling myself to get up, but I can't. I just stay there. I can't move. I think I want to die. How am I going to go on from here?

Will he come back? I don't know how long he's been gone, but I do know that if he were to come back, I don't want to be here. That thought is the motivation I need. Somehow, I manage to get up to a standing position. I hobble to the entrance of the woods. There's still no one around. The rain beating down on my face, as if it knows I feel dirty. It's coming down very hard now, washing the mud off, washing my hopes, my dreams, and my future along with it. How could I live after this?

THOSE TWO LITTLE WORDS

Looking down, I can see that my dress is torn in several spots. Pulling at it, I try to make it cover up my body. I want everything covered, but I know there isn't a way to accomplish this. I need to get to my room. Slowly, my feet move me toward my building. Still shaking, I look over my shoulder with one thought replaying, him coming back to kill me. I saw his face and he knows I did. I just can't place where I've seen him before. I need to get inside as quickly as I can, one foot, then the other. I'm closer now. At this point I realize that I don't have my bag with me. I need my keys because on that key chain was my card, the card that I need to swipe at the door, so I can get access to the building. I don't know what to do?

As I approach the door, I look around. There's no one here. Maybe someone came back to my room. Moving over to the intercom, I raise my hand to push the button. A shooting pain cascades down my arm. I need to get inside. What if he's behind me now? Help. I need help. My mouth is open, but crippling fear paralyzes my vocal cords. This place is usually crawling with people, why not tonight when I need help? I'm so afraid. I start pounding on the door with my other hand. Bang, bang, bang. No one.

Let me use my other hand and try the intercom again. I punch in the code.

"Help, is anyone home? It's April. I need help, please let me in." My voice chokes out. There's no response. Let me try again, desperately, pushing the button.

"Help, please if you're home, please let me in." Those last two words come out in a high pitch, not recognizing my own voice. I don't know what to do. He said he knows where I live. He knows my name and he could be coming back. I can't go back and get my bag. He could be there waiting for me. Maybe he took my bag. Maybe this was his plan, to leave me here with nothing. Maybe I was meant to die. *Help. Please God, help. Did you leave me too?* Desperation pulls at my insides. I can't stop shaking. My head hurts. I take my good arm and touch my scalp. When I bring my hand down I look at it and all I see is blood. My vision starts to blur and my body sways.

Chapter 37

Ifeel someone touch my arm. Panic rips through my heart. "Don't touch me! Leave me alone!" I scream as loud as I can. I try to run, but my legs are being held down. I try to open my eyes, but they won't cooperate.

"Help, someone help me!"

"April, it's okay. I'm here, it's Janice. I came as soon as I heard your voice on the speaker. I ran down the stairs and opened the door as fast as I could. When I saw you, I called an ambulance. Right now you're on a stretcher. That's why you can't get up. You're safe now. I'm right here." She holds my hand and keeps on whispering in my ear, like an angel. Jesus loves me. I could hear a child singing to me also. What a sweet voice, it must be another angel.

"April, I'm Sheryl. I'm an EMT. I'll be in the ambulance with you the whole way to the hospital."

"What's wrong with me? I don't want to go to the hospital. I just want to go to bed." Weeping, I hope she understands.

* * *

"What's wrong with her? Is she going to die?" Janice asks with a quiver in her voice.

"We need to get her to the hospital. She has a head wound and looks like a broken arm. Let's go," she shouts to her co-worker.

"You can meet us at the hospital, if you want," Sheryl says over her shoulder as she races to the ambulance. As Janice turns to run inside to call a taxi, a policeman stops her.

"How do you know April?" he asks as he taps his foot loudly.

"She's my housemate and friend."

"Where did she go tonight?"

"She drove all of us to the club down on Wicker Street."

"Please, give me the names of everyone who went," he demands.

And on the questions went for about a half hour. After Janice answered what appeared to be all of his questions, she hopes she can ask her own. But before she has the chance, he asks her the question that has been plaguing her since she found April.

"Who would want to hurt April?" he questions.

"I was just going to ask you that. I don't know of anyone who would want to hurt her."

A few cops start yelling and waving to the man that's questioning her. He starts running over to them. They're all heading into the woods. Janice follows. She isn't sure if he's finished asking his questions yet and she doesn't know what to do. As she approaches, the four men are talking about this being where the attack happened. They're pointing to April's car in the parking lot, and then they say something else I miss about the man who grabbed her at some point, before entering the woods. Janice doesn't know how they could figure this out, but the scene before her was startling.

April's bag was in the mud and everything that was in it is now scattered on the ground. Instead of picking it up they were taking pictures. The officer that called them over here is saying how this was the spot where he raped her. Rape. April was raped? That couldn't be true. As Janice pictured it, her stomach churned as her dinner presented itself.

"Not April. What happened?" she asks as her knees buckle.

"You're in shock, Janice. You passed out for a second."

"I need to get to the hospital. I need to be with April. I never should have left her alone tonight." She starts to panic.

The young man put Janice back on her feet. "I'll drive you over there." He said something to his buddies, and then he starts walking her to his car.

"I'm going to call April's sister and let her know what happened." She isn't sure why she's informing him of that. Nancy's voicemail came on and Janice leaves an awkward message. How does one inform someone that they needed to get to the hospital without causing panic?

"How long have you known April?"

"We have been roommates for four years now. She's my best friend. We grew up together. She practically lived at my house throughout high school. No one has ever done anything to hurt her, except her father. He decided to up and leave the family when April was 12 or 13, but he's her dad. He wouldn't do a thing like this. He never hurt her physically, so who would do such a horrible thing?" Hot tears run down Janice's checks.

"I don't know, but I'll do my best to find out." He pulls into a parking spot. They briskly walk in through the Emergency Entrance.

"We're here to see April Peterson. She was recently brought in by ambulance," Officer Stan states.

"I don't think it's a good time for questioning," a robust nurse replies curtly.

"How is she doing?" Stan asks.

"Not well enough for questioning," the nurse replies.

This isn't getting them anywhere.

"Can I see her? I'm her best friend," I interject.

"Let me go and find out. Please have a seat." Why is this taking so long? She needs someone to sit with her. She must be terrified.

Chapter 38

Ifeel a gentle touch on my arm. My eyes refuse to open. I try to speak, but no words form. The voice asks me if Janice can sit with me. I try to say yes and when that doesn't work, I nod my head slightly. I hope she understands. I went for a bunch of scans when I first came in. The doctor told me that I'm going to be admitted, but he wasn't sure, yet, if I needed surgery. I was about to ask him what I needed surgery for. But it didn't seem important, or maybe I just didn't care. I should call my mom and sister, but I don't have the energy to do that. Maybe someone will help me. I have a lot of help now, but I still feel alone and afraid.

Sharp pain has been running through my head nonstop. Maybe he'll operate on that and make it stop. I want to sleep, but the pain keeps me awake. I want my mom. I can hear voices, but I'm not sure who they belong to. I hear a moaning, but maybe that voice belongs to me.

"It's okay, dear," a nurse says.

"April, it's me Janice. I just talked to Nancy. She and your mom will be here soon. The doctor wouldn't tell me anything about how you are, but they are letting me stay here with you for now."

I hear more moaning.

"Nurse, can you give her something for the pain?"

"I already did, it should start working any time now."

"Thank you," I hear Janice say.

"April, your arm is very swollen, but it should heal fine. I'm not a doctor or anything, but that is what I think. You don't have any deep cuts on your face, so I think you should heal well. I wish the doctor would tell me more about how you're doing, but he says only family. I should have told him I was your sister. I'm close to you like a sister, but I couldn't lie. You know, you are going to be up on your feet in no time at all. You're a fighter. I bet you'll even be better for mid-terms." A struggled groan escapes April's lips.

"Sorry, April. I shouldn't have brought that up. You are a fighter though. It's what you do best, so you keep it up and get better.

"I rode over here in a cop car. The cop's name is Stan. He wanted to come in and ask you a bunch of questions, but the nurse ran him off. She said that you were too tired to talk. He persisted and said it was really important, but she shooed him away like a cat. She let him know that you're not able to talk yet, but when you are she would call him. I wish you could talk though. Not to talk to him, but so that I know you're okay. I heard the doctor tell the nurse to get the scans of your head and arm. It sounded like you might need surgery, but I'm not sure. All my information comes from eaves dropping. I know it's not a good thing to do but when it concerns you, I'll do it."

"You look thirsty. Let me ask the nurse for some water." Another moan.

"Don't worry I won't leave you, the nurses' station is right outside your room. I could yell to them and not even leave my seat if that's what you want. But knowing you, you would want me to ask politely. I'll just walk to the doorway."

As Janice opens the door, she leans her head out and raises her voice a little, "Excuse me; can I please have some water for April?"

"Yes, I'll be right in."

Within a minute, she's bringing me a glass of water. She gently explains what she is doing. Her voice is very soothing. She tilts my head in such a way where the water goes into my mouth and doesn't trickle down my chin. I moan for more and the nurse gives me some more. This goes on until the glass is finished and I'm able to say, "Thanks." And I mean it!

"April, you can talk. How are you feeling?"

"Not so good." My voice is hoarse.

"I'm really sorry to hear that. I wish this didn't happen to you."

"Thank you for getting me water. I really needed it."

A nurse stands by tapping her foot impatiently.

"April, I'm Martha, your nurse for the next four hours. You have been beaten badly and your arm is very swollen. You have a concussion and a broken arm."

"Do I need to have surgery?"

"I'm not sure, but the doctor should be in to talk to you within the next half hour and he'll be able to answer that. He's looking at the scans now."

"Okay, I'm going to sleep now. Please wake me when he comes. I want to know…the…answers…well…maybe…."

Chapter 39

My mom and sister arrive at the same time the doctor does, which is a good thing because my jaw is hurting and I don't think I can talk much. Everything is hurting. Why me? Why? Janice is right, I am strong, but I don't want to be. I like being independent and now I have to have people help me with everything. I can't even get myself a glass of water.

"April, how are you, sweetie?"

"Mom, I hurt all over." There's no sense in lying, but maybe I should've. I could hear that she's having a tough time controlling her emotions. Nancy is also. There's a lot of sniffling going on.

"April, I'm Dr. Thomas. I have looked through all your scans and you don't need surgery, so that's a good sign. We have you on pain medication, so that should be helping with your pain. The best care you can give yourself is sleep."

"How long will I be here?"

"For now, we're going to take it one day at a time. You have a huge contusion that we need to monitor."

"What's wrong with me?" Panic races through my heart. Monitors start beeping around me.

"April, you need to calm down. Take a slow breath. Please, try to relax." The beeping stops. But maybe he just pushed a button for that to happen.

"Nancy, Janice, and I are right here, April. You're going to be al-right," Mom says.

"Please, don't leave me, please. Please don't let him touch me again."

"April, I won't. I'm not leaving you again." I can hear the strain in Janice's voice, the tears falling on to my hand as she squeezes her reassurance.

"Thank you for keeping me safe. I can sleep now."

"You're safe now, April. You're safe." She holds my hand and with her finger strokes the back of it. The little jester comforts in a big way. Rest comes finally.

* * *

I was running as fast as my body would allow.

"Ahhh."

"April, it's okay. You're safe, I'm right here. I haven't left you. Wake up! It's just a bad dream."

"Mom, it was so real. It was happening all over again."

"I'm right here. You're safe now. You're safe now." My mom sits on the bed and lifts me slightly, placing my head on her lap. As if knowing exactly what I need, she begins to sway back and forth like she used to do when I was little. And I feel comforted. I'm safe in the arms of someone who loves me. To know I'm loved brought about a hope in me, one that makes me think that maybe I can survive today. Maybe I can see a life beyond this point. Maybe I'm going to make it, just maybe.

Chapter 40

Days pass. My head is back to normal. My arm is still sore, along with a large portion of my body. But I'm healing physically. I can walk to the bathroom on my own, which I'm thrilled about. My body will recover in time. According to my heart and mind, healing isn't possible.

The cops came by several times, each time to ask more questions, but never to say that they caught the man. He asked me if I'm disappointed, but I couldn't utter that I'm actually terrified. With him out there, knowing who I am and where I live changes the way I have to think. A normal life is questionable. I don't want to constantly live in fear of him finding me again, but now I have to.

Dr. Thomas told me this morning that I can go home tomorrow. I started to cry and he misunderstood. He thought I was happy about the news. But in truth, I haven't stopped shaking since he spoke those words. I'm a defenseless young woman. I can't even move my arm now. Then I had no strength to use against that man with two good arms. No matter how hard I tried, I couldn't get free. But now, I only have one working arm.

Janice and the other girls talked to all my professors. They all said I could take the summer to finish up my assignments and come in later to schedule all the exams. I don't know if that's a wise move.

The campus police came to visit also. One man said if I choose to come back to school this semester, he and his buddies will personally escort me to and from my car and anywhere else I want to go on campus. It was a relief to hear they would be willing to do that. I also wonder if they think they might catch the guy if they're around me.

My mom and sister want me to go home and stay with them. I want to do that also, but I'm so confused. What's the right thing to do?

A woman by the name of Ellen came to visit me yesterday. Ellen said I need to go to counseling. She was saying that I've been through so much hurt that I need help to process it. I personally didn't want to talk about it. I just want to forget it happened. It was like she was reading my mind because the next thing she said was that what happened will continue to haunt me until I get the help I needed. I asked her how she knew this and she patted my hand and with a sad look on her face she said, "I know because I've been right where you are." I didn't say much after that. I didn't want her to be right. She left me her business card and told me that I could call her anytime I wanted.

I felt compelled to put the card in my wallet, so I was thankful when the police returned my bag earlier this morning along with all the items that they could find. They said it looks like I wasn't robbed and I said, "Oh, but I was." I put Ellen's card in my wallet and hoped that nice woman was wrong.

My mom asked me if I wanted to sell my car and she would help me find a new one. I agreed. So Nancy drove it back to Windham and put up a For Sale sign. They didn't have to say what they were thinking about. We all knew that the evil man knows what my car looks like. I don't want it anymore. Nancy said she would clean it out and bring all my stuff back to me wherever I wanted to stay. I asked mom about my younger sister. She said if I wanted her to come for a visit, she could. She thought it was best that she stayed at a friends' house while they were with me, so she could go to school. I think she was just protecting her too, which was fine. I understood. I know I don't look my best right now.

My face is covered in bruises. I'm not sure how many different shades it's going to change into, but unfortunately I'll find out. I'm tired of the dark purple look. My right arm is going to be in a cast for six weeks. I can write a little, but it starts to hurt after a couple of sentences. Typing is a little easier because I can use my left hand.

I don't have much time left now to make my decision. Where should I go to live? Would my dad protect me if he were here? Would he have taught me how to defend myself if he stayed around? Would he come back, if he knew what happened? Maybe my mom will let him know.

My mom needed to go back to work and so did Nancy. They wouldn't be able to stay with me at their houses. At school I'm almost never alone and the security inside the building was very safe. Also, the campus cops said they would walk with me. I can also ask two of my guy friends to help out with that for a couple of my classes. I think I would be safer on campus because he implied that he knew me from my past. That probably means he already knows where my mom and Nancy live.

I still need to work. Someone at work can walk me out, and then I can have someone meet me in the parking lot. At home there would just be my mom, Ella, and me, which really means mostly me. My mom works all the time and my baby sister has a boyfriend.

THOSE TWO LITTLE WORDS

I want to finish school. I'm almost done and then I'm going to move far away where no one can find me. I'll stay in touch and visit, but I won't let anyone know where I am. Two more months is all I have left to endure this dreadful place, I can do it. That will give me just enough time to make a solid plan for my new life, one where I can live as if this never happened. Away from the people who've come in to visit with their long faces of pity. They don't know what to say to me, nor do I to them. I wish we could all forget it happened and pretend to go back to the way life used to be.

Chapter 41

My arm is healing nicely, or so the doctor says. I'm glad because not having full use of it has been challenging. I haven't figured out how to shower without getting my arm wet. I've needed to get the cast changed twice now because of that. My face almost looks like it used to. No more swelling and the bruises are easily covered with foundation. Many people have commented about my eyes though, something about them not sparkling anymore. I think that it's better that way anyway. I don't want to attract any attention.

My roommates wanted to know why I gave them lots of clothes last week. I went through my closet and took out anything that was form fitting. I'm never going to wear these items again. I gave them away so they could be used, and now I won't have to move them when I leave this city.

I can't talk to anyone about how I feel. They wouldn't understand. They make comments about how I choose to live my life now. They understand the buddy system I put into place and are more than willing to assist me in it, but beyond that, there isn't much understanding. It's alright, I'm moving on. I don't want to forget my friends, but I think it's inevitable. We don't click anymore. It saddens me because these were my closest friends. Why can't they just act normal? I walk into the room and they all stop talking. They treat me like a freak, like I'm a glass vase teetering on the edge of a table. I'm made of stronger stuff than that. I'll bounce back, but they won't have time to see it because I'm leaving in less than two months.

I found a new friend throughout this experience, it's my wall. Not a real one but one I've strongly built so I'd have a place to lean when I was too weak to stand. It doesn't talk back or pity me, but what it does is shield me from those sad looks and awkward conversations. It's an emotional crutch, one I don't envision leaving my side. I can count on it to keep others out, as it protects me from unwanted intrusion.

The west coast sounds appealing. It's far from my family, but I'll visit them often. I hope Nancy forgives me. She'll be livid, but hopefully her feelings will fizzle over time. I can get a job waitressing as soon as I arrive, and then spend time choosing a job in my field. I would like to work with children, maybe as a teacher. Over the next few months those details will work themselves out. For now, I need to save every penny from waitressing because my bank account has been depleted. The car selling is my ticket out of here.

Chapter 42

"Janice, what's today's date?" My voice wobbles with the panic I feel.

"Today is April 30ᵗʰ. Why, April?"

"No reason." But she knows. She looks at me and we know. My life will never be the same again. She pulls me into a hug and we cry together for over an hour. How am I going to go on?

"Let's take a pregnancy test," Janice urges.

"I don't have one."

"I do," she says.

"Why do you have a pregnancy test, Janice?"

"I bought it for this very reason."

"Oh." We walk to the bathroom and she reads the instructions for me. Three or four times I almost look before the three long minutes are up. Janice says it's time and we look together. It says positive. The confirmation causes dizziness to rally through my brain. Pregnant? Pregnant!

"Janice, I don't know anything about being pregnant. This jerk told me if I was to get pregnant that I couldn't raise the baby." Sniffling, I go on to tell her a few of the details that night, my wall slowly forms a window. "He said to have an abortion or put the baby up for adoption. He said if I kept the baby, he would know and he would come back and kill me. I'm afraid. I don't want to be pregnant." Exhaustion floods my head. My eyelids are too heavy to hold up. Difficulty moving follows. Why me? Why do I need to go through this? Wasn't the abuse enough? Now I don't even get to make my own decisions. He still has control over me. Help me God, please help! I get up and make my way to my own bed. Janice and I share a room. She understands me. She doesn't say another word. She just watches me.

I take out a pen and a paper and I write down my three options, parenting, adoption, and abortion. Under parenting I write down the word death because he said he would come back and kill me if I keep the baby. Under adoption I write down separation and heartache, but a saved life. And under abortion I write down, termination of two lives. My options aren't good. I cross out parenting because it's clear that I can't choose that one. Now I have two choices. I don't know anyone that has given their baby up for adoption before, but I have met a couple of people that were adopted and they both only had positive things to say.

One woman, named Lucy, told me that she went and found her biological mom and she was so thankful that she was put up for adoption. She said her biological mom was very young when she had her and she didn't have any money, or a job at the time, and she had no idea how to support herself, let alone a baby. Lucy described the conditions that her biological mom lived in as filthy and that day, Lucy thanked her for giving her up. She said it was a great act of love, and Lucy greatly respected her for it. She also thanked her for going through the condemnation she must have felt because she was pregnant out of wedlock. Her biological mom said that wasn't necessary because she found out too late that she was pregnant and an abortion wasn't an option for her. Lucy was mortified, but then the lady said to her, 'I was young but since then I have thought of you often, and I thank God I found out too late, because your life was worth saving.'

Adoption is an option, but I also have abortion as an option too. I wrote 'two lives terminated' there. I remember a girl in high school talking about having an abortion. She didn't say much. What I do remember was that she was very social in school before the pregnancy, and after she was more withdrawn. She walked around as if she lost something valuable and she didn't know how to get past that. Can I give up the life growing inside me? Or can I kill the life inside? I cross one of my options out and circle the other one.

I can do this, there's a way. Janice will help me also. The plan starts to take form in my mind. This monster isn't going to harm me anymore, nor is he going to tell me what to do.

"Janice, please don't tell the others. I need your help. I'm not sure who this man is, but I can't risk him finding out that I'm… you know, so please don't tell anyone."

"April, you can count on me. I know how to keep secrets and you know I will. How many secrets have we shared over the years? Too many to count and I haven't told one of them. Well, I did blurt out one, but that was a total accident and it won't happen again. Anyway, I can help you. I will."

"Thank you. I know I can trust you. It's not that I don't trust the other girls. It's just that I can't risk it slipping out. If this man finds out what I'm planning to do, he'll kill me for sure." I whisper to Janice.

"I know, April. Whenever you want to talk about your plan, please let me know."

"Soon, I'll let you know soon."

"Great. April, I've decided not to follow the other girls when we graduate. I'm going to move close to you. Maybe I'll even be your housemate again, if you want."

"That means so much to me, Janice. I'll add that to my plans then, okay?"

"Yes, that's fine with me. That's why I told you as soon as I decided."

"Are you sure you want to go wherever I go?"

"Yes, I'm sure."

"Thank you." My voice is barely audible. I know my family will help me, but I never thought Janice would give up her future like this. She was very excited about living together with everyone. I'm grateful for Janice. It's wonderful to have her as my best friend.

Unfortunately, I need lots of help. As I lean to pick up the phone, I glance over at Janice. She's studying, but she'll understand why I don't take this call in the common area. I punch in Nancy's number.

"Hello."

"Nancy, it's me, April."

"How are you doing?"

"I need your help, I'm pregnant."

"Oh, April, no," Nancy breathes.

"Yes, and I need your help. I have a plan, but you will need to sit down for it."

"Umm, okay, please tell me quick, you're scaring me." And I did tell. I told her about what that evil man said to me. She wasn't handling the news well. She was yelling and crying and ranting. If I could see her I would think she was clutching the phone tightly in her hand and pacing back and forth. Nancy has taken care of me for a very long time. She will do almost anything for me, so now is my time to ask.

"Nancy, I have a plan. Please, sit back down. I believe that man knows about me. I believe he knows where I live and even who my family is. I want you and Phil to pretend you're having a baby. I'm going to rent an apartment close to yours and you are going to go through the motions of pregnancy. We can even have a baby shower for you. It's all for you, when I go into labor you come to the hospital and we make everything legal. You and Phil will be the legal guardians of my baby, but I want to be his or her mom. You would need to do most of the parental things, but I'll be very close and come over all the time. I don't want to give up my baby, Nancy. Please help me. This is the only way."

There was no sound coming from the other end.

"Nancy?"

"April, I want to help you anyway I can. Please let me talk to Phil tonight and I'll call you back. While you look for a place near mine, please come home and stay with me. We do have an extra bedroom."

"I think I will."

"Oh, by the way. Your car sold this morning for $1000. Do you want Phil to look for another vehicle for you?"

"Not yet. Nancy, thank you and I have to go. Love ya. Bye."

Janice comes over and hugs me again.

"If Nancy says no, I'll do it. I'll have your baby."

"Thanks Janice, but you need to be married."

"Oh, but if he doesn't know it's yours...."

"I don't want to leave any room for him to come back."

"I'm sorry, April. I was just trying to help."

"I know, I didn't mean to be short with you."

"It's okay."

I need an answer from Nancy. There was nothing else I could do until I know her answer. I think I'll study, so that I can get a good job to support my baby.

Chapter 43

"April?"

"Yes, Nancy?"

"Phil and I had a long talk and we want to be the legal guardians for your baby. I'm going to call my boss tomorrow and see if I can change my hours, so that we can work out an arrangement where the baby is at home and not in daycare. Would it work for you to come over every day to watch the baby too?"

"One minute please…." I put the phone down and grab a bunch of tissues and pick the phone back up.

"Thank you, Nancy. I want to watch her as much as possible so that should work out well. I'm not sure where I'll be working. There aren't many options up on the mountaintop, but I'll find something."

"Phil and I are wondering if you could just move in with us."

"I want to Nancy, but I can't risk that. I don't even think I should be seen with her in public."

"Do you really think it's a girl?"

"Huh, what do you mean?"

"You called your baby a 'she' twice."

"Oh, I didn't mean to. Anyway, I want everyone except Mom and Janice to think that this is your baby."

"I think we should let Phil's brother and parents know also, but everything else sounds fine. Just let me know when to start wearing a pillow under my shirt."

"I will and thank you, Nancy. Please thank Phil for me also."

* * *

My new way of life is growing on me. I'm glad that I have some control over my decisions.

My cast comes off tomorrow. I have had it on for six weeks now. Having full use of my arm is going to be beneficial, because I'm moving home in two weeks. I found an apartment two blocks from Nancy and Phil's house. It's very small, but Janice and I are used to small. The rent is cheap, but, unfortunately, the neighborhood isn't great. No matter where I live I'm going to be uneasy when walking alone, probably for my whole life. I don't know how to get used to the feeling of someone following me. It's creepy. The cops said that they haven't gotten a single lead. They also said that he was just trying to scare me and that he doesn't know who I am. When I reminded them that he knew my name they said he must have seen it when he looked through my bag. That's possible, but how can I believe that he isn't out there following me still?

* * *

Somehow I manage to ace all my finals. I don't know how that happened! Maybe my professors took pity on me. I'm not sure, but I'm glad either way. My GPA is a 3.9. I'm glad I did well, but I'm not going to get to use my degree anytime soon. I found a good waitressing job close to home. I take the bus most days, but when Janice and I leave at the same time, she drops me off. She's amazing, moving here with me so I can raise my baby. She would be making a lot more money, as would I, if we took the job offers we had by the other girls.

I can't change the past and I need to stop thinking about all the 'what ifs'. It's hard not to. I had a dream life planned out. I wish it could've happened that way. My mom said that it still could if I wanted to give the baby up for adoption. She said it's okay if I do. Some days I'm on the fence about my decision. My mom is right. I could have it all back, well most of it. I still have nightmares and I have a tough time falling asleep every night, but I could make a nice living for myself if I give the baby up.

Now I'm stopping several lives with my decision to keep her. Yes, it's a girl. I just found out yesterday. Sometimes I have horrible feelings, like why would I want to keep a baby that is part him? What if she turns out just like him? Then I think about how she's part me and how innocent she is. He must have had a rough childhood or something traumatic to make him want to do something like that. His actions have no bearing on how my child will be. She won't ever meet him whether or not I give her up. A strong part of me wants to protect her and raise her to hate men, but I know that not all men are like that.

* * *

I'm almost eight and a half months along. I'm hiding it well. No one knows at work. She moves around constantly.

"Bye, Doreen."

"Bye, April. Are you doing alright?"

"Oh, yes, I'm fine," I say as I try to straighten up. I've been having contractions on and off throughout my shift. The last half hour they have been hard to ignore. I'm glad it's time to leave. I told my boss that I needed three weeks off around this time when I started the job. She agreed and didn't ask questions about me not knowing the exact date. She's a great boss, but this isn't what I thought I would be doing with my life. Another contraction comes, this time accompanied with a trickle of liquid down my leg. I guess this is it. I have Nancy on speed dial just for this reason.

"Nancy, I'm ready."

"Ready for?"

"I'm ready to go to the hospital."

"Really? How long have you been in labor?"

"I'm not sure, on and...off…." My breathing is getting heavy and it's hard to talk.

"Nancy, the contractions are close together. I think I waited too long. I'm at work, please pick me up. I've been having them all day, but the past half hour has been difficult."

"I'm already in the car. I'll be there in ten minutes. Do you want to stay on the phone?"

"No. I'll wait for you outside. I'm going to call Janice now."

"Okay, sit tight. I'll be there really soon."

"Bye." I want to get off the phone before another contraction comes. As soon as this one ends I'll call Janice. What was it that I'm supposed to do now? Ohhh, I think I'll try to walk through this one. My fist is squeezing the phone. Relax. I think that's what I'm supposed to do? How do I do that? As the contraction eases, I dial Janice.

"Janice, where are you?"

"I'm at home. Why what's wrong?"

"I'm in labor. My water broke. Nancy is coming to get me."

"Good, I'll meet you at the hospital."

"Bye."

Nancy pulls up just as another contraction starts. She jumps out of the car and races around the back of it to get to me. She helps me through the contraction and then places me straight into the passenger seat.

"My water broke. Do you have a towel for me to sit on?" She was already back in her seat and ready to start driving to the hospital.

"You're already sitting on it. Don't worry. How do you feel?"

"I feel like I'm hiking a mountain I didn't train for."

"Well you look like you're doing well. The hospital is only five minutes from here, so we'll have an idea how far apart your contractions are."

I don't want to be rude to my sister. She was helping me so much but I don't feel like talking anymore? What if the baby looks nothing like me? Should I give her up then? Maybe I should, who do I think I am? I'm not fit to be a mother, even though she'll be living with Nancy and Phil still doesn't make me fit for this. I have the number for an adoption agency in my bag. I haven't called yet, but I will after she's born. First, I need to concentrate on relaxing.

Fear pulls me in the opposite way with my next contraction. I can feel my body fighting against itself. I didn't work through many of my emotions prior to today. I tried on my own, but it was useless. Ellen, the nice woman, was right. I need the help of others who have already been through this. I need a group, a safe environment to talk about what he did to me and how that affects me now. I'll call her as soon as I can, if I can find her number.

* * *

The circle of people in my room spun my head around 'till I was queasy. I've been at this for hours, too many to count. My three main people came, and waited, and left, and came back again. Now everyone is here. The nurse says that I should start to feel an urge to push soon. I ask her what would happen if I missed the urge and she says, 'Oh honey, you won't miss it. Trust me, you'll know!' And with that I can feel a change in my body. I yell for someone to hold my legs and I push and push until my mom screams that she sees the head. And then she says the head's gone. It went on like this for an exhausting 30 minutes, but with my next push, out she comes with a joyous noise or so my mom calls it. She cries so loud I wasn't sure what to do. The nurses are moving back and forth with her. All I want is a look, but I don't seem important in this process. I did all that work and they ignore me.

"Hey, bring me my baby. I want to see her now."

"She's beautiful," Nancy says with tears in her eyes.

"I want to hold her NOW." This time the nurse listens and brings my baby to me. As she places her in my arms, my anger diminishes. It's truly amazing to me that something so beautiful can come from such a horrific act. She's perfect and there's no way I'm going to give her up. Everything that has been wrong over the past 8 and ½ months has just been turned right in this single moment. How can someone so small affect me so greatly and in such a healing way? I don't understand it, but I thank God for it. I'm smiling! I haven't truly smiled in a long time.

"Hi, Alyssa," I whisper.

"Is that her name, April?"

"Yes, her name is Alyssa Hope."

"She looks like an Alyssa Hope. I think it's a perfect name for her," my mom says and as I look up I see Janice and Nancy bobbing their heads in agreement. Many tears fall in the next few minutes, healing tears, tears of joy. A nurse comes in and says there's a man outside. I jump, and the nurse says his name is Phil and he would like to come in when it's okay.

"Oh, he can come in now."

We had a wonderful evening, but after an hour, I drift among the noise in the room. There are many arms wanting to hold little Alyssa. I know she's safe in this place.

Chapter 44

I started attending a group for women who have been sexually abused. It's a small group. I can relate to their feelings and they can to mine. The violation and the anger are prevalent, but the fear is what I talk about the most. It's gripping hold that walks with me everywhere. It is present in my days and present in my nights. It haunts me in every face I see approaching me on the street. I've ran full blocks to escape it, but no relief followed. In my apartment, I bolt all the doors and windows and before I leave a room, I double check to make sure they're all locked. I get up at least once a night to check again and I pace with a bat in my hand until the fear ebbs.

The women hear me when I talk, but they don't know what to say to help because we all, in some degree, have our own battle with fear. It creeps into other areas of my life too. I only go out when I need to. I don't want to risk a chance of anything happening to me. If I step foot outside my door I take a risk that most days I don't want to take. This fear has control over my comings and goings, over my friendships, and even enters when I eat. I think that if I eat certain foods I might choke, so I avoid them. I wait and only eat when Janice is home or when I'm at Nancy's and she and/or Phil are there, and when they are there, I eat a lot. I'm gaining weight and to me that's alright. I don't want to be attractive anymore. I want to cover myself up as much as possible, so I can be invisible in this world. Less attention is better.

I try to focus on Alyssa. I spend most of my day with her at Nancy's house. She's such a joy to me. She has brought a new hope into my heart that I never thought would be there. I thought my life was over that cold night, but with the brightness of day, I can see that my life will go on. I'll give it my best for this little girl who has wrapped herself around my heart and has shown me how to love. I have a long battle ahead of me, but with this baby in my arms, I'm willing to fight. That's why I go to the group, for her, because I know if I continue on with my ways, I will cut myself off from everyone around me. For her, I won't let that happen. For her, I will continue to breath and hope that with each breath my life smells sweeter.

THOSE TWO LITTLE WORDS

My mom suggested I start dating. I laughed it off, but how can I explain to her that dating is something I will never do again. I have no desire to share myself with another man, in any area. It might be fear striking again, but I have too many other areas in my life to focus on instead. My personal life can be left void for all my years. My focus is giving my little girl everything I didn't have. I want to be present throughout all of her growing years. It's odd to have Phil and Nancy as her substitute parents, but it's working out so far. Nancy has struggled with her role in this arrangement. I don't blame her. I put her in a difficult situation and one that doesn't ever end. I hope Alyssa grows to love us all, no matter how confused our arrangement appears.

It's best she calls Nancy 'Mom' and Phil 'Dad', but I also want to be called 'Mom.' I have some time to figure out how to make that happen. I love my little girl and even if I need to give up the title, I'll do it for her. I'm not giving her up, just the title. An important name, but I know who I am.

She looks exactly like me when I was a baby. She has my nose and my chin. I'm not sure about her hair yet. She doesn't have much so it's hard to tell.

Chapter 45

Ihaven't slept in three days. My wife is out there somewhere and I can't find her. I don't know where to look either. The same question keeps on coming to my mind. Why come back? After all these years, why now? It doesn't make sense. Normally, rapists don't come back seven years later and kidnap their victim. He has an attachment to her. I need to figure out how, and then, maybe, I'll be able to find him.

"Nick, I need to talk something through with you. I have an idea," I say through my Bluetooth.

"Sure, in person or on the phone?"

"In person, I'm on my way over."

"Do you want me to meet you somewhere?"

"No, we need to protect April's family. I want you to think back to high school. Take notes and remember back to all the conversations April had with guys."

"What do you mean?"

"You know, conversations she had with anyone of the opposite sex or that any guys had about her."

"I heard you, but I don't see how that's going to help us find her."

"It might not help us at all. I just have a hunch, so please do it."

"I'll do it, but I think it's a waste of time."

"Thank you." I push the off button and drive with a purpose. I'm going to get this man. I can't let my mind think of how badly I want to beat him. Focusing on vengeance will distract me from what I need to do.

Pulling into my mother-in-laws driveway, I complete my mental list of conversations and there were a few that peaked my interest.

Agnes opens the door and lets me in. Nick and Nancy are sitting on the couch, Nick with a pen in his hand. He finishes writing and tosses me the pad.

The front of one piece of paper is filled and the back empty. It isn't much.

174

Skimming it, I learn that nearly the whole basketball team spent time talking about April. The problem was that she didn't care to talk to any of them. She actually made most of them mad, by ignoring them.

"Nick, tell me, who had a crush on April back then?"

"Ryan, come on, you know as well as I do, that everyone from the team wanted to date her."

"Why?"

"Ryan, why are we going over this?"

"Please Nick, help me talk this through." Nick puts his hand through his hair and growls at me. Why is he so upset over the past? What's he hiding?

"Fine, you know as well as I do that April never talked to the guys. She was the most beautiful girl in her class and the guys were furious that she wouldn't flirt with them."

"All of them?"

"Pretty much, I can't think of one of the guys who didn't want to date her, yourself included."

"That's true, so let's write down all the names."

"Why?"

"Because I've been thinking about why her rapist would come back after all these years and the only thing I can come up with was that he had a history with her. Now we need to go back and sort through her history."

"Urgh, I think this is a waste of time." He's irate. I try not to get distracted by his defiance. I believe I'm on to something.

"Carl, Blake, Dan, Frank, and Sam were the five basketball players from our grade besides you and me, so that makes seven people."

"Ryan, yes, that makes seven players, but you must be forgetting the other 20 something guys in her class, who also looked at her. This is pointless!"

"Not pointless, we need to start somewhere. I think these seven are who we need to start with."

"Why?" Nick yelled.

"Because the basketball team members were the strongest boys in our school and with that strength, came great arrogance. April rejected all of us and with rejection, for some, came anger and maybe with one came an uncontrollable urge to get what he wanted. Why? Because he was used to getting what he wanted!"

"Ryan, that's a great theory, but we could come up with a good theory for most of our class. This is a waste of time." Ignoring him comes easily with my mind replaying endless conversations about April.

"Nick, what about Rick?"

"Rick got kicked out of school when we were juniors."

"He did, do you remember why?"

"He was arrested for sexually assaulting a cheerleader after a game on school property." Nick stands up from his chair and he starts to embrace my line of thinking.

"I remember that night. We lost the game because of Rick. He traveled the ball repeatedly, and then missed five of his six foul shots. He messed up big time. He was cursing in the locker room and said someone was going to pay for it. He wasn't making sense really, blaming everyone who crossed in front of his locker. He assaulted that girl and that was the last time we saw him."

"Do you remember him ever having a crush on April?"

"He was mad at her for not giving him the time of day."

"Yeah, but more than the other guys?"

"I don't know. His whole family moved away after that. I never did hear where they went."

"Neither did I."

"Can you call Carl at the police station and see if they can find out anything further?'"

"I'm on it."

"Good. I'm going to the kitchen to ask Nancy and Agnes if they can recall anything."

Wonderful smells filled the kitchen. Unfortunately, it's wasted on me because I have no desire to eat. The kitchen is an eat-in with just enough room for a large table at one end.

"Nancy and Agnes, do either of you remember any boys from high school making threats to April?"

Their lists are a lot longer than Nick's. Maybe Nick was right and this is a dead end, but at least I'm doing something.

Chapter 46

Her chest is barely rising and her breaths hiss out weakly. Her skin is pasty pale and her lips are accompanied with a bluish hue. He's not a doctor, but death seems close. If she dies, his plans are destroyed. He can't let that happen. He needs a new plan. Didn't someone he knows become a doctor or a nurse? Maybe a drink will help clear his mind.

His daughter really loves her mom. She hasn't left her side since he brought her here. He wonders if she would love him like that if he becomes involved in her life. April lost consciousness a couple of hours ago, but Alyssa hasn't left her. He needs to find someone that Alyssa would trust.

"Alyssa do you know of a friend of your mom's who is a doctor or a nurse?"

"I don't know a doctor, but mom calls Aunt Janice a lot when she has questions. Aunt Janice is a nurse, I think. She must know a lot because Mommy calls her about stuff like that. Can we call Aunt Janice? Do you think she would know how to make mommy better?"

"Let's call Aunt Janice now, you and me. You tell her Mommy is very sick and I'll tell her the rest."

"Okay."

"Do you know her number?"

"Yes, Mommy has me memorize all the important numbers just in case of an emergency. This is an emergency, so I'll tell you. It's 555-1212."

He dials the number as his heart starts beating fast. This could be fun.

"Hello." He put the phone to Alyssa's ear.

"Hi, Aunt Janice."

"Alyssa, is that you? Where are you?"

"I'm in the ac...." He pulls the phone away from her and pushes her hard to the ground. She let out a yelp. He'll deal with her later. How dare she change the plan!

"Janice, your friend needs help badly and you are the only one who can help her now."

"Where is she? How...."

"You listen to me. No more talking. She needs medical attention, so pack all your drugs and tools and meet me at Brandywine's on Main Street in 10 minutes. If you call the police, your friend and her daughter will die. Do you understand?"

"Yes, I understand. I'll be there." Click. This is going to be a fun night.

* * *

She's not sure what she should do. Would he really kill her? Would he know if Janice made a call? Should she take the chance, and what was Alyssa trying to tell her? Janice is a note taker, so she quickly jots down all that she's thinking. She adds drugs. It took two minutes to write, and three to pack, and now she's out the door.

The wind is ripping branches off trees. The gusts push her forward, sometimes lifting her off her feet. She's about one minute away. She should make it in time, but she's being stupid for not calling anyone. She thinks she'll send Ryan a text. He didn't say not to text. First, she turns off her ringer and as the air blows her in front of her face as she types. 'At Brandywine's, heard from Alyssa. April is bad, going to help.' That's what she meant to text but she's not sure she spelled everything right. Her eyes are tearing from the cold and her fingers are going numb. She can't chance him seeing her with her phone. Should she toss it? No, that would be unwise. Maybe she should put it in her boot. Can the police track her phone?

Before she could ponder her next moves, a blue Sedan pulls up. He leans over to the passenger side and opens the door. A gruff voice yells, "Get in."

Really? This is straight out of a movie.

"Where is she?"

"You'll find out after you get in."

"How can I believe you?"

"If you don't get in within the next five seconds, I'm leaving." She doesn't recognize the voice or the car. He had himself tucked too far into the car for her to get a visual.

She didn't see another choice. April's life's on the line. She closes the door and he takes off. She doesn't want to know who he is because she knows once she does, he's going to kill her after she helps April. She wants her last thoughts to be on how she can help her best friend. This monster next to her doesn't deserve to even be acknowledged.

He drives for about three minutes and then pulls over. He hands her a bag and tells her to put it over her head. She does so, without saying a word. He surprisingly starts to drive again. She can feel the car sliding as they work their way up a hill. She's lived up here most of her life, so she's very familiar with the country roads that seem to lead to nowhere. She thinks they must be driving up toward the old Morghon's farm, wishing she could text with her toes. How can she get to her phone to let Ryan know? There has to be a way, she just hopes she figures it out before it's too late.

He slams on his breaks and demands that she hands over her bag. She doesn't keep any of her work supplies at home. It sounds like he's quickly searching through her belongings, then tosses the bag back.

"Empty your pockets." She pulls old tissues and a variety of other junk. He grabs it. "Where's your purse and your phone?"

She hands him her purse which she had clutched in her hand. There isn't anything of value in there. She left her credit cards at home. The annoying grunts cue her into his awareness of that fact.

"Where are your credit cards and phone?"

"I left them at home."

"If I find them on you, I'll shoot you between the eyes." Wow, she wonders if that's how she's really going to die. Instead of panicking, she focuses on the task. God has had her in April's life all these years for a reason. She's her best friend. She has benefited from their friendship more than she will ever know or believe. She hopes she's alive when she gets to April. This man is desperate. There is no way Janice was a part of his original plan.

He comes around and yanks her door open, then proceeds to grip her arm so tightly tears leak from her eyes. He's strong. The cold weather freezes them to her cheeks before they can fall. He leads her into the building and down a hall. She can hear him jingle some keys and with a breath, he opens the door and tosses her in. She lands on her side, her bags hitting her in the head and shoulder. She hears him close and lock the door. She takes the bag off her head and her eyes quickly scan the room.

She's shocked to see April, or who she assumes is April. There isn't a single mark on her face that reminds Janice of her. She was beaten beyond recognition. Alyssa was asleep next to her. After a quick scan, she assesses that Alyssa is fine, so Janice turns her focus back to April. Was she breathing? Barely. She doesn't have oxygen. She examines her from head to toe. She has several broken bones. She hopes there isn't any internal bleeding because if she's here, that means he isn't bringing her to the hospital. Janice decides her most pressing injury is the head wound that's still bleeding. She cleans and wraps the wound as best as she can. She's spiking a fever. She takes out her liquid pain medication and tilts her head back. She's not sure how much makes it down her throat, but hopefully it will ease some of her pain.

She can't believe that it's April. She looks close to death. Janice isn't sure she can save her. She knows if she could talk, she would tell her to save Alyssa. Shoot, she forgot to send a message to Ryan. She quickly pulls off her boot and grabs her phone. She types, 'We're at the old Morg.' and stops because she hears the keys rattle in the doorknob. She tries to press the button 'send' as she shoves it back into her boot. She hopes she gets her boot on in time. As she pulls it up, she leans over April.

"How is she?" comes his hoarse whisper from the door.

"She might die. She needs to go to a hospital. I can't do much for her here without the proper equipment."

"Why are you out of breath?" He takes a step forward.

"I've been racing around April, trying to help her." Alyssa wakes and reaches for me.

"Aunt Janice you're here. I'm so glad. Mommy needs help. Can you help her get better?"

"I'm trying Alyssa. How do you feel?"

"I want to go home." And with that statement a lot of tears flow. Janice doesn't want Alyssa to cry, but her tears chase that man out again and for that she's grateful. She hugs her tightly. She doesn't know how to protect her, but she'll try her best. God will give her wisdom.

"Alyssa, has he hurt you at all?"

"He hit me and pushed me down."

"Did he do anything else?"

"No, he brought me here and told me that my Mommy was coming here too, but then she didn't come. He told me I had to wait. I told him I wanted to go home, but he said no. Then, he brought Mommy here, but she doesn't look like Mommy. She talked to me for a while, but she hasn't woken up for a long time. I tried to wake her, but she wouldn't wake up. Make her better, Aunt Janice."

"Honey, I'm trying, okay. I need you to stay strong. I'm going to try to find a way out of here."

"I already tried. It's all locked," she whines.

"Then we need to ask God to show us." She looks back at April, who looks the same, horrible.

"God, we need you badly. Please help us get out of here, alive. Please." Her throat grows tight. She doesn't want to scare Alyssa with her crying, so she stops. She needs a miracle right now. Her phone, she still has her phone. She slides it out of her boot. She quickly dials Ryan's number. Ring, ring, ring, come on, pick up. She starts tapping her foot. Maybe she should just call the police.

"Hello."

"Ryan, it's Janice," she whispers. "I'm with April and Alyssa. April isn't doing well." The doorknob starts to turn. She jams her phone into her pants pocket.

"We're leaving, now. Help me pick her up." He points to April.

"Are we taking her to the hospital?"

* * *

"No." And that is all he says. I hear them grunting under April's weight, or so I thought that's what was happening. Janice, say something. Nick and I are in the car. We left the moment we received Janice's text. We're about five minutes from the old farm. Janice needs to stall him. I'm not sure what the best plan of action is, but Nick is on the phone with Carl, the police officer.

"Who are you anyway?" I hear Janice say, but I don't hear any response. "I said, 'who are you?'" Still nothing. I hear a car door open and a lot of ruffling sounds. "You can't throw her in like that," Janice shouts. My heart is racing. How dare he hurt my wife! When I get my hands on him, I'm going to beat him and if no one stops me I'll keep going. My hands are sweating even though I could see my breath in front of me.

"You're a beast pushing around a defenseless woman. She isn't even...." I hear the slap through the phone. I step on the gas, but realize that it's already down as far as it can go. I can hear him start the car. We're so close, he can't get away. I have to ease off the gas because the ground is quite slick now. It was when we left, but now I can see icicles hanging from the trees. The snow falling on the road instantly sticks. I need to slow down to keep my car on the road. He can't be that far in front of me.

"Why are we going down the mountain? Are we going to a hospital?"

Janice you're a genius, now I won't waste time going up that steep road. I turn the corner and pass the farm.

"Where are you going?" Nick asks. "I told Carl to meet us at the farm house." I hold my hand over my blue tooth and whisper, "Janice just said they are going down the mountain." Nick presses redial.

The back tires skid out. I pull the wheel and we begin to spin. We go in a circle two times before I'm able to stop the car. I look around and we are the only car in sight. I point the car in the right direction and thank God that we aren't in a ditch. We really should be stuck on the side of the road, but instead we're still heading toward the… "Nick look, I think that's them." We are close to the car.

"What's wrong?" I hear Janice say.

"We're being followed," he says and that's when I know who we are following. I've heard that voice before. When I get my hands on him…he's a dead man.

The ground has about five inches of snow. Icicles hang from the trees, flowing with the wind. It appears to be swaying back and forth as if saying, 'No, don't go any further. Turn back now, it's too dangerous.' I need to catch them but I don't want him to do anything stupid. We're passing Point Look Out on our way down Windham Mountain. You can see five states from this spot. The view is gorgeous on a sunny day. But on a day like this, crashing into the guardrail could be fatal. There's only a single guardrail keeping one from an unending fall. I ease off the gas. Distance is what will keep April, Alyssa, and Janice from leaving the road. This mad man is determined to get down this mountain. I have to pull my steering wheel to the left a bit because the wind is pushing me hard to the right. A snow and ice mix pelts the windshield, making it hard to see. We are about four minutes from the bottom of the mountain when the car in front of me starts to spin. Come on, hold the wheel tight. He starts to straighten it out, but the car doesn't want to fully obey. It must be hard for him not having control over this situation.

The car spins out toward the rail. Nick shouts, "One, two, three, stop." The blue sedan spun three times and then crashes into the rail. I ease on the brake stopping about 20 feet from them. Nick and I jump out, running as fast as we can. The front of the car is sticking over the rail.

"Nick, the car is teetering, be careful. We don't want to send it over," I shout to him. As we approach, we can see a man fighting with Janice. He's pushing her and pulling her hair. It seems like he is trying to drag her out of the car. Nick goes to the driver's side and I open the back seat. There lay April on the floor. Alyssa is screaming. I pull Alyssa and wrap my arms

THOSE TWO LITTLE WORDS

around April. A rush of adrenaline helps me lift them both out. I carry them to my car and gently put them inside. I turn back to see Nick leaning in the car. His arms are moving so fast, but beyond that I can't figure out what's happening. I tell Alyssa to lock the car.

"Please don't leave us, Daddy, please!" That was the first time she's called me Daddy. My heart melts and all I want to do is hold her in my arms and let her know that everything is going to be alright, now that Daddy has her and that I'll keep her safe from now on. But that isn't what I have time to do. I lean in and tell her that I'm just going back to the car to get Janice.

"I'm not leaving you, Alyssa. Okay?" She nods and then locks the doors.

Nick is running out of time. The car rocks twice. I break into a run, but I don't get there fast enough. The car goes over with the next gust of wind. Nick pulls his body out of the car holding someone. The body goes over the edge, but Nick is still holding on. He's close to falling with them. I reach out to help pull. The three of us barely make it. The ground is slippery and the nickel sized ice hits our heads.

A police car screeches to a stop. I look at Nick and we both look at who we pulled over the cliff. It's Janice, panicking and near hysteria. I leave the two of them there and make my way back to the car. I have to check on my girls. April isn't breathing. I cradle her in my arms and give her two short breathes. They go in.

"I need help. Hurry!" I yell and then put her on the ground. I start CPR. This is my wife and I need to save her. She is the love of my life. I just keep chanting these phrases over and over. The cold doesn't matter. The numbness has already set in. I don't care. I will continue until an ambulance arrives and if that takes all night, then I'll just keep going. This is my wife and I need to save her.

A police officer wraps a blanket around April. Janice is huddled inside the car with Alyssa. Sirens pierce through the air. Two men jump out before the ambulance comes to a sliding stop. They take over April's care. They continue the chest compressions. I'm helplessly unsure of what to do. I walk to Alyssa to explain what's happening and before I could get back to the paramedics, they're closing the doors to their vehicle.

One shouts that they are taking her to Albany Med. I get into the car. Nick slides in right after me. We follow the ambulance. The roads are still slick. We pass two cars in a ditch. Normally, I would stop to help, but not today. When we make it to the Thruway, the snow stops as if the clouds know to hold their precipitation. The roads are clear and the ground is dry. The change in weather is drastic. I don't want to speak my thoughts. Why haven't they put on their sirens? This is an emergency and we should be racing to the hospital.

There is only one answer that comes to mind, but I will not think about that. There is hope for April, but why aren't they going faster? The drive moves in slow motion, each mile marker painstakingly creeps by. The drive is eerily quiet, only interrupted by occasional whimpering. I wish I could just hold Alyssa right now. She needs loving arms around her, letting her know she's safe. Alyssa was not going to be okay for a long time. She had just endured more trauma then 90% of the adult population. I think we'll all be seeing Helen for a very long time.

The vehicle holding April puts on its blinker and exited at Exit 21b. We are supposed to get off at Exit 23. What's going on? The ambulance is still driving slowly compared to the speed we should be travelling in a crisis like this. The driver pulls off onto a dirt road and keeps on driving. Wait a minute, could Dan have escaped?

"Nick, did you see Dan fall with the car?" I don't want to scare Alyssa, but I have to know.

"Yes, I saw him fall with...." He turns to me and his eyes grow large. We are thinking the same thing.

"Step on it!" but I already am.

He isn't that far ahead of me to begin with, so it doesn't take long to catch him. There isn't much to this dirt road. It's only one lane, but if one needs to, they can squeeze two. And right now there is a need! I jerk the wheel to the left and slam down the gas pedal. Alyssa and Janice both let out a muffled scream. I have no choice, I have to find out who is behind the wheel. Nick rolls down his window, anxiously waiting for an opportunity to look at the driver. We are about three feet away.

The ambulance veers in our direction causing me to move further into the edge of the road. I avoid the collision and the driver straightens out his wheel. We are now four feet away, but I'm hopeful to minimize the margin quickly. Three feet and still gaining.

"Come on, Ryan, hurry it up."

"I'm trying."

Two feet.

"What… are we… doing?" Alyssa sobs.

"I'll explain everything soon."

One foot.

A loud rumble erupts from the mountaintop. Alyssa continues sobbing and my heart is breaking all over again. Janice wraps her arms around her and they cry together. The sound only grows louder. It distracts Nick and me from our task. I refocus and see that we lost a foot. I'm tired of this game. I gun it and we close the gap in seconds. Nick realizes what I'm doing and sticks his head out the window to get a better glance.

'They're up too high, I can't see in from here. All I see is his shoulder and the back of his head." It doesn't matter though. I can't stop it. I wouldn't risk April getting hurt more than she already is. I've failed her. She needed me to protect her and I failed her. I couldn't rescue her in time. Her life is slipping away before my eyes and here I am unable to help. I'm weak right now. I have no power to make this right. God is her only hope. Thank God for that. I let the car slip back behind the ambulance.

The noise increases. My heart takes over faster than my head and I start to pray. I ask God to take control of this hopeless situation because He is the only one who can turn this into good. And my tears cascade down my cheeks as my spirit groans for me. I pray for God to be in control and that no man could change God's plan for April's life.

We turn another corner and a huge clearing spreads out before us. April's ride turns and a rumbling helicopter lands. The back door opens and Nick and I jump out. We are ready, for what, we don't know. A man I've never seen before jumps out of the back and I wish I had my gun on me. It appears that Nick doesn't have his either. I forgot to tell Janice and Alyssa to lock the doors behind us. I can't go back now.

The man seems dispassionate toward Nick and me as we approach him. He turns his back to us and I brace myself for the turn of gunfire. Nick perches down. He starts pulling on a large object. He must not be able to hear us over the chopper blades. He's moving fast and before I can reach him, he pulls out the stretcher that's carrying April.

I run and am at her side in seconds. She isn't awake. She doesn't look like herself. Her face is bruised and swollen to the point where her features are flowing from one to the other. My girl must be in a lot of pain. I reach for her hand. I look up and Nick's gone. I'm glad he is going after the bad guy. Right now I need to be with my wife. A second man jumps out and starts pointing and shouting franticly. I can't hear him over the noise. I yell back and he turns and goes back into the ambulance. Should I follow him? I can't leave April alone, so I stay right by her side and even though it is too loud, I lean my mouth to her ear and whisper my love to her. I tell her about the life we are going to have together. How we're going to paint the house any color she wants and how we are going to see all the chick flicks she can get her hands on. How we are going to raise Alyssa together, but first she needs to fight for her life. I tell her about all the children we are going to have, whether it will be through adoption or from us.

I'm not ashamed of my tears falling next to her face and I tell her that I will hold her hand through all our life's challenges. I will walk beside her no matter how difficult the path becomes. Lastly, I tell her how much I love her. I feel her squeeze my hand and that makes me tell her over and over again. Maybe I imagined it, but in that moment it felt real and that is all I need.

The man comes back and hands me a piece of paper, then proceeds to push the gurney toward the helicopter. I race to April's side and grab her hand again. He points to the paper. I lift it up, but I refuse to let go of her hand. I can't read it in the dark. When we reach the chopper, I see that the pilot and the two EMT's are the only people here. I need to find Nick. They're starting to push April into the helicopter. I lean over and kiss her on each eyelid and tell her how much I love her and that Alyssa is safe. I pull the note out because I couldn't let them leave without knowing what was going on. Using the light coming from the chopper I read:

'Your wife is in really bad shape.
We need to airlift her because she's running out of time.'

I realize then that Nick and I are chasing a ghost. He must have figured it out also because his arm wraps around my shoulder and he leads me back to the car. I go with him because there's nothing else for me to do. The chopper already took off, leaving us in a wind tunnel of debris. I couldn't make eye contact with Alyssa. She would figure out how bleak our crisis really is, if she looks into my eyes. I turn the car around as Nick explains the basic reason for our change of plans. We make our way back to the main road and continue on to the hospital. Alyssa falls asleep.

I slow my pace, hoping it isn't noticeable because I don't want to explain. The longer the drive takes, the more time I have before receiving the news that awaits me at the hospital, news that would churn my stomach for the rest of my days here on earth. Yes, I can wait and hope to wait for a very long time.

Fatigue pulls my logical reasoning sideways.

Chapter 47

The frozen hours sloth by. I pace, I sit, and I pace some more. Alyssa and Janice are staying in a hotel a mile down the road. Agnes, Nancy, and Nick silently sit in their chairs, staring at nothing. We don't say a word to each other. We don't need to. We just wait. They seem more patient than I am, but still we all just wait. About every hour, one of us asks the receptionist if there is any news and she would always say that they will let us know as soon as there is.

When we arrived, they informed us that she was in critical condition and not able to breathe on her own. That was it. They didn't say if she needed surgery or if they were just watching her.

I should look at this as a good sign, I guess. She's still alive. Otherwise, they would have come out to tell us, right? The woman behind the desk asks us if we want to go get some sleep. We all shake our heads. She mentions that it could be hours. Again, we all shake our heads.

I'm not paying much attention to anyone without scrubs on, so I really don't know how long the man in the corner was standing there. I'm surprised when Nick goes over to him. He isn't far away, so when they start talking, the rest of us can hear their conversation.

"Hi, my name is Nick. Are you waiting to hear news about a loved one?"

"I'm here waiting with all of you," the man replies.

"Huh, I'm confused."

"I'm waiting to hear about April also." Who is this guy? I've never seen him before.

"How do you know April?"

"From high school, but she probably wouldn't know who I am."

"What do you mean?" Nick asks.

"All the guys had a crush on April in high school."

"And you were one of them?"

"Yes, but that's not why I'm here. I was one of the men helping look for her and I was the driver for the EMT's tonight. You followed me for a while until you, or maybe it was him, tried to run me off the road. That was rather bizarre behavior if you ask me. Your wife was in there. I was just trying to drive the ambulance to the clearing." I think it's my turn to intervene.

"I'm sorry about that. We thought you were the kidnapper. We were just trying to get a look at your face."

"It's okay, but does that mean you know who he is?"

"'Yes, we do." And that's when we told him the story, the story we knew and thought to be true, but only April will be able to fill in all the gaps. Only April can fill in a lot of voids, voids all of us felt in this room. The driver's name was Gabriel. He was four years behind April in school, so that explains why we didn't recognize him. He said he was concerned for April and came to find out how she was. He wants to help us in any way we need. He's a nice guy, too nice if you ask me. I grow weary of his questions and leery of why he's asking them. He wants to know too much. I give Nick a hidden tap and he gives me a slight nod.

I drift back to my corner while Nick makes small talk. I know he understood not to give out any more information, and as I know the back of my hand he must be working on gathering his own.

I'm not sure why he's so interested in April. I need to find out what happened in that ambulance. Maybe there was more than one man involved. Exhaustion swallowed my ability to think reasonably. I haven't slept in three days, I think. I'm not sure. I might have napped, but that doesn't matter.

I need to protect Alyssa. I thought we had our man, but maybe we don't have him at all, and if that was the case we need to keep this man here while we get someone to protect Alyssa. I'm torn, how can I choose between my wife and my daughter? I can't be in two places at once. Nor can I protect them both when they are in two different places. Who can I trust? Can I even trust Nick? I'm not sure. He hasn't been accounted for, for several hours yesterday and the day of the kidnapping. Normally, I'm good at discernment, but I know that fatigue is camping out in my brain presently, and now I'm questioning myself and the integrity of my best friend, and the man he is talking to. Nick is spending too much time conversing with him, and after I walked away they started whispering. I need to go somewhere to think. I need to see April and I need Alyssa with me at all times. I know she is with

Janice, but I'm her dad now and I need to be the one protecting her. April would want that. She would want me to put everything aside and protect her, just like she did for all of Alyssa's life.

I have my answer and with all my strength, I push myself off my chair.

"Nancy and Agnes, I'm going out for a little bit, please call me as soon as you hear something."

"We will," Nancy replies. With each step, I remind myself that I'm doing what April would ask me to do. I'm loving her in the best way I know how, by loving her daughter, my daughter, who needs her dad right now. The loss this little girl has faced was tremendous. She has matured way beyond her childhood years. In a way, she might try to be the comforting adult for me but I'm not going to let that happen. I'm going to be her dad. I've played the role as friend and uncle, but now I'll make the transition to loving father. I'm not sure how yet, but my God is with me every step of the way. I just need to remember to ask him for the help.

The hotel wasn't far and when I knock on the door, I can hear that they are both awake. Alyssa opens the door after looking in the peep hole three times and asking who it is twice. Her voice quivers as she says 'hi.' I slowly scoop her up and hold her in my arms.

"Daddy's here, you'll be okay now." My voice catches on the last word. She clings to me and I know, through the cloudiness of my mind, that this is the right place to be. I sit in a chair with her head on my shoulder. I whisper a prayer in her ear and she starts to relax.

I'm not sure who fell asleep first, but I awoke to a knock on the door. I didn't want to startle Alyssa so I motion to Janice, who is already on her feet going to the door.

"Who is it?" I ask quietly.

"It's Nick and some other guy." I didn't tell anyone I was here so he wasn't here for me. Why would he come here? I motion to her not open the door. I gently put Alyssa in the bed. Judging quickly is something I'm not accustomed to, but the lives of my wife and daughter are at stake and I need to consider every possibility. I decide to see what they want, but in order to do that I need to leave. I wouldn't leave physically just give the illusion that I'm not present.

"Janice, I'm not sure why they're here, but they don't know I'm here so let's let them think it's just you and Alyssa. Okay?"

"But this is Nick you're talking about."

189

Please work with me on this Janice.

"I know this doesn't make sense, but…."

Someone knocks again.

"One minute," Janice says.

"You're right, this doesn't make sense, but I'll just play along. I'm too tired to argue."

"Tell me about it," and with that I hide behind the bathroom door. Janice opens the door and asks what they want. Nick introduces the man with him as the EMT driver who brought April to the hospital. He then says that he wants to look at Alyssa. Why? She was looked over at the hospital when we first arrived.

"She's sleeping and the doctor told us to let her sleep as much as she wants, so I'm not going to wake her."

"Oh, right, we don't want to wake her," says the EMT. "Maybe we can come back later."

"I don't see a need for that, but thank you. The doctor did a thorough exam and said she was free to go home."

"I understand, okay. Thank you." Janice seems to be understanding where I'm coming from now. I inch closer, in case he decides to make a move.

"Why are you really here?" I throw my fist into the air, go Janice. She always did get right to the point and didn't care who she offended along the way.

"Uh."

"It's okay, if you don't tell her, she'll never let you see Alyssa."

"I'm Dan's little brother. I just want to talk to Alyssa to find out if it was really him." He starts to cry. "I can't believe he would do something so horrible. I've known him my whole life and never thought he was capable of …it. You know what I mean."

"I do know what you mean, because he also kidnapped me."

"Did he hurt you?" His voice pleading for a no.

"Not in that way. He did scare me though and he hit Alyssa. She was having a tough time with all this, especially not knowing what's going on with her mom." He seems genuine, but I'm still not sold. Maybe I just need a full night's sleep. I even thought Nick was involved. My best friend, someone I consider close as a brother and I thought he might be connected somehow.

"I'm so sorry my brother did all these horrible things to all of you. I wouldn't have guessed he was capable of such horrific behavior, my own flesh and blood. Please, please, I'm begging you, please forgive. I knew he had a crush on April. He liked her all through high school, but she would never even glance his way. I know because I also had a crush on her, but not like him. I remember one day he came home in a horrible mood. I asked him what was wrong, but he just yelled at me to leave him alone and then slammed his door. I only heard him say one thing as he moved about his room and that was, 'How dare she disrespect me! I will not tolerate it anymore. She will pay.' I thought he was referring to our mom. If I had any idea what he meant by that, I would have done something and none of this would have ever happened. Please forgive me, please."

"This isn't your fault, please don't think it is," Janice says.

"But I could have prevented this."

"You are not in control of someone else's actions, they make their own choices. Your brother made his own choice and you are not to be blamed for it. There is nothing to forgive you for, nothing." Janice stands firm and after they talked for a couple more minutes, they leave saying they are going back to the hospital. There still wasn't any word on April.

As the door clicks shut, I step out of the bathroom. Janice doesn't say anything as I enter the room. She just turns around and busied herself with, well, I'm not sure, she looks occupied which is fine with me. Alyssa is still asleep. I hear Alyssa mumbling something in her sleep. I step closer, it sounds like she's singing. I hear the words, Jesus and me. Then I hear the next line clearly, Jesus loves me. Goosebumps fill my arms and legs, but most importantly warms my heart. I move to the chair and begin to pray. After finding out where God and April want me to be, left one thing. I need to lift her up to the only One that can save her. The strength is not my own and I'm thankful that I'm able to talk freely with my God who wants to know my heart. I tell Him how afraid I really am. I don't want to lose my wife before we are able to spend time in love. I'm afraid for Alyssa, of her never getting an opportunity to live under the same roof with her mom. I cry out to Him, and I know He hears. My heart aches with unbearable sobs. And He hears me. My mind reels with undesirable future possibilities. And He hears me. My body longs for my wife. And He hears me. My emotions crave her correspondence. And He hears me. My future hopes for her presence. And He hears me. My little girl cries for her mommy. And He hears the small voice of his child.

SAMANTHA KEATHLEY

I wipe my eyes on my sleeve and wrap my arms around my girl. I'm not sure if my prayers woke her, but I'm thankful to share this moment with her. My hope has been restored. No matter what our future holds, my God is in control and I trust Him, I do.

The phone rings and Janice, who's sitting right by it, picks it up. I wish she could put it on speaker. I almost grab it from her, but she understands before I say anything and repeats everything that was said.

To me she says, "Nancy's on the phone."

To Nancy she says, "Okay." Maybe she didn't understand, I want the phone.

"Okay." This is the longest minute of my life. Then she adds, "Here, talk to Ryan." I grab the phone and look at Janice's face to get an idea of how April is. She's wiping tears from her eyes and then she walks away. Do I want to know? Are these my last seconds of her being with me here on earth?

"How is she?" I ask through a cracked voice.

"She's in stable condition."

"Really? She's alive?" My heart is pounding so hard right now. I need to be aware of Alyssa too. This is her mom we're talking about. She clings to my leg and as I look down, I see the pleading in her face.

"Mommy's doing okay, Sweetie." And she holds tighter. She knows we are waiting to hear if her mom was still alive, yet another hardship for such a little one to endure.

"Go on, Nancy."

"The reason they didn't say anything for so long is because they weren't sure if she was going to make it. The doctors wanted to give us good news instead of the uncertainty they felt for hours. They had a tough time bringing her back, but over the past hour she has really turned a corner for the better. They're saying it's a miracle because she was pretty much gone when she was brought in and she wasn't improving either, but this past hour she made a tremendous comeback. They said you can go in to see her when you get here. They think Alyssa should wait though, but that decision is up to you."

Okay, we're on our way." I look at Alyssa; she's already putting her shoes on. I don't know what the best decision is, but God will let me know when the time is right for her to see her mom. *Thank you, God, for this miracle!*

THOSE TWO LITTLE WORDS

We half run to the car, Janice is with us, and I drive to the hospital. I try to stick within ten miles above the speed limit. I know that if I'm pulled over, it would take A LOT longer to get to my April. So I push, what I feel, is the max without getting pulled over. Alyssa is talking a little. I was starting to get concerned because she has barely spoken since she came home to me.

We arrive at the hospital and find her floor. We see Nancy and Agnes in the waiting room.

"She's only allowed one to two people in her room at a time and only for ten minutes. We went in right after we got off the phone with you because we wanted you to be able to go in as soon as you got here. Alyssa can wait here with us."

"No, I'm going to see my Mom."

"I understand you want to see her, but she really doesn't look like herself yet." Grandma Agnes starts to explain. "We want you to see her when she looks better."

"No, I was there when he hit her and I was there the whole time she was sick, so how is this any different. I want my Mommy." Alyssa is not going to stand for any of us to tell her no, and frankly I don't blame her.

"Alyssa, I'm going to leave this choice to you. If you think you can handle seeing her, than you can come in with me. If you decide to go in and change your mind when we get in there, then I'll bring you back to Grandma, Aunt Nancy, and Aunt Janice. So what do you want to do?"

"I'm going in with my Daddy, to go and see my Mommy. I miss her, and I'm sorry I yelled at you Grandma."

"I forgive you, Sweetie." Grandma Agnes slowly gets down on her knees and looks Alyssa in the eyes. "I love you Sweetie, and I want you to know that I'm so proud of you. You were so brave with that bad man. You did such a great job taking care of your mom too. You are the bravest girl I know!" With that she pulls her into her arms, so she wouldn't see her tears running down her cheeks and she holds her until Alyssa asks if she can go now and see her mommy. I'm glad Alyssa spoke up.

She takes my hand and we walk to the nurses' station to find out the room number. The nurse is polite and points down the hall, as she informs us of the number. We find it on the right not far from the station. I slowly open the door and pray that I made the right decision by bringing Alyssa here. I couldn't deny her. Not this, she's right, she already saw her in an unrecognizable state. And that was how we found her. Her face was swollen to double it's normal size and with a wide range of colors. I couldn't believe it. She didn't look like my April. I almost questioned if it was. And she doesn't look like April now either.

Alyssa on the other hand has no doubt. She gently picks up her mom's hand and starts to sing Jesus loves me. I couldn't keep my tears away. If someone asks me a question, I won't have the ability to answer. My daughter is an amazing girl. Her life has touched so many, and here she is nurturing her mom. To think of life without Alyssa would be unimaginable. I'm glad April had her and I'm proud to call her my daughter.

I reach for her other hand and kiss it with my lips. I notice that she has a cast on most of her right arm up to her shoulder. I lean in and whisper in her ear like I did before she was put on the helicopter. Alyssa doesn't ask why April hasn't talked or opened her eyes yet. She has a grown understanding of this situation. She doesn't ask questions, she only loves. We stay like this longer than we're supposed to. A nurse comes in and tells us our time is up.

"When can we see her again?" Alyssa asks.

"In an hour if the doctor says it's alright." Then she turns to me, "And the doctor would like to meet with you as soon as Alyssa is enjoying time with her aunt and grandma." Alyssa starts to speak, but changes her mind, so we walk to the waiting room with the nurse in tow. Alyssa sits down and stares off into space. Too much burden for a girl her age to carry and, sadly, there is nothing I can do to change that.

With Alyssa safely with her grandmother, I begin to brace my heart for the news the doctor has for me. I follow the nurse to what appears to be another waiting room. She tells me to wait there and I take the example of a very brave girl and didn't bombard the nurse with questions before the doctor arrives. I take my seat and wait. I know that my April is alive. I saw her breathe with my own two eyes and I thank God for each breath she takes.

Chapter 48

After twenty minutes, a balding short man, who I guess to be in his sixties, comes in. He walks straight to me, so my assumption of him being the doctor I'm waiting for is correct.

He extends his hand and says, "I'm Dr. Williams, April's doctor. There are several of us, actually, who have been overseeing her case, but I'm the man in charge." He gets right to the point.

"Hi, I'm Ryan, April's husband."

"I'll get right to the point. When April came in, her heart wasn't beating. The EMTs didn't give up the whole time they had her in the ambulance and in the helicopter. They're the ones that saved your wife. Because the drive was so long, most paramedics would have given up, but someone in there was a quick thinker and arranged for the chopper. They were exhausted when they arrived here yesterday.

"Your wife is a fighter. All throughout the night she was not able to breathe on her own. She has a broken arm and a dislocated shoulder. She also broke five ribs and has some internal bleeding. We are monitoring all of this, but worst concern was her lungs. It appears that she was kicked or hit with something very hard. It broke several ribs and one of those ribs punctured her right lung. She also has pneumonia and the combination made breathing very difficult for her. At some point she died. Sorry to put it that way, but she did.

"The miracle is that she was rescued in time and you performed CPR shortly after. We won't know if there's any permanent damage until she wakes up, and we do believe she will wake up. We don't know how long she was without oxygen unless the other two victims in the car remember. They weren't here last night, so we couldn't ask them. Her recovery will greatly depend on that answer."

"She was breathing on her own again when I was with her, before she went on the chopper."

"She crashed shortly after getting in the air and the paramedics were working on her the whole time before in the ambulance. We need to know what happened before you started CPR."

"I'll ask Janice and if she doesn't know, I'll somehow manage to ask my daughter."

"Good, you can let the nurse on duty know what you find out. Now for the other news."

"There's more?"

"Yes, rape." The room begins to sway and my legs grow heavy. I've never fainted before, but when grayness sweeps through my line of vision and I feel nauseous, I know what will happen next.

"Ryan, Ryan, wake up." Startled, I try to focus my eyes on who is talking to me. It's the doctor standing over me. Why am I on the ground? Oh, right. He was about to tell me that April was raped again. Nausea rushes in again. I hold my head between my legs unable to hear what the doctor is saying. Slowly his words make it through.

"Ryan, you didn't let me finish. I was saying that she was badly beaten, but I wanted you to know that she wasn't raped."

"Oh, really? Are you sure? You really scared me for a minute."

'I'm sorry about that. I've never been known for a good bedside manner. Anyway, your wife is in bad shape, but she has been showing signs of improvement, which makes me hopeful that she'll make it. You and your daughter are free to visit her at any time. You two also don't have a time limit anymore. Other friends still have to abide by the visiting hour rules. I'll be in touch each day to give you an update."

"Thank you, Dr. William's."

"You're welcome. Have something to eat. I don't want you passing out again. You have a wife and daughter that need you well right now." And with that, he turns on his heel and exits the waiting room.

I sit in my chair trying to digest all the information he gave me. She wasn't raped, thank God. He also said I could see her anytime. Why am I sitting here? Racing back to the waiting room, I find my family eagerly awaiting the news.

I fill them in on most things, but didn't want Alyssa to hear all that the doctor had to say. When I got to the part that Alyssa and I could stay with April, she starts pulling me toward the door. I didn't resist at all. I wave as we get to the door, and then let Alyssa lead me to the room. We are happy, the two of us. April seems about the same. The day passes by quickly and April still hasn't woken up. A kindhearted nurse wheels in a cot for Alyssa.

"You can use the second bed to sleep in tonight. Actually, you can use it until there is someone else who needs it."

"Thank you. I really appreciate it."

"You're welcome, Ryan. We're all rooting for April and we feel that both of your presence will help her pull through, so we'll do our best to help that happen." She turns quickly, but before she completely looks away, I see her eyes fill up. She cares and that touches my heart. This nurse's name I don't even know, but she cares about my wife and my family. It's amazing to see people who put others before themselves, truly loving.

Chapter 49

Days pass. April's face starts looking more like the woman I love. I've whispered my love into her ear, but she still hasn't woken up. I'm not sure she hears me and Alyssa is struggling with not having her mom awake. I've spent the past three days trying to be a good parent, but I feel that I'm failing in this area as well. Alyssa has thrown several temper tantrums that seemed only appropriate for a two year old. I don't know how to handle her. I've made sure she was getting plenty to eat, even though I myself have lacked these past few days in that area. Maybe I've been testy also.

I noticed Alyssa hasn't been sleeping well. She tosses and turns and cries out sometimes. The nightmares haven't forced her to wake up, but maybe she's replaying what happened to her over in her mind when she's awake. I think it's time to give Helen a call.

"Ummm."

"Yes, Alyssa what is it?"

"I didn't say anything."

"If you didn't then," and we both race to April's side. Her eyes are shut and she isn't moving. Her heart was beating at a strong steady beat and her color looks good. The doctor came in this morning and said that there was no swelling in her brain and that her scans this morning looked good. Her arm and ribs would take some time to heal, along with the nasty gash in her head. She had 50 stitches, but that also was healing well. He saw no reason why she couldn't wake up. It all depends on how long her heart was stopped in that car ride. Janice didn't know and we gently asked Alyssa, who also didn't know. We were hoping for more than that, but there wasn't anything else we could do.

And so we waited, for three days, we waited. Many people came and went. More than we wanted to greet. That might sound ungrateful and I guess it is, but we're tired and don't have the answers that most of the people coming to visit wanted. We made small talk and repeated the doctor's words over and over. And then we waited some more.

198

Alyssa and I are losing hope. Here we are standing at her bedside. I thought I heard a noise, but it wasn't from Alyssa. No one else is in the room, but the three of us, so if it isn't April then it had to be me. Maybe it was me. I'm averaging four hours of sleep a night. I wake up several times in between those four hours also. As I start to turn around, I hear it again.

"Ummm."

"Was that you, Alyssa?"

"No it wasn't, did you say that, Daddy?" Alyssa asks.

"No I didn't," I say.

"Then it has to be Mommy, right Daddy?" Wide-eyed and waiting for my response, I nod to her. That was the same conclusion I drew, so we stand and watch this time, staring at her lips. We long to hear her say our names and to see her beautiful eyes. And there it is, movement. No words, but a very slight twitch. Alyssa doesn't say anything, I'm not going to either, just in case she doesn't notice it. Then, April stretches, and we watch with our mouths a gap. Her eyes open and Alyssa and I move closer.

"How long have I been asleep?" Tears blur my vision, but I can still see her smile.

"Well, how long?"

"Mommy you've been asleep for days."

"What?"

"You're healing fast and, and I'm so happy to see you."

"Wait, I'm confused. What happened?"

"Mommy, we were kidnapped by that mean man. He hurt you and you were sick for a really long time."

"I remember that, but how did we get away from him?"

"Daddy rescued us. He's my hero." April raises her brow and gives me a half smile. I'm not sure what that means, but I'll have a life time to find out.

"He's my hero too, honey. Ryan, I have a list of questions to ask you. Janice and I wrote them a while back and I'd like to know the answers to them but I can't remember them now. I need to find that list."

Chuckling, I say, "April, I'll answer any question you have for me, any question at all." It's wonderful to hear her talk.

Chapter 50

Over my stay in the hospital, Ryan took the time to explain everything that happened. It turned out that I was asleep for three days and needed to stay in the hospital for three more. During those three days, many people came to visit. Lots of friends and family came to tell me they were praying all along. They told me how over two hundred people were praying outside the church for Alyssa and me to come home safely. They told me how Ryan was so distraught over not being able to find us and how he couldn't and wouldn't picture life without me in it.

The stories kept pouring forth and I personally loved the ones with Ryan in them. He sounded like my knight in shining armor and that's probably because he was. We haven't had time alone, yet. Alyssa won't leave my side, which I understand and prefer her right where she is. Ryan and I will have time together at some point, but for now, the three of us together has warmed my heart. I don't remember much after Dan hit and kicked me, except that my mind felt like it was constantly singing. I remembered that Jesus loves me and that He is my strength and I held on to that throughout my unconscious state. It's hard to explain, but I knew that He held me in His palm the entire time. I never felt closer to Him than when I was kidnapped and taken to where Alyssa was. He kept me strong, and even if I didn't live, He still had me near his side, taking care of me. I'm thankful to Him that I can now continue life with my family. For the first time, we are a mom, dad, and child, and we will all be living under the same roof!

The police also came in a few times over the past three days. They told me that Dan's body was found at the bottom of the mountain and it was confirmed that he was the kidnapper and the rapist from years ago. My heart has changed toward him. For years, I ran and lived in fear of him finding out about Alyssa. For years, I thought every man was like him, angry and needing to control what rightfully was not theirs. For years I shut myself off from those that loved me the most because I couldn't face my fear of being hurt again. And, for years, I let him continue to control me from a far.

What I have discovered over the past week is that Dan has never been in control. He has never had that right and he never will again. My soul and spirit are what remain and he can never have a part of me, if I don't let him. I've seen that I don't own my life either. Years ago, I gave my life over to the man who gave His for me. He is the one in control. And He chooses to give me and the rest of the world the freedom to choose. With the freedom He has given me, I choose today to give myself to Him by loving Him and His people. Today, I'm going to start with Ryan and Alyssa.

Another change that happened is that I forgave Dan for what he did to me. He violated me in such a sinful way. But I forgive him so that my heart can be free from this burden of fear, anger, and bitterness that has welled up. The heavy load has passed away, and now I can walk with my head held high. I can look at Alyssa and see such great love the Lord has given me through such a horrific act, an innocent child that has warmed my heart too many times to count. She has kept a smile on my face over the years and given me a reason to continue to keep my heart open to love. Without her, I wouldn't have been open to getting married. I know I would have kept men at a distance forever. I might have extended this to all my friends as well.

I thank God that He knows me best. I thank Him for never leaving my side and for loving me when I was unwilling to love back. Most of all, I thank Him for healing my heart and letting His peace rest in me.

Chapter 51

My Mommy is coming home today. I can't wait. The doctor said she needed to rest for a couple of weeks. I didn't tell Mommy yet, but I'm going to be her best helper. I'm going to clean up after myself always and help Daddy cook dinner. I still need to go to school, but not until next week. The doctor wrote a note for me, saying I needed to rest too. I didn't want to tell him that I thought I was okay because I really wanted to stay home with Mommy.

Mommy and Daddy said that I'm going to be seeing a woman, Helen. She's Aunt Nancy's good friend. I'm not sure how I feel about this, but they both said it would be good for me. I wanted to tell them that it was good for me to stay with them instead, but I'll go because they know what's best for me. I can't wait to get Mommy home.

Chapter 52

To see her beautiful face staring at me puts the bounce in my step that a newlywed should have. She's coming home today. I haven't been home to see what needs to be done there. I couldn't leave her side for more than a minute and the only reason I did that was to use the bathroom or get her something. We have spent the past three days together as a happy family, and I have loved every second. I've been saving my vacation time and have decided to surprise April. I'll stay home this week and see how she's doing before I make plans.

It's amazing to look back and see where we have come from, I, a man in love with a girl from high school going through the years pining for her attention. She, a girl hurt by men, first her father and then Dan. I've wanted to rescue her from her pain for years, but she never gave me the opportunity. She wouldn't even give me five minutes of her time. We saw each other often over the years or more like, I've seen her. She was my brother's sister-in-law. My brother and I tried over the years to combine family gatherings to include both sides, but April would have nothing to do with it. She was the only one who opposed and she stood strong. One day I'll ask her why, but for now the look of happiness on her face means the world to me. All I've wanted was to make her happy. I never dreamed she would be my wife, not recently anyway. Over the past year I've grown content in where God had me, single with no one in the picture. I enjoyed the times I was able to spend with Alyssa and cherished the fact that April didn't object.

Now, I'm here in this hospital room looking out of the window thankful that God has brought these wonderful changes into my life. I didn't want to trap April or trick her into marrying me. I wouldn't hurt her that way. I was surprised Nancy's letters made it into our hands, but I'm glad we found love through it all. I've had a love for her for years and now to look into her eyes and see love for me brings tears to mine. How awesome is God to care about me and my feelings all these years. To know that He heard my cries, and even though I didn't think He would have put us together this way, He allowed it and worked it out for His good, and for that I'm touched.

Chapter 53

“April,” Ryan says as he turns his head and looks down into my eyes. The look takes my breath away. How can he love me so much? I secretly had a crush on him in middle school and I would have melted if he looked at me with such love then. Maybe I'll let him know about that someday, but for now I'm going to continue to enjoy being in love with the best man I know. He has always been special to me. That was part of why I've kept my distance. I was afraid he would steal my heart and leave me after he had it. I know now that he's not that type of person. I can trust him with my heart. I know at times I'll panic some because I'm a work in progress, but I long to spend those times learning and growing with Ryan.

“Umm, Yes.”

“What are you thinking about?” he asks as he wheels me to the parking garage.

“You.” I know he's going to want more of an answer than that. It will take me time to open up and share more of myself, but for him I'm willing to do it. I have never depended on a man before and now I have two that I can trust, my Jesus and my Ryan.

“Good thoughts?”

“Yes,” I say as I squeeze his hand. He parks the wheelchair.

“I'm going to pull the car around, are you and Alyssa okay waiting here?”

“Yes, we'll be fine. Thank you.”

He opens his mouth to say more, but decides against it because he turns and runs toward the car.

“Mommy, I'm so glad we're going home. I can't wait to live in the same house as you and Daddy. I can call him Daddy now, right?”

“Yes, Alyssa you can call him Daddy now.”

“Good, because I already started. I have always wanted him to be my daddy. He has always been kind to me. Not like that other man who said he was my real daddy. There's no way he is, Ryan's my daddy. Mommy, this is like one of those fairy tales where you find the prince and live happily ever after, but I found a daddy instead.”

"Yes, honey, you did." And I found the prince. He is too good to be true. I never wanted to give control of my heart to someone that could easily hurt me and I wouldn't if Nancy's letter didn't trick me into it. I would have lived my personal life alone rather than risk loving someone, someone that could choose to leave me at anytime, but now I see how loving him is worth that risk. To love and be loved is a wonderful thing and I thank God for sending the right man to me. I have seen the wrong men over the years and through my unfortunate circumstances I have experienced great pain due to them, but now with Mr. Right, I'm also starting to experience great happiness.

Ryan pulls up and before I could stand, he's there helping me to my feet. It hurt, the pain shooting through my whole body. My first steps are challenging. I don't know why I'm not recovering as fast as I thought I should. I shouldn't need help walking, but I do. Alyssa opens the door and as I ease into the seat, she's buckling herself in, anxious to get home. Ryan closes my door and as he walks around the front of the car, I notice his smile. His lips are… I can't believe I'm picturing myself kissing him. How far have I come in such a short time? These thoughts are ones that I will share with him soon.

"You look happy," Ryan comments.

"Actually, I'm very happy. I'm enjoying being married to you." Ryan put the car back in park and turns to me.

"Really?"

"Really." His expression speaks volumes. I don't know if I'm ready for what it looks like he has in mind, but I know he'll be patient with me.

He puts the car back in drive and gently takes my left hand in his. He strokes the back of my hand with his thumb. We occasionally exchange smiles as we listen to Alyssa's banter. She's recovering well. I know there will be times when she has memories of these horrible days and I know we will all have long talks about everything we went through, but importantly I know that God will give us the wisdom we need to get through those times. I trust that He will. He promises to never leave me and I know that to be true. He held my hand when I was walking to my dorm many years ago and He cradled me when I was forced into situations against my will. He dried my tears when I let them fall and He walked quietly next to me throughout my years of anger I had toward Him. He never left me and when I look back over this past week, I know He was there every step of the way.

Ryan pulls the car into the garage and Alyssa jumps out. She's quite bubbly.

SAMANTHA KEATHLEY

"Come on, Mommy. Let's go inside. I can't wait to see my new room. Daddy was telling me all about it when you were sleeping in the hospital. He told me that I can decorate it anyway I want. Well, he did say you needed to approve, but I know you will. I've thought about it a lot. I don't want to paint it pink. I was thinking of orange. What do you think Mom? Isn't orange a great color?"

"Ugh, we'll talk about it after dinner, okay?" I'm expecting a little argument from her, but she grows surprisingly quiet. Ryan unlocks the door and pushes it open for me. I'm unsure where the light switch is, but as I reach for one Ryan leans over and starts to whisper in my ear.

"I just thought of this now, but you have been through a lot of frightening stuff and I don't want you to get startled, so that's why I'm telling you. Alyssa and lots of others have planned a welcoming home party for you. They're all waiting in the living room." I reach down and squeeze his hand.

"Thank you. I would have been terrified entering a room with lots of people screaming."

"Come on, Mommy and Daddy. Let's go look at my new room." Alyssa's voice rings loudly, alerting the guests that we have arrived. I'm thankful Ryan told me. I'm glad people came over, but I'm appreciative that my husband cares enough about me to think about how I would react in this situation. He's protecting me, loving me in a way I've never felt loved before. We continue to walk toward the living room, Ryan holding my hand and turning on lights.

"Welcome home," chorus a bunch of friends and family. Ryan doesn't let me get swept away into the crowd. He leads me to the couch. I'm exhausted from that walk, but happy to see everyone. These are only a handful of the people who have been praying for me and I'm blessed to have them in my life. I'm going to be more open to letting friendships form.

Maybe, it's time to go to the mini college reunion too. The girls get together once a year, but I've never attended. Some changes are good, I'm realizing. All the police officers that were on the case came over and told me how hard my case was and how happy they were with the outcome. Some apologized for not figuring it out. Two were guys from high school. I reassured them that it wasn't their fault and I thanked them for all their hard work. Next, the pastor and his wife along with many other well wishers come over. I'm fatigued by the time most people leave the house. Helen, laughingly, reminds me that we still had a few meetings left. I'm not sure if she's joking about having them, but I tell her that it sounds like a good idea.

My Mom hugs me gently and cries softly into my hair. We embrace for a long time. She prays into my ear, thanking God for saving me and bringing me home.

"Mom, how about when I'm better we go shopping together, just the two of us."

"I would love that, really." She wipes her eyes. Nancy stays back. I could tell she wants to feel closure about what she did. We haven't had time to talk about it since she came out of surgery and Alyssa was kidnapped. Without her saying anything, I've already forgiven her in my heart, but she doesn't know that.

"April, I'm so sorry. Please, forgive me. I didn't mean to trick you. I couldn't sleep the night before the surgery so I stayed up writing those letters. He, Dan, sent me threatening letters and he called me again the day of the accident. He said he was going to take her if she didn't have a dad. He said he was her dad and had every right to take her. I called you, but you didn't answer. I was trying to get to you to tell you when my brakes stopped working. I hit my head pretty badly in the accident and I broke my leg. I couldn't remember anything about that day until after surgery. I knew when I was writing that there was a reason I wanted you and Ryan to get married. I was on a very powerful pain medication and honestly regret all that I wrote. Please forgive me. Helen let me read the letters she has and she summed up the letters you have. I'm so sorry." At this point, Ryan stands at my side listening too. I look at him and we exchange a smile.

"Nancy, thank you."

"What?"

"I never would have taken the risk to marry Ryan. Without your crazy letters I wouldn't have found the love of my life."

The shock on her face is priceless. "Really, you love him?"

"Yes, I do."

She starts to hug me, but then remembered the pain I'm in.

"Nancy, don't you want to know how I feel about this whole thing?"

"Ryan, you don't need to say anything. You've been in love with April since middle school."

"Ha-ha. I guess I was a little obvious over the years," Ryan comments.

"You're right, but not just a little. April, another day I'll tell you story after story about Ryan and his love for you."

"I'll look forward to it," I say.

"Hey, that's not fair," Ryan replies.

"Why not?" Nancy asks.

"Because… because, oh, fine. Go ahead and tell her."

"Good, I will." As they joke around I realize that there is still a piece to the puzzle that hasn't been answered yet.

"How were the letters mailed?" I want to know.

"I don't know how you got them." By this time everyone in the room is listening.

"I saw that Nancy left some letters in her room addressed to Helen, Ryan, and April, so I mailed it to them that day when she went into surgery. I didn't want to sit and wait. I wanted to do something, so I mailed it to them," my mom says.

"Helen opened it and read the letter saying that if she receives this package then I must have died. Where is Helen?" Nancy asks.

"In the kitchen refilling the chip bowls. Alyssa can you…." In walks Helen.

"Helen, we were just talking about the letters I sent."

"Yes. I know you're not that type of person so I knew you were just preparing for the worst, and somehow the letters were mailed by accident. Am I right?"

"Yes, but how did you know that?" April asks.

"I heard you say it, as I was walking back in." Everyone laughs.

"So I guess I'm the one that should be saying sorry then. I had no idea what was in the envelopes. Wow, Nancy please don't take those pain meds again," Mom says.

"I agree! I don't want to know what you'll come up with next," Janice adds.

"Oh and Nancy, I forgive you. I think Ryan and I might start from the beginning of the letters and follow the steps again." I turn to Ryan, "I think it might be fun this time, now that I like you."

"That might be fun. Maybe we should write a letter for Nancy to follow also," Ryan adds.

"Nice try, Ryan," Nancy scolds.

"I'm serious," Ryan states. "Oh, and what was that about when April and I called the hospital and Ella said Nancy was gone?"

"Ummm," Ella shyly says, "that wasn't all I said. I said, 'She's gone,' and then I took a second to swallow the bite of my sandwich that was in my mouth when I picked up the phone and after that I said, 'down to surgery again.' When I asked April if she was coming to the hospital, she wasn't on the phone. I tried to call back, but there was no answer," Ella finishes.

"Really?!?" Ryan says. "So no one but Helen, April, and I thought Nancy was dead. Wow! Unbelievable, I'm very glad you're alive Nancy, and now I'm married to the love of my life, all because of a bunch of miscommunications. Amazing!"

I love some miscommunications too, and I love that my family gets along well. I curl up on the couch and listen to them talk as I slowly drift to sleep.

Epilogue

Ryan waited on me for the past four days. I'm moving better today and I can walk with hardly any pain. It's great to feel normal again. Ryan says he wants to take me on a real honeymoon. We both have reservations leaving Alyssa, so we arrange for a family gathering at Niagara Falls. We figure we all need a vacation and this way we have many babysitters available to us. My mom, Nancy, Janice, and Alyssa are all in one car and you'll never guess who volunteers to drive. Nick, of course. My in-laws, with a couple of their friends are in the second car and Ryan and I are driving the third car.

The drive is nice. Ryan and I are still getting to know each other. When we arrive at the hotel, Ryan and I walk hand in hand as we go to check in and next to the reception area a sign reads, 'Ryan and April Wedding Room 2.'

"I wanted to have a wedding to remember. I know we'll remember the first one, but I wanted it to be your choice to marry me so…," he starts to say as he gets down on one knee. "April will you do me the honor and be my wife?" His hand is shaking as he holds out an engagement ring.

"Yes." And that's all I could say as he puts the ring on my finger. Tears spill over my eyelids, happy tears because the truth is I really want to marry him, again. He stands up and hugs me.

"I have to admit, April, I was nervous asking you."

"Ryan, why would you be nervous asking me out?" I can't hold a straight face with that line nor can he.

"So when is the wedding?"

He looks at his watch and says, "Three hours."

"What? How am I supposed…." He puts his finger up to my lips. Leans in and whispers that he took care of everything from the dress, to the hair and make-up as well as all the food. "I did delegate those details because I wanted you to have the best, so I hired a woman here. She's going to meet you in four minutes in your room."

"You're a confident man, Ryan. What if I said no?"

"I would have been crushed."

"And so would I, I don't want to hurt you again. I love you, Ryan, and I look forward to being married to you. Please lead me to my room. I can't wait to say those two little words, again." I look up into his eyes as he looks down at me. He slowly lifts his hand and cradles the back of my neck. As his lips part, he leans down and covers mine with his. We stay that way for a while, until we realize we are still standing in the hotel lobby.

Giggling, we walk up the stairs to our suite. I have to get ready for my wedding. I'm amazed by this man. When did he have time to plan this? He was by my side the whole time.

Coming Soon

Book Two in the Quick Decision Series: *All over Again*

April and Ryan are back with another life altering quick decision. Unfortunately once its made they can't change their minds even if one of them wants to. Do they come to an agreement or will this tear them a part before they really had a change to begin?